VARSITY
Heartbreaker

GINGER SCOTT

Cover Design by Ginger Scott, Little Miss Write LLC

Photograph by Wander Aguiar Photography

Print ISBN: 978-1-952778-03-2

For Autumn.
You so get me.

CHAPTER ONE

I t's quite a thing for a girl to watch her future go up in smoke. I suppose I'm being a little melodramatic, given that it's my mom who lost her job, not me. And honestly, I hate how dependent my dreams are on her hard work. I've never found it fair, but there are a lot of things in my life that I consider unjust but nonetheless are sewn into my fabric. What's one more?

My mom worked at Tiny Prints Studio in the mall at the edge of Allensville, our town that's like a pimple on Indianapolis's forehead. We're a nice zit, but economically? Full-on parasite. Most of the department stores closed when the huge outlet mall opened off the turnpike a year ago, and the empty spaces taken up by a charter school, pawn shop and thrift store. Other than the few remaining fast food joints, the photography studio was the only original business still operating in the plaza . . . until Tuesday.

Rent on the studio was too much for the couple who

owned the business, and retirement was far more inviting than negotiating. They gave a few of the oldest pieces of equipment to my mom, sold the rest, then rode off for warmer temps in some retirement burb near Phoenix. Meanwhile, Kristen Mabee is once again working the wedding circuit, shooting weddings all over the tri-state area so we can stay in this shitty house full of shitty memories of how my shitty dad decided to walk out on us.

And me?

Well, no more Montessori school, for starters. It's not posh private-school expensive, but it does cost, and public school is nice and free. And anything beyond community college is out of the blueprint too, unless the bowling alley gives me a hundred-dollar-an-hour raise. Not likely. In my immediate future, though, I wish like hell there's a way I could borrow my mom's photo tech to touch up the photo on my ID before my first day back at Public. I seriously miss the warm cocoon of the tiny Montessori school I got to go to for junior year.

"June, it's fine!" My best friend Abby rips the card from my hand and tosses it into her back seat. It's a mess back there so I'll be lucky to find it before school starts on Monday.

"I'm cross-eyed." I sigh, pulling the visor down and flipping on the light for the mirror. Am I always that way or just for this one picture?

"Nobody will ever see it. I promise," she says.

I flip the visor back up, not convinced that I don't actually look that way in real life, and flop back into my seat. Six people have already seen it, and the school photocopied it twice for registration. At this rate, my high school ID photo is in line for billboard placement any day now.

"You promise I'm going to know people at this party?" I'm not great with socializing. It was part of the appeal of going to a small school for the last year. The closer we get to the D'Angelo house, the more ill-fitting my T-shirt feels. I swear it shrank in the wash. I don't buy belly shirts, but I see my flesh when I raise my arms up halfway. And the top of my jeans is folding in on itself. It makes the zipper part bulge like I'm some jock with a huge cup. I squirm in my seat and shimmy the tight black pants down my hips while simultaneously tugging the black and white striped T-shirt toward my waist.

Abby glances at me and laughs.

"You're being nuts. You look great. And it's everyone you remember from sophomore year. It'll be like you never left." She pulls into a free space at the side of the road about four houses down from the twins' house. Cars line up both sides of the street, and we can hear the music thumping the moment Abby opens the driver's side door.

"I don't really *like* everyone from sophomore year. And I did leave for a reason." Perspiration builds at my neck despite the coolness of the late summer air.

"You left because you thought people didn't like you." She actually rolls her eyes when she says it, which pisses me off a little. She makes it seem so insignificant. She's always thought most of it was in my head, but a few things were plainly undeniable. The dog poop left on the hood of my car about a dozen times when it was parked at school was just the tip of the iceberg.

"Abby, someone literally picked my car up and moved

it into the middle of the drainage area by the school. Being a dick like that takes a coordinated effort. That's a bit of a sign."

"Yeah, I know. But people at this school are just dicks, like, unilaterally. To everyone." She nods in halfhearted acknowledgement, flipping her own mirror down to touch up the red on her lips. She turns to me and holds out the gloss. I recoil and she shrugs. Abby is pin-up beautiful. Her hair is this caramel color that lightens every summer, and her skin is a rich, cocoa brown. She got curves in eighth grade, and her skin is expensive and flawless. Her mom got her into modeling when she was young, and she's been landing some big print ads lately. At a thousand dollars a gig, the money in her college account has grown to Ivy League proportions over the years. I've always been her alt-friend with near-black hair that I sometimes wear in braids on either side of my head because it's literally the only hair style I know how to do. My friend has always said she'd trade me her hair and curves in a heartbeat for my green eyes. I wish trades like that were a thing. Done deal. Enjoy the lanky body with knobby knees and size A cups.

"Look, everyone has gotten older," she begins, flipping her mirror closed and flicking her long-nailed fingertips toward my door handle in a gesture that urges me to get out. My hand grips the handle, but I can't seem to bring myself to open the door. "You're living in the past too much. People don't care about pranks and childish things like grudges or whatever."

"You mean bullying," I correct. A grudge would mean I did something wrong, and I would know *who* I wronged. I've never known any of it. It's just these little things that always came out of nowhere and built up. And yeah, maybe Abby is right—our school is full of immature pranksters. I've seen others get hit with the fallout, too. But for me, it wore me down.

"Fine, *bullying*. All I'm saying, June, is we're going to be eighteen this year—all of us. This is it, the last moments of unabandoned freedom and youth! We're supposed to party and stay out late and maybe even—*gasp!*—fail a class that doesn't count on our transcripts. And there are so many boys we need to kiss! I *know* you wanna kiss boys at parties, June."

I hate that I blush when she teases me. I get out of the car just to escape her conversation, but it only delays the inevitable. She's going to bring this all back to Lucas Fuller. It always comes back to him.

I've been in love with my neighbor since the day he moved in at the start of our sixth-grade year. We were instant friends, though admittedly, my attraction to him was heavily dimples and blue-eye driven at first. Our moms took turns with school carpool duties. We swam together in the same summer league. We wasted away afternoons licking sticky grape-flavored popsicle juice from our arms while we sat in the sun on the roof of the old Buick my dad stored in our back yard. Technically, Lucas Fuller was my first kiss—it was an eighth grade dare in the back of a field trip bus. Our lips were puckered, there was zero tongue, and our eyes were wide open. Even after that awkward kiss, not a single day passed without us either hanging out or texting each other good night. I made my mom drive me two hours away once to watch his freshman football game, and I was always the one yelling the loudest for his home ones.

Mostly—more than anything—Lucas Fuller was my person. I'm shy, painfully so, but never around him. We had a pact that we would never lie, and there would be zero secrets.

Now, that's all that's left.

The summer after our freshman year, it all just stopped. Everything—no rides, no glances in my direction, no acknowledgement of my existence. I called and texted and left so many unanswered messages. When I went to his house, nobody opened the door, even when I knew they all were home. My parents divorced around then, and my grandmother moved in because she got too sick to live on her own. My mom worked and took care of her, and when she couldn't, I did. Hospice came and went, my grandmother's belongings were set out in our driveway for people to pick through so we could collect quarters and dimes to piece together enough to cover her last few expenses. My world was falling apart, and my best friend, the one person who swore we would never keep secrets from each other, was both right next door and a million miles away. That's when Abby and I got closer. She'd been through a lot of the same things I was going through, and she's the kind of person who insists on helping.

Dragging me out to this party, though? It doesn't feel much like help. It's more of the torture variety.

"And would you look at that. It's a black Nissan pickup truck with . . . oh! FULLER1 license plates!" Abby points in the direction of an oversized tire as if I don't know it's Lucas's truck she's talking about.

"He's at every party, Abs. And no, I'm not going to talk to him. It's not like he doesn't know where to find me. If he wanted to talk, we would have by now." I look down at my feet while I push my fists into my pockets and shuffle along the blacktop. After a few steps, I run into my friend's waiting palms as she grips me by the shoulders and shakes me until I meet her gaze.

"Maybe you should just finally move on and spend tonight talking to someone—hell, *anyone*—else." Abby's eyes plead with mine for a non-verbal agreement that I'll try to be a normal high school senior for just one night.

"You're someone else. I talk to you," I quip. I'm only partly teasing.

Abby shoves off me and walks backward a few steps, giving me a challenging stare before spinning on her heel.

"I meant someone with a penis. And no, before you make another joke, I do not have a secret dick tucked away in my pants." Her pace picks up, bringing us closer to the front door of the party house. I laugh a little, silently, because her penis joke was funny, but by the time her hand is firmly on the D'Angelos' doorknob, my amusement has shifted to a need to vomit.

"Ready?" she asks.

"No." Her mouth twists to say "tough shit," and with one push, we're inside.

Competing music blasts from two separate rooms, the hard thump of indie punk trying to drown out rib-shaking hip hop beats. Faces I don't really recognize nod at Abby then me as we walk through the crowded living room toward the kitchen area. Two girls face each other over a coffee table littered with beer cans and vape pens, yelling about who is disrespecting whom. The overwhelming cacophony ratchets up my urge to run. Abby must sense it because she grabs my hand and tugs me close, keeping me right at her side until we get to the open doorway that leads to the back yard.

"Why is this fun again?" I say close to her ear. I'm still not sure she can hear me.

She bends down and flips open a red cooler filled with freezing water and melting ice. She fishes her hand around, coming up with two beers.

"Here. You're drinking one," she says, pulling back the tab then pressing the lip of the can to my mouth as if I'm a baby needing to be fed. I shake my head and step back, taking the can from her hand.

"I don't like beer."

"You've never tried beer," she retorts.

Our mini staring competition lasts about two seconds before I give in and take a small sip. Her mouth ticks up with satisfaction, but when she tips her head back to take a drink from her own beer, I spill a little of mine on the rocks and let my mouth sour. Beer is gross.

"Oh, my God, is that—? No. It couldn't be!" I recognize Tory D'Angelo's voice without having to turn and face him. His presence motivates me to take another drink of my beer; I suddenly regret pouring so much out.

"June Mabee!" He snakes his hands around my hips as he steps in behind me. I spit out what's left in my mouth and move away from him with a jerk of my elbow. We aren't close. In fact, the only real interaction he and I have had was when I let him copy my science quiz answers during freshman science. I hate myself for letting peer pressure work on me. I should have let the asshole fail.

"Aww, maybe Mabee, what's wrong?" He's drunk, which amps up his assholeness a little. He's been teasing me about my last name since junior high. So clever, saying it twice.

"You were right, Abby. Everyone's grown up so much," I say, giving my friend an icy glare. Her dry smile puckers on one side but she doesn't argue with my reasoning. Kinda hard with Tory still hovering around us, breaking all kinds of personal space rules. Most girls let him get away with it because, in terms of good looks? He's damn near perfection. While he's smug about it, his twin brother Hayden is nearly oblivious to the power he could have at his fingertips. Bronzed skin, chiseled jawlines, light brown hair that somehow makes them both look like they just got in from a jog along the beach—the D'Angelo boys are Calvin Klein models in the making.

"Don't you have some freshman to hit on?" Bless Abby's confidence. One of the best perks of our friendship is her ability to say those things I wish I could.

"Still sore that I wouldn't let you suck my dick this summer, Abs?" He actually pushes his tongue in his cheek to accentuate his crass reply. What a fool. She's going to burn him to the ground.

"Isn't it more like . . ." My friend takes a thin pretzel stick from a bowl on the patio table nearby and pinches it between her thumb and finger, holding it a few inches away from Tory's face. His eyes haze and his jaw twitches. Even though it's only the three of us here to witness her rip on him, the joke breaks through and embarrasses him. I wish I could trade her my green eyes for *that skill* right there.

"Come on, June. Looks like the cool kids are all over there," my friend says. She purposely ignores the raging bull she leaves standing alone and weaves our hands together to drag me along the deck.

"He's probably going to remember tonight all wrong and think I'm the one who said all that, you know." I step on a wooden beam and lift myself to sit on the deck's guardrail. Abby does the same, but swings one leg over so she straddles it facing me.

"Good. Then you'll have a reputation of not putting up with shit from douchebags," she says, pulling her phone from the small purse she's wearing across her body. She holds it up before I can protest and snaps my photo.

"Why? Why do you always do that? You must have an endless collection of me making dumb-as-hell faces," I protest. I start to laugh a little, too.

"If it didn't work on your foul moods so well, I wouldn't do it." She takes one more shot before tucking the phone into the zipper pouch of her bag.

That she has hundreds of those pics scratches at me a little. It means I've been in a foul mood hundreds of times. I had to come back to Public because we couldn't afford the Montessori school anymore, so maybe it means I get to reinvent myself a little. Maybe Abby is a little right in saying that we are all getting older—none of us are the same people we were two years ago. *I'm* not the same. At least, I don't have to be.

"I'm sorry." I half shout the words to my friend because the music is still making it hard to hear. I'm probably not going to be able to apologize to her more than this one time, so I have to make sure she hears it.

Her mouth curves slowly and she flits her thick black lashes at me before leaning forward enough to push gently at my shoulder.

"Aww, June. You're getting all mushy."

I squeeze my eyes shut in playful shame.

"Apology accepted. I'm not sure what you're apologizing for, but I'll save it up and cash it in when I feel like it," she says.

"Okay." I laugh, opening my eyes as my friend tips her head back and drinks the rest of her beer. When she's done, she leans forward again, reaching for my can to test the weight. It's still nearly half full, even with the portion I dumped, so I give it to her reluctantly.

Her eyes haze with suspicion.

"One of us is driving home. Let it be me, okay? I'm not a big beer girl anyhow." I hold her stare as we each grasp the cup between us. She hasn't fully committed yet so I don't let go.

"Abby, I promise. I'm going to stay, and I'll have fun, just not with the beer, okay?"

Her eyes squint a little more. She's still not buying it.

"How about this? Whatever they're doing in there, on the sofas"—some stupid game I would normally make fun of—"you take my beer and I'll go play that game." I regret my offer the second the cup leaves my grip. She gulps nearly half of it down before wiping her chin along her forearm and kicking her leg over the beam to stand on the deck.

Shit. We're going to play a party game.

"Well, all right then," she says, threading our fingers together and tugging me forward until I lose the balance battle and fall to my feet.

Not wanting to look as though I'm being dragged into this—even though I am—I loop my arm around my friend's and smile at her. She isn't convinced. She tosses her head back in laughter, but lets me save face while we make our way inside. At the huge sectional sofa , people are tossing dice on a giant trunk-style coffee table and picking small papers out of a bowl depending on the number they roll. Abby and I kneel on the floor behind a few of the others.

"I'm not next. You're next!" One of the many faces I don't know but recognize shoves playfully at another vaguely familiar girl. In their fit of nervous giggling, the one holding the dice glances in my direction.

"New girl! Your turn." Bile shoots up my throat and burns.

"Oh, no." I hold up a palm and shake my head as if refusing hors d'oeurves.

"She's being shy. She'll play. What's the game?" Abby takes the dice and plops them in my palm, which she has to pry open after lifting my fist from the carpet.

I make wide eyes at her while I hold my breath, but she shakes me off.

"You promised," she says, holding up the rest of her beer and tipping it back with an "*ahh.*"

I inhale deeply while the girl who volunteered me explains the rules. "You roll a number and pick out that many dares."

"So, I could have to do twelve dares?" I ask this as though I'm really going to roll these dice.

"Oh, my God, no! You pick them and then the last person who went gets to pick which one you do. Like, Naomi made me walk to the kitchen and back in her bra!"

This game seems incredibly complex for what it really is: Truth or dare, sans the truth part. I'd like to make a motion that we add the truth part back in, but that's because I'm painfully boring.

"So, who gets to pick my dare?" I'm still acting as if I'm really planning to play.

"I do." I recognize the voice without turning around. Of all of the faces I don't recognize here, that voice belongs to one I know I will. For as long as I have loved Lucas Fuller, Ava Pryor has hated me. I'd blame her for all the lame pranks I endured sophomore year, but overt bullying isn't her style. She's more of the "burn you with a glare" kinda girl, and that glare has this amazing power to make a person feel insignificant with a bat of her lashes. I glance over my shoulder and that stare is ready and waiting to zap my ego—what little there is of it—to shit.

"Lola went last," the girl I've identified as Naomi says.

"That's because I had to refill my beer. Scoot." Ava flits her fingers and the girls slide apart to make space for her on the center of the couch. She steps between Abby and me on her way to sit down.

"I'm not doing this," I mumble to my friend. She's already taken the dice from me, though, and thrown them on the table.

"It's time to stand up and show some balls." I meet her eyes, trying to plead my way out of this, silently begging her to take my turn, but with the slight cock of her chin I can tell she's going to make me walk through this fire.

"Four," Ava says, a tinge of disappointment in her tone that I rolled such a low number.

"Okay, so I just . . ." I reach toward the bowl and Ava taps it toward me with the toe of her white canvas shoe.

I pull it toward me and search the contents, hoping to find clues in the poorly folded strips of paper, but it's no use. It doesn't matter how deep I dig into the plastic snack bowl. I pick out four from the top of the heap and toss them on the table as I sit back on my heels.

"Let's see," Ava says, leaning forward and rubbing her palms. I'm sweating watching her meticulously unfold the first paper and drag her gaze along the scribbled line. She's twirling a lock of her white-blonde hair around her finger while her mouth moves slightly with the words. I stare intently at her face, trying to read her lips. She stops and flits her thick black fake lashes up to stare at me from underneath. Her mouth curves up on one side.

"This one." She tosses it on the table, but before I can grab it, Abby does.

"You didn't read them all yet," my friend says, looking at the paper and chuckling lightly.

"Don't need to. That one's the winner." Ava leans back on the oversized sofa cushion and folds her arms over her chest while crossing her legs.

"You afraid of the dark? Spiders?" Abby flicks the paper toward me with her index finger. I pick it up and read.

SPEND FIVE MINUTES IN THE GARAGE IN THE DARK

"Uh, not really . . . I guess." I feel as if there's probably a trick so I'm not going to boast confidently. There's a catch. I know there is.

"Good, then the time should just fly right by," Ava says, both sides of her mouth curved into an ominous grin. She glances down the darkened hallway behind me, toward what I assume is the garage door.

"Now?" *That sounded stupid. Of course now.*

"Uh huh," she says, flitting her fingers at me with the same nonchalance she had when she forced the girls to give up their seats. Ava is a stereotype. That stereotype is bitch.

"All right," I say through a sigh. I get to my feet and tug up my jeans a little, my shirt now feeling like a goddamn halter.

"Atta girl," Abby says, slapping my ass just before I make my way to the garage. Naomi is quick on my heels, probably to lock the door behind me. Do any of them realize I can hit the button inside?

The escape plan zips through my mind just as I open the door, but then it's quickly replaced with panic and dread so toxic that my knees buckle a little. Naomi pushes me inside and slams the door shut. The lock clicks behind me, and Lucas meets my stare. He's sitting on a folding chair with his phone in his palm.

"Oh, fuck me." Disdain slips from his mouth the moment everything goes black. *This* was the catch. Five minutes in the dark, locked in the garage, but not alone.

With Lucas Fuller.

I spin around and flatten my palms on the wall, feeling in search of a switch or the garage door opener. Something stabs at the side of my palm as I slide it closer to the door.

"Shit!" I mutter under my breath and feel along my skin. It's damp. I cut myself on something. My phone is in my back pocket, so I take it out awkwardly with the opposite hand; it slips from my grip and bounces at my feet. I want to cry. I also want to punch things.

I'm mid-squat when the glow of a phone light brightens the ground a few feet in front of me. I glance up and squint at the flash from Lucas's phone.

"Thanks," I say. I feel humbled, and mortified. My phone is just underneath the front end of one of the cars. Lowering myself, I reach out until my hand lands on it to drag it closer. The garage goes dark again.

Tapping on my phone with the hope it still works, I rest back on my legs, resigned to this pathetic position for the remaining four minutes I'm stuck here. The cracks on my phone screen take up most of the surface, and one of the corners is badly chipped. With my luck, I'm sure I'll find a way to prick my finger on it . . . *again*.

The metal chair Lucas was sitting in screeches along the floor, so I glance up to see whether I can see him. I can make out his form. His long arms stretch upward, and I bet if he jumped just a little, his fingertips would graze the ceiling. He's wearing a light T-shirt and jeans, a flannel tied around his waist. It's too dark with only my phone light to tell whether he's looking at me or not, and I'm not sure which I prefer.

As his feet slide closer, I let my body relax into a sitting position, legs folded around each other like a pretzel. I cup my broken phone in my lap and graze my fingertips along the screen to send shouty-cap swears to Abby. The dome light from the car flickers on at my right, and from my periphery, I see Lucas lean inside. He taps a button near the rearview mirror and the garage door lifts.

I stand to brush dust from my knees and ass, and flip my hair back just in time to come face-to-face with the source of that sharp pain I sometimes feel when I look out my bedroom window. Those blue eyes still glow like sapphires, even in the faintest of light, but the boyish dimples have given way to harsh angles and a set jaw framing emotionless lips. Lucas has always been three or four inches taller than me, but that difference feels even greater as he stares down at me.

"I didn't know you were in here." Fuck, I haven't spoken to him in two years and the first words I say are a pathetic apology for being in a garage at the same time. I roll my shoulders and force myself to stand straighter—taller. His head cocks to the side ever so slightly and he lifts his hand, holding the garage door opener out for me to take. I do, and I hate that I do. This is not how this conversation between us was supposed to go. *He* was supposed to apologize, not me. And he should be giving me flowers, not some taped-together garage clicker from one of his asshole friend's cars.

"Tell Ava she's a dick." He doesn't stick around to wait for my response, turning and taking long strides out of the garage with his hands shoved in his pockets and his pace evident of just how much he wants to get away from me.

There's a little more than a minute left on my time in here, assuming those assholes plan on sticking with their own dumb rule. By the time Lucas disappears around the bushes at the end of the long driveway, I've made up my mind to take his last bit of advice. With the garage remote in my hand, I leave the same way Lucas did and reenter the house through the front door, elbowing through the people gathered in the front room. I toss the opener into the bowl of paper dares, and the gossip fest that's probably going down on the sofa ceases immediately. I feel my best friend's eyes on me without having to look. My focus is set on the ice princess leaning forward and folding her hands on her pushed-together knees like she's some sort of lady.

"You're a dick, Ava." I hold her stare for a breath, just long enough for her to understand that I mean it, and I'm not afraid of her opinion of me anymore. I don't know where the chip on her shoulder came from, but I didn't put it there. If she wants to keep it, that's on her.

I glance down to where my friend is still sitting on the floor, and the approving grin that has spread across her entire face tells me two things: one, I've just entertained the shit out of her; and two, she's giving me a gold star for the night.

"This game is juvenile. Next time, I'll bring the games to the party, ladies, and we'll have some *real* fun." Abby winks at Ava as she gets to her feet and walks right through the middle of the group of girls still huddled around the scene. She reaches into her pocket and hands me her keys, then links our arms together as we turn our backs on only the first dose of drama we're bound to see this year.

I don't say a word and she doesn't ask questions as our feet hit the blacktop and we cut through the rows of cars lining the street. I notice that Lucas's truck is still here about a second before his headlights flick on and the engine roars to life.

"Looks like someone else thought that party was pretty

lame, too," my friend says. And because she's my rock, and because I don't lie to her, I tell her everything.

"He was in the garage. And he's a dick, too." I save that last part until we're walking right next to his unrolled window. I glance his way after I say it, and our eyes meet for a brief moment. When Abby and I get another full car length away, his tires peel out as he takes off.

"Well, if this ain't a new June Mabee," she says, swaying her hip into me. I gurgle out a faint laugh and smile with tight lips. My smile falls as soon as our arms part and my friend walks to the passenger side of her car.

Sure, I'm proud of what I did. Doesn't mean I don't wish like hell that none of it happened.

CHAPTER TWO

I guess I made a name for myself, beyond "that girl who lives next to the Fullers." That's what I'm usually called, especially by the girls who had crushes on Lucas in junior high and our freshman year. A few times, his groupies have tried to befriend me just to worm their way into a sleepover so they can stare at him through my window.

Joke's always on them. I don't have sleepovers, except with Abby, and she doesn't count because she's like family. That's my mom's rule. She's funny about having strangers in the house. Even more so since my dad left. I think maybe she's become really distrustful. I guess I have, too.

I wonder how many sleepover requests I'll get now that I'm "the girl who told off Ava Pryor." Maybe it was a deterrent for others. Though, judging by the fact I'm now walking through the halls of Public with not just one, but *three* other people, I can't deny that calling Ava a dick had some sort of quantum effect.

"So, where did you move here from?" Naomi, my first friend from the party, asks.

Abby laughs hard enough to spit out her iced latte. Her mom runs a coffee shop so we start every morning there. Even when I went to a different school, we both got up thirty minutes early to have our coffee talk time.

"You've known each other since fourth grade, when *you* moved here, Naomi," Abby says. She and I glance at each other with crooked smiles while Naomi literally stops in her tracks.

"We had the same homeroom freshman year," I add through a crooked smile. I shrug on the outside, but the truth is I only figured that out last night when I looked them both up in my freshman yearbook.

"I recognized her," Lola brags, tipping her head back as she pours the crumbs from her granola packet into her mouth. It's hard to tell whether she's bluffing or not. Lola has a certain cockiness about her, an appealing kind. I don't know her well enough yet, but when I do, I'll tell her she looks just like the girl from *Clueless*.

"I have to check in with the office," I announce at the sound of the first bell. I accept the awkward side-hug-squeeze from Abby. She's pushing the envelope today on the dress code. It's not so much the length of her shorts, but rather the words on her shirt. I'm pretty sure the asterisk filling in for the U between the F and CK isn't going to slide by.

"We all have first lunch, so I'll grab a table," Naomi shouts over the rush of people between us. She's maybe five-one, but she makes up for her small size with large volume.

Slightly bolstered by the fact I've somehow started my final year of high school with actual lunch plans rather than aimlessly wandering rows of tables with my tray, I push through the door without really noticing the body coming at it from the opposite side. If it weren't a glass door, I might have pushed harder, but seeing the familiar deep blue wool and white leather sleeves of Lucas's letterman jacket is like getting hit with a flashing red stop sign shrouded by flares.

"Sorry." Damn it. Back to apologies.

I step back to let him through, but to my surprise, he does the same. I catch the short twitch his mouth makes in amusement. It wasn't quite a laugh, but it was definitely light years from the scowl I got last night.

Not wanting him to change his mind, I push the glass forward and step through. He reaches to take the door's weight just as my hand lets go, and his fingertips run along the tops of my knuckles. It's nothing more than an accident, and I see the slight recoil in his arm when it happens. The effect on me, though, is exactly the opposite. I glow—flush with the shot of adrenaline and long-lost affection. I would swear he cut me, the leftover feeling along my hand is so strong.

"June!" Maggie Williams went to high school with my mom. Not here, ironically, but in Fort Wayne. Her and Mom are more Facebook friends than *real* friends, but Maggie's always been nice. And it's good to have a familiar face in the front office.

"Lucas! Wait!" she shouts, just before the glass door closes. I turn quickly to see whether he heard, hoping he escapes without her making some sort of embarrassing connection, like reminding him who I am even though we're neighbors. But the good student and well-mannered guy that Lucas is wins the battle and he turns, cracking the doorway open to hear her out.

"Can you take June here to your first hour? She's in your class."

I'm pretty sure Lucas and I both vomit a little. There's definitely a pregnant pause. The air is stagnant long enough for Maggie to blink twice with irritation and shake the paper she holds out for me to take. That little movement triggers my response, and I take my schedule from her hand.

"Sure," Lucas says, flashing his classic tight-lipped smile. I know him well enough to recognize that's the one he gives when he's playing nice. He made that face when Tory D'Angelo won MVP at the eighth grade football banquet, and he made it again when his parents told him they were spending New Year's three years ago camping at Yosemite, just the three of them. Those lips are air-tight right now, and that bend is going to break even the moment we step back into the hallway.

"Let me know if you need anything today, 'kay, hon?" Maggie's already answering the attendance line, pen in hand and phone propped on her shoulder. Not that I could ask her to rewind life a hair or two and not mention the idea of Lucas showing me anywhere, but maybe if she weren't swamped I could make up another question or two to stall and let him get away.

I suppose he's doing a fine job of running away as it is, though. For every step he takes, I have to make two. I'm not that much shorter, so I know he's pushing it. Our first hour is physics, the farthest building on campus, which means "I'll be sweaty and breathless by the time my ass finds a seat in there."

I said that part out loud. *Shit.*

"Not my problem," Lucas says over his shoulder. His arms pump as if he's a speed walker. He pushes open the double doors of the A building and flings them open enough to give me a chance to zip through behind him. He was probably rooting for them to close on my shoulders. All I can focus on are his leather sleeves and that it's a little warm, now that we're outside.

"You know, it's like eighty, and humid," I say, somehow halting my words before tacking on a bit about how stupid his jacket is. I also think he's cute in it, which is fucking up my head right now. I'm both physically and emotionally hot, and I want to take it out on that jacket and the ego it represents. I've never even seen him play in a varsity game.

He doesn't respond, and that's probably for the best. Also, either I'm getting faster or he's slowing down because the gap between us is tightening. Students rush past us, probably taking up all of the seats in our class, which is still a good four hundred yards away. I'm almost in sync with his steps when he turns and stops in the middle of the walkway.

"We don't have to do this, you know." He points at me then to himself. I have no idea what he means, and my expression must say so because he explains. "Pretend we have some bond or shit. You have your life, I have mine that I've built here. Just go to class, hang out with your friend, get your straight A's or whatever."

"Friends," I cut in.

He shrugs and wrinkles his brow, annoyed.

"You said I should hang out with my *friend,* but I have *friends,* Lucas." *You used to be one of them.*

"Sure. Just . . ." He pauses, his jaw stiffening the way it does when he's frustrated. So many of his nuances are etched in my memory bank. With a slight shake to his head, he glances up and takes a deep breath, letting his shoulders quickly lift and fall. His gaze leaves the sky and lands back on me. "I'm just saying, it's not like we really know each other now. That's all."

He turns and continues down the path, but I don't bother to keep up. I let him get several feet ahead, far enough that the doors to the science building close behind him while I have many steps to go. I let him go in case I have to cry, but really, I'm just pissed. The clenched sensation in my gut makes me want to scream. My hand flattens along the bar for the double doors, but I stop before pushing and check my reflection in the tinted glass. I don't want to look the way I feel. While I don't really *know* people here very well, they know enough about me to put together the crush I once had on the guy who just walked into Physics. I'm already chasing him in there. I don't need to look upset about it, too.

With one heavy exhale, I push the right door open and slip quietly inside. The bells have sounded and the classroom doors are closed. I'm holding this golden late pass of a new student's schedule, though, so I can take my time. My steps are measured, a fraction of what they were outside. Might as well also take advantage of this time to cool down. I let Abby talk me into wearing my hair down straight. It feels like a damp warm blanket on my back and shoulders, though, and I'm pretty sure my flat iron work to smooth out the kinks has all been undone. My hair isn't curly, but it's far from perfectly straight. It's more tousled without the supermodel image that word conjures.

The class door flies open easily but I manage to grab the handle before it flings into the wall. My entry still catches most everyone's attention. I focus on the teacher, an older man wearing a shirt like my dad owned—collared and polo-style with a single breast pocket. Today's color is orange. *Vivid* orange. I wonder what the rest of his closet looks like.

"I'm sorry. I'm new, and I had to stop at the office," I explain, diffusing the disgruntled look forming on his face. He wasn't here my freshman year. I knew all the teachers, despite only knowing maybe six students.

"Oh, yes! Miss Mabee." A few snickers are poorly masked by fake coughs. People my age are so amused by alliteration. He takes my paper and tips his glasses forward on his nose. He has a thin comb over, and the gel he used to swipe the hairs from right to left is still fresh. It glistens.

"I hope you're all right with a front-row seat," he says, bending at the edge of his desk to sign my form. He points with the tip of his pen to the only open seat in the classroom. I've already noticed it though, and the six-foot-something pissed-off jock sitting behind it.

"Here you go," the teacher says, handing back my paper. I keep my focus on the teacher's name on the page rather than the desk I'm sliding into. He didn't say it when I walked in, so the pronunciation is still a mystery to me —*Slatvka.*

Situated in my chair, I lean forward, elbows on the

small desktop so my hair doesn't tangle itself with anything Lucas-related behind me. I'm so obsessed with that fear that I reach behind my neck and sweep it over my right shoulder, entwining it with my mechanical pencil and flinging it around like a rogue swing set.

"Oh, my God," I whisper just as the pencil falls loose and onto the floor, bouncing backward of course. I run my fingers through my now-tangled hair, flattening it over my shoulder before I lean to the side and slouch in my seat in an attempt to reach my pencil. Our teacher is writing a list of the things we need to purchase for class on the board, and he's about to hand out the syllabus, which means I have about three more seconds before he turns around and spots my contortionist act. The rest of the class is already privy to this spectacular view. I'm nearly flat in my seat, head practically resting on Lucas's desktop behind me while my hand flails about, fingers stretching and pinching desperately at the floor but coming up with nothing but air.

Lucas groans and taps on the top of my head with a flick of his finger.

"Sit up," he says, leaning to his right while I do, and easily picking up my pencil. I twist just enough to glance at him sideways, taking the pencil in my hand. He doesn't let go right away, holding on for an extra two or three seconds to make sure I feel the burn of everyone staring at me. It irritates me, and the *thank you* I was preparing to say gets swapped out for an entirely different response.

"You could have picked it up sooner." I give my best glower, and he lets go of the tip, pulling the eraser out and tossing it back on the floor where it bounces a good four or five feet away. I breathe out a faint laugh then look back at him before turning around for the final time—*ever!*

"Good thing I don't make mistakes," I say, holding his gaze for a beat then turning to greet Mr. Slatvka just in time to take the syllabus from him.

I busy myself copying down the list of items that I plan to get tonight at the office supply store, feeling pleased with myself for how I handled that little interaction. When our teacher makes it to the back of the classroom, Lucas leans forward on his elbows and brings his mouth close enough to my neck that I feel the tickle of his warm breath.

"June," he says, breathing out my name. Both the sound and the feel of it along my skin force me to stop writing and pay attention to the prickle of every hair on my body. I blink at the words typed on my paper. "You are so far from perfect, you have no clue."

His weight shifts against the back of my seat where his desktop touches my chair, and I shake with the blunt force of his shoe on the leg of my chair as he rests it there, pushing me forward an inch or two.

This isn't one of those moments when I don't have a response. I've got one. It just wouldn't put him in his place. I say it in my head instead of giving him the satisfaction.

I know exactly how imperfect I am.

CHAPTER THREE

The day just gets better and better. And by better, I mean complete nosedive into a shit pool.

I had the option of getting out of school early this year. I earned enough credits, and none of the last hour electives appealed to me. I hate cooking, so culinary was out. I've already taken photography—*and* I live with a photographer—and the thought of being in the weight room with half of the football team trying to *bulk up* sounded like torture. But Abby has to be here for the full day, and she begged.

She begged, and I caved.

I figured being a teacher's assistant for the last hour would be a cake walk, and I'd be able to sit in the back of the class and fly through my homework in an hour. I'm assigned to a freshman algebra class, so the only work I'll have to help with is making copies and handing out paper since student grading isn't allowed. It looked promising, until Tory was camped out in Mr. Newsome's chair when I walked in. He's Mr. Newsome's favorite, because Tory

D'Angelo and his brother Hayden are the one-two punch on Public's basketball team, and Mr. Newsome is their coach. I could have been assigned to any classroom for this hour, and somehow, I'm doubling up with him.

"Why the glum look, Mabee?" Tory twists side to side in the office chair a few feet away from me. I've been pretending to ignore his existence while I review the stack of class rules and instructions I collected today, and jot down lists of other teachers I can potentially assist.

"No glum look. Just relishing how comfortable this box is, and what a gentleman you are," I say without peeling my eyes from my work. I'm sitting on a large storage bin filled with donated school supplies like note cards, hand-wipes and tissues. This class is full and there are no extra chairs. Tory hasn't moved from his seat—too busy playing solitaire on the teacher's laptop.

"Oh, I'm a gentleman. I offered to share." He swivels so his knees are square with me then pats his thigh.

"I'm not sitting on your lap," I say, my tone flat and head tilted. I've twisted my hair into a knot and poked two pencils through it to hold it in place. It's slipping a little, so tiny hairs stick out in all directions and tickle my face. I pull the pencils free to retwist.

"You should leave it down," Tory says. Ignoring him, I continue to twist, holding one pencil in my hand and one gripped by my teeth.

"I'm serious," he continues. I give in with a sideways look as I poke one pencil through my attempt at a bun; once I feel it's secure, I take the pencil from my mouth and maneuver it around my head.

"I'm waiting for the misogynistic joke that usually

follows everything you've ever said to me." I wiggle the second pencil until everything feels secure then let my hands fall flat to my lap, my focus still on Tory.

A few seconds pass without him saying a word, and while I partly brace myself for a doozy of a comeback, a piece of me also feels guilty for laying into him after a compliment. He eventually shrugs and turns back to the computer, clicking away at card graphics while wearing a flat line on his mouth.

"June, can I get a hand with these?" Mr. Newsome asks. Delighted to leave the close quarters with Tory, I unfurl my legs and stretch to a stand as I take a stack of stapled papers from the teacher. Rather than passing several at a time up the rows, I drop one at every desk, mostly to stretch the activity out a little longer.

There are a few packets left when I get to the last student, so I hold them up to signal I'm done. Mr. Newsome nods for me to leave them on his desk, and I head back to my box-seat only to find it occupied by Tory. The desk chair is turned to the side for easy access, and my papers are stacked in front of the laptop. The asshole makes me grin a little and I glance down at where he's slouched on the box, back against the wall, as I pass by. He looks up from his phone for a hint and our eyes meet.

"Yeah, yeah. Don't say I never gave you nothin'," he says with an uneven smile and shift of his eyes. His thumb scrolls through a series of Instagram images like he's playing roulette, and my mouth forms the shape to utter "thank you" back to him. Before the words come out, though, he stops on a picture of a woman in barely-there lingerie, and I decide to just be smug about this. Might as well let this class period end with his nice gesture rather than open an opportunity for him to show me all of his sordid follows on social media.

The bell is mid-ring by the time Tory is up from the box and headed to the door. He holds out a fist to pound with Mr. Newsome, who suggests he only go half-speed in football practice and save yourself for the sport that really matters.

Tory laughs quietly and nods, leaving the room without looking back to where he left me the comfortable seat. I wait for everyone to clear out so I can pitch an idea to Mr. Newsome, but as the last few students leave, Lucas slips in and I practically sprint back to the chair. Pulling the pencils from my makeshift bun, I let my hair fall to my left side to shade my face and provide camouflage.

"You have a sec? I need help on something, and I'm not sure how to handle it." It's a different tone from Lucas than I've been hearing; this one is more like the boy I grew up with. There's an uncertainty to it, and respect. Our interactions have been far from courteous.

"Sure, you wanna step outside?" I tense at Mr. Newsome's response. Clearly, he means it's not private in here.

"No, it's—" I turn my head and my hair slides apart like a veil, and my eyes hit Lucas's for a breath. He holds his stare on me and responds. "It's fine. It's not anything private."

Emboldened by being allowed to stay, I tuck the hair behind my ear and offer an apologetic smile that's quickly dismissed when Lucas turns his shoulder to me and shoves his hands in his pockets. I blink away and return my focus to my papers, drawing the same doodle of flowers and leaves that I started earlier in the day.

"What's going on?" Mr. Newsome's tone is lowered, but I can still hear every word. *I should leave.*

"It's about Tennessee," Lucas says. I'm guessing it's college. Even though I quit attending Public games when I quit going to school here, it was impossible not to hear about them. Lucas started as a sophomore, and they went to state last year. Plus, he's always been smart, so I imagine his college options are plentiful. A lot bigger than the tiny list I'm left with now that we're surviving on wedding photos. Not that I have any clue what I want to study or become. I just want to go somewhere different; reinvent myself a little.

"I see. You know how I feel about it, but it's up to you, really," Mr. Newsome says. I can't help the eavesdropping, and the exchange has my curious mind buzzing. Tennessee isn't that far from here, maybe a five or six-hour drive. Not that I'll be driving there to visit him or anything. The time I spent on that calculation was wholly unnecessary.

"If it were up to me, I wouldn't be here, would I?" Lucas laughs lightly, but it sounds frustrated. I tilt my head in time to catch him running his hand through his thick hair then rubbing both palms on his face. "Gah! Maybe I should just flip a coin!"

Mr. Newsome laughs at the joke, but Lucas doesn't. I turn my head to the side again to inspect his face, in search of those little tells he's always had that once served as windows into his true feelings. For the briefest moment, his lips twitch, almost as if he's about to be sick. He's angry, maybe trapped, but it washes away in a flash when he catches me looking.

He sniffles and his eyes flit back to Mr. Newsome.

"You know what? I'll figure it out. I gotta get to practice." He lightly pounds his left fist against the door frame as he takes a step back. Our eyes meet one last time, and I can tell he would rather I wasn't here for whatever this conversation is really about.

"Let me make a call, talk to him." Mr. Newsome's plea does little to break through the guards Lucas has already raised.

"Maybe. I'll let ya know. Whatever, right?" A deep raspy laugh comes from his chest as he disappears around the doorway. Mr. Newsome steps out, holding the door open with his foot while he throws a Hail Mary.

"It might help! Lucas?" Mr. Newsome's fingers rap against the door frame, counting down the seconds it probably takes Lucas to walk to the end of the hallway and out the double doors. His chin eventually falls to his chest, and he mouths out "damn it."

I gather my stack of papers and relocate my doodle to the bottom of the pile along with my list of alternate teachers I could help this semester. It doesn't feel like the right time to ask.

I'm pushing in the chair when Mr. Newsome turns his focus back to the inside of his classroom, his eyes flashing quickly with shock as he remembers I'm in here, waiting.

"June, sorry. You know Lucas, right? From your freshman algebra class?" He lets the door shut behind him and moves to one of the desks that face his, leaning back to sit on the desktop. I give him a crooked smile and short laugh.

"Yeah, he's hard to forget," I say, not mentioning all the ways Lucas and I have history. Even if our relationship was drawn from our time in Mr. Newsome's class and nothing else, Lucas would have made an impression. He took our extra credit math games so seriously, leaping with pounding his chest when he scored the most points and earned credit he didn't need. He tested out of geometry and second-year algebra and went right to pre-calc. I'm smart, but I don't enjoy math, not like Lucas did . . . *does*. At least, I guess he still does.

"Kid has a chance to go to MIT." He mutters the words under his breath, but probably louder than he realizes. Lucas is choosing between MIT and Tennessee. He shakes his head out of a semi-trance and palms both his cheeks, clapping them lightly. "Sorry, I was just thinking out loud. What did you need?"

My thumb runs along the edge of my stacked papers, feeling for the staple on the last form, the one I wrote my backup list of teachers on.

"You have two assistants." I'm hemming, hawing, hedging—all of it.

His head falls back with a belly laugh, and I pause with my thumb on the top of the page I need for reference.

"I guess you could say that, but Tory D'Angelo isn't much of an assistant. I just like keeping an eye on that kid, keeps him out of trouble. I was glad they gave me two of you. I promise I won't overburden you." He leans forward and cups the side of his mouth. "I know some of you like to use these gigs to get homework done."

A nervous laugh shakes my chest and shoulders.

"Yeah, umm." I mash my lips together and kick myself inside over what I'm about to do. "No, I was just going to say I hope it's okay that I stay, even though you already have Tory. I . . . I like it in here. It's quiet enough."

He punches out a laugh and pushes off from the table, leaning forward to the stack of papers Tory left behind. He rolls them and slaps them against his other palm.

"If you can find quiet with Tory in the room, then you have Zen secrets I need to learn." He holds up the roll of papers. "The guy had one job today, to make sure he took these things home."

"I can give them to him," I volunteer, clearly having some out-of-body experience.

Mr. Newsome lowers his head and holds the roll out toward me, his head cocked to the side.

"You sure? I don't mind hassling him. It's one of my favorite hobbies," he jokes.

I shake my head and smile. "No, really. I don't mind." *Yes, yes! I do mind. What is this being that has inhabited my body and is making me do things I am loathe to do?*

"Great."

And in less than a minute, I go from fixing the debacle that is my last hour of the day to walking out of Mr. Newsome's class with a sweaty stack of papers from teachers who probably don't expect Tory to follow instructions anyhow.

After I exit the building, I unbend Tory's sheets and stack them with mine, noticing culinary on the top. At least I don't have to cook with him.

"What took you so long?" Abby swings her feet out

and leaves the comfort of the short cement wall that weaves between the math building and library.

"Overachiever," I say, handing her the stack of papers. She scrunches up her face and taps on Tory's name with her thumb.

"You are? Or he is?" She's joking, of course. I take the papers back and feel for my keys in my front pocket. Tomorrow, I'll be bogged down with a heavy bag and folders.

"I'm stuck being a TA with him in Newsome." This is actually the first lie I've ever told Abby. I comfort myself with the logic that it's a slight exaggeration. I'm not stuck. I just blew my chance to get *un*stuck.

Abby lets out a slow laugh that starts like a trickle but becomes a fire hose of amusement as she crosses her arms and has to pause to catch her breath.

"Holy shit, you have the worst luck! The only person worse to be stuck with is Ava." I smile into the air while I press the unlock button on my key fob.

"Yeah," I hazily agree. Though that isn't really true. There's one person who would even top her on the list, and I can't seem to get away from him. Even when we both try.

CHAPTER FOUR

T his marks the second time I've been to the D'Angelo house in three days. That's a record for me, one I had no intention of setting. I figured coming here now, though, during football practice, would spare me having to see the twins or any of their friends.

Lucas.

I've never prayed harder for my little beater of a car to not break down. It's idling pretty high as I crawl along the D'Angelo's street. My fifteen-year-old Honda may be approaching two-hundred-thousand miles, but it got me through a year of back-and-forth to my other school without fail. It was loyal by me, so I'm loyal by it.

As if I could get a new car.

The white brick home with black trim and fancy shutters comes into view as I slow at the side of the opposite curb. This place looks a lot different in the daylight. I'm pretty sure there were condoms hanging from the huge oak tree in the center of their front yard when I left Saturday night. I wonder whether the twins took care of the mess or if their parents deal with it, chalking it up to the price of having two popular teenagers in the house.

I kill my engine and lean forward to kiss the top of my steering wheel, a superstitious gesture I started a month ago when the pinging sound became louder. I'm busy separating Tory's papers from my own when I notice someone moving toward the back of the wide driveway that winds up the side of the property and to the infamous garage at the back of the twins' house. A bolt flashes from the back of my neck straight to my gut, my heart pounding with a dose of adrenaline. I'm not even sure what I saw, but just being here after what happened in that garage two days ago puts me on edge. Without pause, I sink down below window level, my knees bent as far as they will so I practically rest my shins on the gas and brake pedals.

No matter who it is, I now have to stay here until I'm sure they're gone. I won't be able to climb out gracefully, and I'm not certain I didn't just make a scene. My car sorta sticks out, what with the patch job on the driver's side fender and the two-tone blue paint from years of enduring Indiana winters and salted roads. But from across the street I'm not immediately visible, and I intend to stay that way.

I slow my breathing to hear what's happening outside, but it's no use. I'm basically panting like an overheated golden retriever. And my makeshift bun has fallen to shit yet again, so I'm swimming in a web of my own hair. When I hear what sounds like the rumbling of a nearby vehicle, I brave lifting my body just enough to see out my driver's side window. A small trail of exhaust puffs out from behind the retaining wall. Someone is probably pulling out of the garage, which means if I wait another moment, I can drop these papers at the front door and put a rock on top of them, call it a day.

I swallow and flinch when I see the chrome bumper, but hold steady, feeling pretty well-hidden. A deep gray truck rolls into view then pauses again, no more exhaust to obscure the details. For a moment, I think maybe someone forgot something inside, but even as I rationalize, I know better. I'm glued to the scene, and I don't think I could not follow through, merely to confirm this awful gut feeling. I don't want to be right, mostly because this is something I don't want to be burdened knowing. It's too late, though. Really, I knew it the second I saw the color of the truck. It's too easy to put together.

I *know* that truck.

I see it every night.

In the driveway next door to me.

Still, even in the face of this blatant evidence, I hope there is something else happening, another explanation. The truck continues its path backward, the dark silhouette of the driver just vague enough that it could still be explained, could be anyone.

But the license plate—I know that plate.

The brake lights trigger more panic, and I tuck myself a little lower in the seat, ready to duck out of view, but the truck is idling again. Waiting.

For someone padding down the driveway in bare feet.

Mrs. D'Angelo isn't wearing much. It's mid-afternoon, and I don't know whether she's a stay-at-home mom or if she goes to an office every day, but I do know Lucas's dad does. He works in Indy at a big law firm. And whatever he is doing at the D'Angelos' house right now doesn't look like business. It also doesn't look neighborly. It looks like a secret, the kind I'm certain my dad had. The kind that rips families apart.

Her T-shirt rises up the length of her thigh as she lifts up on her toes and reaches through the driver's side window. They kiss. That much I can infer. She takes his hand and he lets her as she falls back down to her heels, the white sleeve of his dress shirt rolled up to his elbow. I wonder if he even bothered to tuck it in. A sourness coats my taste buds at the image, and whether I want to or not, I superimpose my dad in the same position, of leaving some woman's house who isn't my mom after having . . .

They hold on to each other in the way people in love linger, only this . . . it isn't love. It's a scandal. It's four in the afternoon, and I've seen way too much.

The truck's brake lights go dark again so I duck low in my seat, completely hidden. There's nothing more to see. Now, it's only time to wait. I'm tempted to sit up tall enough to catch Mr. Fuller's face as he drives away, but I don't know what I'd do if he saw me. I'm already sitting in a car he could recognize. If he sees me here, I'll be living with more than knowing this secret, I'll be living with knowing that *he* knows I know.

That's messy.

Messier.

I feel sick.

The truck's engine fades into the distance, the familiar turn up ahead signaled by the change in gears just before I hear nothing. I can't fathom Tory's mom hanging around the front of the house in the thinnest, shortest T-shirt in the world, but maybe she is, so I stay hunkered down for almost a full three minutes. I lift myself up slowly, my legs cramping from the awkward position, and I rub at my knees and thighs as I get up high enough to scan my surroundings.

The street is quiet. The house is quiet. I glance to my right, to the seat where my school papers are splayed out with Tory's on top. He doesn't really care about any of this. And he won't do anything with them if I give them to him. I promised Mr. Newsome, but really, what do I owe that guy?

I might be tipping the scale in the direction I want, but who cares? I crank the engine, thank every god I'm aware of that it starts, and drive home the long way so I don't have to turn around and risk being noticed.

I told Abby I would be over today, but all I want to do is hide and figure out how to emotionally sort this new baggage. I want to donate this baggage; give it away. It's not mine, yet here it is, taking up *my mental space!*

I can't stop diving into my life of two years ago, my dad explaining to me that sometimes people grow apart while my mother sobbed and slammed doors upstairs. His quick departure. His quick engagement. How young the other woman is. How disappointing my father had become. How much it hurt to go through. It would hurt Lucas, learning this. He wouldn't believe me because, well, we don't talk. But eventually, he would have to.

I . . . could hurt him with this.

I shake my head, hating the satisfying feeling that

45

thought leaves etched in my chest. This is not the person I am.

My trip home isn't long enough, and the punk music I turn up loud enough that my nearly dead speakers buzz doesn't do shit to distract me from processing all of this. I'm not stupid—people cheat on other people all the time. My father included. But that was *my* life crisis. I had no choice but to suck it up and push through to the other side. Seeing Lucas's dad having an affair forces a choice on me like a ton of falling bricks. It's this heavy wet blanket that suffocates me. I have a choice: tell Lucas, or keep this to myself and try to simply forget. It's that I know *why* I would be telling him that eats at me. I would be telling him to watch him go through everything I did. And then I'd step back and watch him do it alone.

He and I aren't friends. We don't talk, though I will see him every day for the next several months. If I tell him, he probably won't believe me, and he'll hate me for being the bearer of the news.

Nobody knows what I saw. I'm the only one who has to live with this. If it ever comes out some other way, the fact I kept this secret won't be relevant. Nobody will care, because I am nothing to Lucas Fuller. He said as much. He has his life, and I have mine.

Resolved, I pull into my driveway and put my car in park without even a glance at the house to the left. Kicking the drip pan under my car, I purposely walk sideways, avoiding any temptation to check the other driveway, to inspect the garage, or to change my mind. I move to my passenger side and grab my papers from the seat, taking Tory's too. I'll just buy two of everything and set him up with supplies for the semester. I'll pick up a shift at the bowling alley to cover the cost.

I make it to our garage door, to the keypad, type in my birthday followed by my mom's, and duck to get inside faster. Mom is out with the van, so I halt for a moment in the center of the garage, giving myself one more chance to weigh my options. My gaze lands on the extra remote taped to the wall with Velcro. The higher the garage door rises, the more defined the remote becomes thanks to the light. What are the odds? Me and the D'Angelos have the same goddamn garage opener.

I blink at it once then curl my right hand into a fist, the memory of the one Lucas handed me vivid in my memory —that night, the look on his face, playing in my head like a hi-def movie. I push aside the temptation to retaliate, hurt for hurt, and leave the burden of what I witnessed behind me on the garage floor. Then I march forward and slap my hand on the remote to close it off behind me. I push through the door and head straight to the stairs, not bothering to stop in my room before stripping away my clothes and turning on the hot water for a shower. I'm numb as I step under the falling spray, and don't really want to clean anything. I just want to stand here for a while and think, or rather try *not* to think. It's inevitable, though. As small as my world feels sometimes, right now, the box is closing in. I heave a sob—just one—and press my palms into my eyes. I tilt my head back to let the water wash away any evidence along with the renewed rage I have for my dad. Opening my mouth to let water fill the space, I test my voice in case I need to scream. The urge is gone, so I right my head and spit the warm water out.

Football practice isn't over until 6:30. I could go out for my supplies and be back without ever having to see anyone from that house about a hundred feet to the west of me. My body is listless, though, so with a towel wrapped around my hair and another wrapped around my body, I pad out the door, leaving steamy footprints on the wood floor.

There's this strange pain in my heart that holds me to the bed. I want to see him. Both of them—Lucas *and* his dad. I'm not sure why. Whatever the reason, I don't think it says anything good about me.

She started calling about forty minutes ago, and eighty-one missed calls means I probably slept through a lot of vibrations on my phone. Amazing, since it's stuck to my face. My head aches from the pull of the towel still wrapped around my damp hair. The towel on my body is still loosely held in place. I catch Abby's current call right before she hangs up (no doubt only to try again).

"Yeah, I know. Sorry." I've learned that it's better to head her lectures off at the pass. I sit up and unwrap my hair to relieve the pressure and see what kind of mess I've made.

"You know, I thought you were dead." She's exaggerating—by a lot. She must need something.

"Surprise! I'm not," I say, clutching my towel together at my chest while I drag my body and the discarded wet one from my head back to the bathroom. "I think I figured out how to make beachy waves, though."

Combing through my hair with my fingertips, I wait for the big ask that has to be coming any minute now. After several seconds of silence, I stop noodling with my head and hold my phone out to see if Abby hung up.

"You there?"

"Yeah, I'm waiting. Beachy waves," she says, annoyed I haven't told her yet.

I cough out a short laugh and go back to pushing around loose hairs. My head is still super wet, but maybe an entire night in the towel would do the trick.

"I was kidding, sort of. I slept in a towel," I say.

"Oh. Well that's not a very big breakthrough. Look, I need you to do me a favor." And there it is.

"Sure," I agree. This is a mistake.

"Awesome. So Friday, after the game, we're going to this place off the Interstate about fifteen miles or so. The road is dirt, so if your mom will let you take the van—"

"Hold up," I break in, snapping out of the beachy waves trance to realize the details of what she's signing me up for. "No more parties. I did a party."

"June, you *barely* did a party. And senior year is not a single-item checklist," she says.

"Yes, it is." I'm quick. "And that last party was pretty close to a low point."

"Ha, no way," she says. "I refuse to let you diminish what you achieved."

My friend is moving around while she talks, and sometimes her face muffles her words, but I get the gist of her argument from a few keywords—"stood up to her" and "made friends."

"I made some enemies too," I argue. I'm being contrary,

but I also just woke up and everything from a few hours ago is resurfacing in my thought pool.

"You already had those enemies, so nothing new. Now, Friday. Do you want to pick me up and drive us to the game? Naomi and Lola are in too, and there's a lot of room in the van. That way we can go right to the creek—"

"Abby!" As if shouting her name has ever gotten her to give up a fight.

The line is silent for a few seconds. I finally accept that she is not going to give in and I am going to another party.

"You know minivans aren't off-road vehicles, right?" I wait through more silence from her, finally giving in with a sigh. "Yeah . . . I'll pick you up before the game."

"Stellar. Okay, see you in the morning." She ends the call without giving me a chance to reverse course.

The smell of burnt tomato is carrying upstairs, which means my mom must be home and attempting to cook. My dad was a griller. He still is, I guess, for another woman and kid in Florida. When he left, he took everything remotely culinary with him, which was fine because mom and I really only know how to make sandwiches and heat things up. Over the last year, though, Mom has been ambitious, with little to no improvement on her cooking skills.

I drop my towel and slide into my favorite sweats and long-sleeved T-shirt, then stop in my room to put on some flipflops and grab my keys and wallet. I have my supplies list memorized, so I leave the papers behind and rush down the stairs in time to move the pot from the burner before marinara sauce bubbles through the lid.

"Mom! You ruined dinner . . . again!" It's not a mean thing to say. It's a common thing to say.

"Damn it! Sorry!" My mom's voice is faint through the garage door.

I turn the burner off and note the still water in the pot she never turned on, curling my lips on the right side in amusement as I shake my head. A thud against the garage door pulls my attention away, so I leave the burnt sauce to cool and open the door for my mom, her arms weighed down with two cases of water. I take one from her and plop it on the counter just inside.

"Thanks. They had a two-for-one so I stocked up. I booked two shoots this weekend! One wedding and one family session." Her grin is so high it lifts her eyebrows. She's proud, and so am I.

"That was fast!" I say.

She nods after dropping the second case on the counter near the other one. Hands on her hips, she blows up at the dark brown cut of bangs that's grown long enough to hide her eyes. They part with her breath and she turns her focus to the stove, sighing.

"I'll order in," she says.

"Actually"—I touch her shoulder just before she moves to the drawer that holds our takeout menus—"I have to run out for school supplies. I'll pick up. Pizza?"

"Perfect." She looks relieved, and tired. She's spent the last few days calling every client she ever had at the studio and putting cards and flyers in every coffee shop within a ten-mile radius. My mom is incredibly talented at portrait photography, but the hustle part of the business doesn't come naturally. Hustle ranks right up there with cooking. Two jobs in one weekend—that's huge for her, and vital for us.

I leave my mom as she's pulling the smoldering pot away from the stove, slipping out the door before guilt tricks me into offering to clean that, too. I hate wet food, even crusty sauce bits singed onto metal.

Not paying much attention on my trip out the garage to my car, I press the unlock button on the key fob, triggering the honking sound and scaring the father-son duo playing hoops in the driveway just a strip of grass away from ours. The ball bounces away from their game, through the grass and toward me while they both stare. I stop it with my foot and glance up to meet their uneasy eyes.

I'm one-hundred percent certain this is weirder for me than for either of them. I was never really close to Lucas's dad, Todd, mostly because of his work schedule and how little he's home. But I would wave, he would wave, we'd pass pleasantries and make jokes and say hi. That little bit of banter ceased when Lucas pulled away. They're like a team, but I don't get the game we're playing. Every accidental interaction has been strange over the last two years, but now, I have the advantage of knowing what a scumbag Mr. Fuller is. And Lucas is blissfully ignorant.

I could crush them right now if I wanted to.

Without weighing the post part of my actions, I bend my knee and kick the ball back at them, punting it with the top of my bare foot hard enough that I'm pretty sure a bruise is forming. The airborne ball sails about two dozen feet to the right, up the property line and down the slope of our back yards into the thick weeds that Mom and I need to pull someday. It gets lodged under the crooked bumper of the old Buick my dad left behind, and it's rough arrival sends a flight of birds flurrying out of the yard.

Fuck. That was dramatic.

"Oops," I say, my eyes off in the distance, still watching the last few birds flap their wings and leave the premises. I can't believe I did that. I wonder if this is what my mom means when she utters "hormones" under her breath at me.

Following up my rash decision with another one, I decide the only thing that could make this worse is apologizing, so I continue my trip around the front of my car, get in, and turn the key.

It clicks.

Several clicks in a row.

The same clicks that the van made when we got the news that we needed a new alternator.

I lean forward—still not buckled in—and kiss my steering wheel, sure that the Fuller men are watching and wondering what the fuck I'm on.

"Please," I whisper, turning the key and pumping the gas once like my dad used to tell me. The ignition catches, the vibration of hope rattling my fingers where they grip the switch and key. I press the pedal down just a little more, and the sweet sound of a dozen-plus-year-old Honda firing up fills my ears.

I shift into reverse and peel out backward with my eyes glued to the rearview mirror. The car dips from the driveway and into the road and I crank the wheel with every intention of hauling ass out of this place and not coming home until I'm sure Lucas and his dad are inside. But whatever it is that's growing inside me, this thing that makes me speak up, act out, and be . . . abrasive and bold—it boils to the top. With my car tenuously idling at the curb in front of Lucas's driveway, I turn to my right, drawn to this gut feeling that he would be there. He was.

While his dad was wading through the knee-high crab grass and dandelion, Lucas had walked to the end of his driveway, probably on the off chance he'd get the last silent word. I meet his stare and promise myself not to blink, and not to drive away until he gives first. My nostrils flare, and the evening air chills the breath puffing from his barely parted lips. My window fogs, but I can still see him clearly under the glow of the streetlight—the same streetlight he and I used to beat with spoons to usher in the new year at midnight every January first. Maybe I imagine it, but the longer we hold on to this, the harder his chest heaves with what looks like anger and pain. The more time that passes, the more determined I am to win.

Without interruption of headlights and the heavy blaring of a car horn, I think maybe Lucas and I would have remained here in this dumb power play until the sun came up and my car ran out of gas. But we both blink and jerk our gazes away to the white Chevy Tahoe violently flashing its brights at me. I shade my eyes as if I have to visually confirm that it's Lucas's mom, but my buzzing pulse kicks in my sense of autopilot, and I reverse several feet to clear the Fuller driveway. Shannon Fuller doesn't glance my way once as she pulls into her home, driving straight into the family garage and closing the door the second the Tahoe's bumper clears the line. When I look back to where Lucas was standing, he's gone. I scan the driveway and the deepest part of our properties where our yards meet without a glint of him or his dad.

They've gone inside. Mom came home and the game is over. I'm still here, so I guess that means I won. I look back to the road ahead, the street empty through the next several stop signs, and I drive off for school supplies, pizza, and a handle on my pride.

CHAPTER FIVE

A bby can't fathom why I would go out of my way to do something nice for Tory D'Angelo. It's fair to call it into question, and I can't quite find the right words to explain that I'm not really doing anything to be nice to him; I'm doing it to make a show of being nice to him in front of Lucas.

I accepted the truth last night sometime around the checkout counter at the office supply store when I slid my credit card for seventy-four bucks' worth of binders, paper, labels, and pens. That's a chunk of money and two hours of my time spent on a guy I've never really liked. Yeah, it all sank in right at that moment.

"Your new boyfriend is coming. Go woo him with the protractor and pencil bag," Abby says, making a joke and pointing to the side parking lot where Lucas and the twins just pulled in beside each other.

"You're a bitch sometimes," I say, pushing off from my

front bumper, where we've been leaning and waiting for the last ten minutes.

"Yeah, I know. But at least I don't buy presents for assholes," she shouts at me. It draws a few stares from people hanging out in the lot, but I ignore them. My eyes are focused on Lucas, sitting with one leg out of his truck and his hand resting on his steering wheel. He's wearing a hat today, all black with deep blue AP embroidered on the front for Allensville Public. He's not strutting his peacock feather of a varsity jacket today either. Just a plain black T-shirt that hugs his biceps. No matter the argument I make in my head, the twins just don't fill out their shirts quite the same way Lucas does.

I fight the urge to lower my gaze to my feet when I get closer, and I'm rewarded by catching the moment Lucas notices me and shifts his position in his truck, his arm sliding from the wheel and his body sitting taller as I approach. He's talking to the twins, who stand right beside his truck. He nods out his front window, silently telling them to look my direction, and when Hayden and Tory see me, I put on the performance of my life.

My eyes leave Lucas and greet Tory, all my effort going into an effortless smile I hope breezes across my face.

"Mabee, what's up," the arrogant twin says. He holds out a palm and moves a few steps toward me.

Everything in my body buzzes with caution. This could be a trick. I always assume there's a trick waiting. Nasty words written about me in bathroom stalls, dicks drawn in the dust of my car window, late-night hang-ups from blocked numbers—it's hard to take Abby's word that juvenile shit is behind us, especially after the immature prank I fell victim to at the party.

I take Tory's hand, half waiting for him to pull it away at the last second and laugh like a third-grader. He doesn't. Instead, he tugs me toward his chest and wraps his other arm around me briefly in a hug. It's an odd feeling, being swallowed up by his masculine sent, the coolness of his freshly showered body under a T-shirt, his muscles hard, and his height about the same as Lucas. In a brief lapse of judgement, I indulge and understand why so many girls date him. This . . . it feels nice.

"Hey," I utter out nervously. I swallow down the dry feeling in my throat as we pull apart and glance to the right, to Lucas. It's as if he's watching a television show, concentration and suspicion denting his brow, his chin propped up on the back of his palm as he leans into the center console of his truck. His bewilderment sparks a joy in my chest that paints the richest sinister smile on my lips. I flit my eyes back to Tory and lift the bag. "I come bearing gifts."

Tory's eyes widen and he bares his teeth in a genuine grin mixed with laughter, like a boy being given a toy from Santa. For once, I don't even think he'll make something dirty out of this. He takes the bag from me, a plastic strap in each hand, and opens it wide to look inside. His mouth sours a little and he looks in deeper, exaggerating before popping his view back to me.

"School shit?" His neck shrinks into his shoulders in playful repulsion so I laugh to keep the mood light, shoving at him playfully. Flirtatiously.

"Yes, but you left your list in class yesterday. You left

all of your papers, actually. They're in there too." I make eyes toward the bag dangling from his hands, but his gaze seems stuck on me. I think I've stumped him . . . or he's afraid I'm falling in love with him. Whatever the cause, I think he's going to be kind to me right now.

"Thanks, Mabee. I mean, I probably won't use half of this shit, but . . . yeah. Hey, that was nice," he says, lightly laughing out his words. He opens his arms, welcoming me in for another hug, so I accept, resting my cheek on his hard chest and wrapping my arms around his body as far as they'll go. I look right at Lucas while I'm there, eyes hazed and smile daring him to do his worst.

"You're welcome," I say, letting my hands run along his sides while I let go. Tory tilts his head and looks at me sideways, and that little motion sends a chill through my chest. I'm flirting with fire now, and mixed signals aren't really part of who I am. I ball my hands into fists, shove them in my pockets, and take in my surroundings one last time. Both Tory and his brother watch me with puzzled expressions, Lucas, with his mouth a hard, flat line and eyes frozen cold.

I lift my hand to wave good-bye and turn to head back to Abby, focusing on the pattern her feet make as they kick back and forth from where she sits on the hood of my car. I imagine laughter behind me, partly because I expect it, but it's not real. When I focus, I hear nothing, not even the sound of people walking close behind. My body feels hot and my pulse is pounding in all parts of my body—fingertips, throat, ears, legs. I'm nearly jelly when I reach my friend, and she slides from my car and hands me my black and white checkered backpack, fully stocked with my "school shit."

"That went well," she says, an eyebrow raised. I can't feel my feet.

"I don't know if I have a barometer to measure how that went," I say.

"I don't know what that means." She shrugs. I twist my head to meet her eyes as we walk toward the main doors of the front building. The longer I look at her, the harder it becomes to hold in my laughter. When it breaks free, Abby joins in, and I'm pretty sure she thinks we're laughing because she doesn't know what a barometer is, but that's not what's funny at all. Nothing's funny, really. Things are nuts, way out of my comfort ballpark, but funny? Certainly not. Nervous, tenuous, doubtful, sad—that's what things are. And they're that way because of Lucas Fuller and what he is and was to me.

I part ways with my friend after the first building and begin my trek to the science area, the burning hole in my chest growing hotter the closer I get. My pace is quick enough that I get settled in my seat before Lucas arrives. I'm well into my act of being distracted by reading when I feel him shove his large body into the seat behind me. I jerk forward when his desk bangs into my chair, but grit my teeth instead of engaging him.

"Oops, sorry." His tone is flat and purposely cold.

I put the end of my pencil in my mouth, my teeth squeezing at the eraser with light pressure that takes all of my attention. Most of my attention. Not nearly enough of my attention.

"My dad says you're unhinged." His face is close to the

back of my head. My hair is pulled back into a messy bun today, which means every bit of his breath slithers around my bare neck.

"Your dad's a real good judge of character, I bet," I say just loud enough that I'm sure he hears me. I chomp down on my pencil hard enough to bend the metal band around the eraser and stare toward the door. Our teacher stands outside waiting for stragglers to rush in before he closes it. Being early was the wrong choice. It would have been better to just come face-to-face with him once than having to sit here in this cone of silence where I swear I can hear every breath he takes. I wonder if he can hear my heart thundering.

My chair shifts with the weight of his foot, which is now balanced on the back leg. He taps his toe against the metal a few times, and I refuse to believe he's unaware of how annoying that is. The door finally closing behind our teacher, I bend to my side and unzip my backpack, pulling out my new pack of folders and a notebook.

"You get Tory pink ones too?" Lucas chuckles out his lame tease as he leans forward, his hands gripped around the front of his desk to pull his body close. Rather than respond, I smile with my lips pressed together tightly and meet his glare blink for blink. He eventually leans back in his seat, laughing quietly while stretching his arms over his head, fingers woven together. I wait for him to look away before turning around.

Lucas's little digs stop as soon as our teacher's lecture begins, and the next hour is a blissful lesson on velocity. I'm almost free, the minutes nearing the top of the hour signaling the end of class, when Mr. Slatvka drops a bomb in the form of a giant Ziploc filled with Hot Wheels track and a few cars on my desktop.

"Mabee and Fuller, partners," he says, waggling his finger in a motion to nonverbally link us together. He moves down the line to the next pair before I register what just happened.

"Fuck," Lucas breathes out in a whisper behind me. I turn to match his groan with one of my own.

"I don't like it either," I say, lifting my hand to request to work with *anybody* else. Before our teacher turns to notice me, though, the bell sounds and the classroom erupts into chaos. The final bag in his hand is given to a group of three, the benefit of being near the end in a world of odd numbers. I lower my hand slowly and wonder why all of this is happening to me.

"It's fine. Just give me the bag and I'll do everything for us," Lucas says, pulling his backpack from the side of his desk and slinging it over his shoulder as he stands. His T-shirt lifts up a little when he weaves his other arm through his shoulder straps, and my eyes zero in on the tanned line where his dark jeans rest low on his hips, a red band from his boxer briefs showing above the waistband. At least, I imagine they're briefs. Shit, I'm imagining him in briefs.

"No, I'll do it. Screw you," I say, tossing the bag into my backpack and zipping it inside before standing and sliding my bag over my shoulder.

"Fine, whatever," he says, looking off to the side as he brushes by me and moves out the door. I let the rest of the class filter out to form a human wall of space between us, but my eyes still lock on his position the minute I leave the room. He pushes through the double doors, and the tinted glass does little to dissuade me from stalking him with my eyes until I'm outside, too. I follow in his steps around the media center, toward the gym where I expect he'll peel off and duck inside for weights or some other stupid jock thing, but instead, he fishes out his keys from his pocket and continues toward the front of the school.

He's leaving. And judging by the way he scans to his right and left, he's timing his steps perfectly to catch the front gate before it locks and forces him to exit through the office. He slips out undetected and jogs into the sea of student parking spots, stopping at a red sports car about four rows deep where he ducks inside the passenger door and fades in with the rest of the mundane background.

We're seniors now. Almost eighteen. Adults.

Different people than we were.

I wonder who Lucas has become.

CHAPTER SIX

I'm two days back at my old school and already doing a boy's homework for him. Granted, this is technically my homework, too, but still, there's some tragic irony in this.

It's taken me an hour to rig the tracks in a way that this experiment will work with only one person. By the time my mom walks through the door from a quick grocery run, I'm sweaty and trigger-happy irritable. In case she couldn't tell by the cold shoulder I gave her when she walked in, I drop a big fat F-bomb when the tape gives way under the weight of the cars I carefully balanced on the makeshift bridge from the wall to the table. The only car to make the full trip before the bridge collapses is sailing off the end of the table as my mom steps into the kitchen. It ricochets off of her shin.

"Playing with your old toys, I see?" She rubs at the spot where a tiny Pontiac Firebird nailed her about six inches below her knee.

"I fucking hate this school!" I rip the intact tracks apart in my mini tantrum. I snap out of it quickly and am met by my mom's disappointed stare. "Ducking, sorry," I correct.

Her straight-lined lips curl up on one side as her eyes squint in tepid forgiveness. Our swearing arrangement is we can auto-correct swear in front of each other. *Ducking* gets used a lot.

"Coffee break?" She's still giving me her sideways look as she sets a plastic bag on the counter and pulls out a roll of towels and a package of our favorite brew. It's her silent acknowledgement of my bad mood met with her own warning that I've used my free pass. I breathe in and hold my chest full for a few seconds, then relax my shoulders with a heavy exhale.

"Coffee break, yeah," I relent. I got hooked on coffee after dad left. Mom sometimes got up really early in the morning for no reason, and I'd find her down here before the sun came up sipping on straight black coffee. I acquired the taste after six or seven cups, and now coffee breaks have become our thing.

She fills the pot at the sink and holds up her fingers, switching between one and two.

"Two," I say, answering how many cups I want. "Always two." A pathetic, tired laugh falls from my lips and I rest my head on my arms on our kitchen table. I roll one of the cars back and forth in front of my face while I consider finding this stupid experiment on YouTube so I can copy someone else's results.

Once the coffeemaker starts brewing, my mom leans against the counter with her hands gripping the edge on either side of her.

"So, what is this mini Daytona thing all about?" she says, nodding at the few pieces of track that ended up on the floor. I bend down and pick them up, slapping them on the pile on the table.

"Physics experiment on velocity," I say.

"Ah," she says, the brewer gurgling behind her. She turns to watch it finish. We both like our coffee piping hot, even in the heat of summer. "Seems like a lot of moving parts to do on your own."

"Yeah, well my partner sucks," I let out, not really thinking.

"Already? On day one?" she asks.

"Uh huh," I mutter, hoping that now that she's busy pulling the pot from the warmer and pouring our cups she'll move on to something else. She slides my cup to me and leaves what's left in the pot to keep it warm. When she joins me at the table, cradling her World's Best Mom mug in both hands as she blows steam from the rim, I know she's going to keep fishing.

"Most people met right after school or during study hall, but my partner plays football." I lift one brow and tilt my head to the left, toward the Fuller's house. She studies me a for a few moments then slowly nods, a faint frown at her lips.

"I see. Hence why you couldn't meet up after school. Convenient you live right next door to each other though, so maybe . . ." She leans her head to the right and glances toward the Fuller house. It's been a while since she suggested I do anything with Lucas. I guess after the dozens of excuses I gave her, she got the point.

I laugh, probably harder than she expects. Instead of

getting into it, I take a long sip of my dark night coffee. It's acidic and delicious in a way that has the power to burn away a bad day. I will it to work on this one. My mom takes the same kind of sip, which softens me a little. I forget how hard all of this is on her. I know how tight our bills are. And I know how small the support checks are from my father. He's a con-man. Not literally, but enough of one that he got the judge to believe his salary was a third of what it really is. I think if I weren't so close to graduating, Mom would sell this house and move us into something cheaper. Maybe I should bring it up so we could move into a different school district.

"You and I have never really talked about it, you know," my mom says. I m not sure which *it* she's talking about. There are many—their marriage troubles, the miscarriage I know she had when I was eight, the new woman in Dad's life.

She means Lucas.

"What's to talk about?" I say, testing the temperature of the coffee against my lips. It's no longer scalding so I take a bigger drink.

"You guys were so close." She's inching into the topic so I start to rebuild the track for my project.

"Yep." I'm short. Probably overstepping my free pass to be a bitch but I really, truly, do not want to get into the saga of me and Lucas Fuller.

After a few breaths of quiet, my mom snaps together pieces of track with me, putting them in pairs and passing them my way until I again have one long, twelve-foot strip. We admire our work, finishing our coffee in silence. My mom twirls the worksheet around on the table so she can read the instructions, and I gauge her reaction in her eyes. She's exaggerating a little, grimacing at the calculations and the number of trials I'm supposed to conduct to find averages and means. I know better than to ask her for help. She long ago made the point that she would never enable me from having to face challenges, especially when the adversity was something as solvable as being strong enough to stand up for myself.

It's weird how effective her silence is. The shadows cast across our ceiling are familiar, the same ones I've memorized during football season for the last two years. Lucas's practice is over, the glare of his headlights through our windows lining up right where it should when he parks. The brightness dims, followed by the heavy clunk of a truck door. I glance from the window to my mom, and find her eyes waiting on me. She doesn't say a word, instead reaches for my empty cup, her tight smile holding so much inside.

It's hard not to imagine how different things could be. Like right now, my mom's back turned to me as she rinses out our coffee mugs. In some other dimension, maybe I'm not sitting at this table alone. Maybe my father kept his promise to stay through thick and thin. Or maybe . . . maybe the one soul I trusted all of my secrets with didn't pull away. I half imagine Lucas knocking at our side door and turn my head, wishing to see his shadow at the window.

"So, I have some bad news." My least favorite sentence pulls me back to reality. Just hearing it makes me want to rip my track apart again.

"Hit me with it." I sit back in my chair and brace

myself for something heavy. She does the same against the counter. Her eyes are tired, the dark circles a shade of purple now that they're not hidden by makeup. She cut her hair super short a few weeks ago, buzzing the back and sides. She said she wanted something easy to do, but I think she liked the idea of something inexpensive. It looks nice on her, though she keeps mentioning how much she hates how it brings out her grays. I'll be gray too one day, just like her. Our natural hair color is exactly the same.

"It's more of a good news, bad news thing," she begins, and I relax a little. The last bad news thing was when she lost her job. "You know how I said I booked two shoots?"

I nod, my mind racing with possibilities. *Is it someone famous? It's for a magazine! Maybe a royal wedding?*

"It's in Dayton. The wedding?" I blink a few times, slowly, mentally working through what she's saying.

"We're going to Dayton?" The divot between my brows is so deep I can actually feel it on my face without using my hands.

My mom laughs lightly.

"*I'm* going to Dayton. I have to leave tomorrow, which I know . . . You don't love staying alone. But the family hired me when their original photographer backed out and they want to capture the rehearsal dinner along with a few other things, and the amount they are paying is . . ." She trails off, holding her palms out in front of her to indicate a massive amount.

I smile and reassuringly tilt my head to the side.

"I don't mind staying here alone. I'm really proud of you," I say. Her eyes twitch and gloss quickly, which naturally forces my tough-as-nails mom to busy herself by running a paper towel around the counter to distract me from the emotion creeping up on her face.

"Just four days, four and a half max." Her voice wavers, but she coughs the clue away.

"Piece of cake," I say, stealing a glance out the window to the dark house just two driveways away.

"And I'll still leave you the van for the game Friday," she says. I was hoping she would forget that I asked to use it. My mom and Abby must be in cahoots to force me into some semblance of a normal senior year.

"Well, I need to get everything ready. I'm going to run out to Clicks and see if I can rent an extra light kit for the weekend." Our eyes meet briefly and a silent thank-you passes between us.

I stare out the window while my mom gathers her things and heads out the side door to her van. I stand while she backs out so I can watch her go, and let my gaze get lost on the space she leaves behind. I'm not sure how much time passes, but it's enough that I'm lulled into a deep trance that only the thumping beat of the Fuller's backyard audio system can snap me from. Always with the Kanye. Lucas Fuller listens to Kanye more than *Kanye* listens to Kanye.

The house is dark, which means he's probably just sitting in his back yard drinking one of his father's beers and watching dumb fucking Tik Tok videos while I do our assignment by myself. All because of some childish caste system that we fell into in high school.

By the time I realize I've got a chokehold on the section of track in my palm, the plastic siding cuts into my hand. I relax my hold to assess the damage, a deep red line broken through the skin right along my life line. So appropriate.

Without pulling my focus from the glowing haze of lights in Lucas's back yard, I yank the track into a few manageable pieces, gather the cars and worksheet, and stuff it all into the bag it came home in. I pull the Notre Dame sweatshirt I found at Goodwill over my head and down over my hips, and stuff my feet in a pair of Vans. I leave the same way my mom did, my long strides carrying me across my driveway, the strip of grass between our homes, and up the side of Lucas's house. The music is so loud the bass vibrates in my chest, which only fuels my courage. What a fucking asshole!

With one deep breath to ensure I get the words all out in one go, I round the corner of his home and step onto the brick walkway that leads to the patio. The pool light is on, casting an aqua glow around the yard, but the lounge chairs and hammock I expect to see him in are all empty. My steps slow, a twitch of caution flicking against the side of my neck. The large window that looks out from the Fuller kitchen is just to my left, but the only light glowing inside is the small panel light that illuminates the floor near the pantry. Not that I'd be able to hear anything other than the music, but there is a stillness that eats up my surroundings; it feels as though I'm here all alone.

I hug the project bag to my chest and scan every possible nook as I inch deeper into the covered patio and up the steps to the deck. The fire pit Lucas and I used to roast marshmallows sits in the center, and it looks unused since the last time he and I made treats in the flames. The chairs around the deck are covered. The Fullers don't have big parties like they used to. I run my finger along one of the tarps, drawing a line in the dust, then stop to lean against the railing and blow the particles away in the breeze.

That's when I spot him, and he isn't alone.

Lucas and Ava are lying in the center of the trampoline, barely visible if it weren't for the pool light. My throat burns with fire from my stomach, and the fuming rage that carried me to this house has shifted into dread and panic over being caught. My hands shake and my legs have very little feeling. Despite the near stroke I might be having, I can't look away. Her body is arched, her flannel shirt open to expose her white lacey bra that Lucas is slowly peeling away with his teeth as he holds himself over her from the side. His left hand is sunk inside her unbuttoned jeans, and Ava is writhing with his touch. He's wearing his gray football T-shirt and black joggers that are low on his hips, and is probably seconds from losing his shirt and letting her touch him just as intimately. He moves like a predator, slow and stealthy, and where his shirt rises up, the side of a cut V that traces hard-earned abs dives lower. The scene is so erotic and private yet I'm glued to it, trembling with the threat of tears. I'm so fucking jealous, and I hate that I am because this is not *my* Lucas anymore. This feels like a betrayal, though I know it's not. That should be me lying there. It was supposed to be me.

In a different life.

The music fades between songs and a deep, masculine moan cuts through the quiet. I swallow hard at the familiar voice making that sound, lock my jaw and hold my breath. I slowly back away, just as Ava's hips rise and her hands help Lucas slide down her jeans. I turn quickly when I'm sure I'm out of view, but in my rush, I kick one of the chairs, the metal leg screeching against the wood deck so loudly it's impossible it wasn't heard.

"Shit," I breathe out silently, breaking into a run that turns into a full sprint across our driveways and back to my house. I slam the side door closed behind me, lock it, and fly up the stairs two at a time until I'm in the safety of my room. I close my door behind me and toss the bag to the corner, burying myself under my comforter without bothering to turn on the lights.

A million futures play out in my mind, and none of them are easy. They all come with pain.

I hate this fucking school.

And I hate my fucking neighbor.

I hate that I loved him so much even more.

CHAPTER SEVEN

I wake up early to see my mom off and to bullshit my way through the project I never finished last night. I went the YouTube video route, changing all of the numbers by the same percentage so the results weren't an exact copy.

All of the extra things added to my morning leave no time for a shower though, so I braid my hair into one long weave that runs from one side to the other. I have to lay down to finish because my arms are getting tired. I wrap a band around the end of my braid then let my arms flop to my sides. Staring at my ceiling, I replay what I saw last night in my head, dragging my own hand slowly up my side and over my shirt to my right breast. I look nothing like Ava, all flat in the places where she is round. I touch the soft peak of my breast and run my thumb over my own nipple until it hardens under my long-sleeved T-shirt and cotton bra. I let my hand fall away, trailing it down the length of my body, stopping just above my waistband, too embarrassed to touch myself anywhere else.

I'm a girl playing woman.

It's tempting to call myself out sick today. My voice and my mother's sound eerily similar, and nobody would think I was ditching. Running away isn't supposed to be my thing now, though. Senior year—parties, freedom, courage and kissing. I laugh out once for nobody to hear.

"What a load of crap," I say.

I sit up and drag my backpack toward me, zipping it up after I make sure my fake project worksheet is inside. I tuck my phone in my back pocket and double knot the laces on my boots, then grab a flannel from the hook behind my door before heading downstairs. While the days still feel very much like summer, the mornings and late afternoons are fall and I hate being cold. I poke my arms through the unbuttoned shirt and pause as I look down at the plaid pattern. It's too much like Ava's. Newly committed to being chilly instead, I pull my arms free again and roll the shirt up, tossing it into a deep corner in the laundry-slash-mud room. I really want to throw it away but mom only bought it for me last month.

With my backpack slung over one shoulder, I snag a granola bar from the cabinet and a strawberry milk from the fridge, holding the bar in my teeth while I lock the side door behind me. I'm almost looking forward to my lazy drive to school with my favorite breakfast. I know Mom picked up the strawberry milks so I won't miss her so much. I smile as I twist the cap loose.

As I approach my car, I notice something resting on the windshield. It's mostly white, and almost looks like a scrunchie wrapped around my wiper blade. I unlock my door and toss my bag across to the passenger seat, then reach for the twisted piece of cloth. I realize what it is right before my hand makes contact and I pause, breathing out hard, short puffs through my nose to the familiar beat of the last Kanye song I heard. I pull my keys from my pocket and poke the long one meant for my ignition through the lacey item that's barely within my reach. I drag the material toward me and pinch it to hold up for inspection.

The panties are mostly white with little black hearts sewn everywhere, and the coverage they would provide is minimal. It's the bottom part that matches the bra I got a glimpse of; at least, I'm pretty sure it is. Last night's hurt and fury stirs in my belly. I twist to take in the still house behind me, the garage closed and the downstairs as quiet as it was last night. Lucas's truck is gone, which probably means I am not being watched. I carry the thong—held by my thumb and middle finger—into my car and unzip my backpack to tuck it inside. I back down the driveway, squealing my tires a little when I hit the road.

I buckle up while moving, then reach to zip my bag closed again. There's a chance I missed one of the four-way stops leaving my neighborhood, and I'm not sure how I got to where I am, a block from school. All I can think about are the underwear; it's basically tunnel vision for my thoughts.

Ava's panties are in my backpack. What the ever-loving fuck?

Abby is waiting for me in her car, her music loud enough that I can hear it through both of our closed windows and with my engine on. She's happy. That's her personality. Very little to find fault with in the world according to my best friend, even though she's getting hauled into court again next week as part of her parents' constant and bitter custody battle. Her dad, who has seen her maybe twice since she and I have been best friends, lives in Miami now. He wants custody because he wants the money she earns modeling, and she's not eighteen for six more months. Her mom recently put it all into an S-Corp, Abigail Cortez LLC. My friend is an LLC. Her father wants it dissolved. It's a Netflix documentary-worthy mess.

Maybe having some chick's underpants in my backpack isn't so bad.

I glance at the zipper and give one last thought to what's hidden behind it, then pull the bag into my lap, kill my engine, and get out to wait for Abby to finish crimping her eyelashes. She's still singing the last few lines of the song when she gets out and joins me on the hood of her car to stare at other people and make judgements about them we would never say to their faces. That's a lie. *She* would say it. Me, never. Except maybe . . .

"Ava Pryor looks like she had a boob job," my friend says, both of our necks craned to the left, watching the platinum blonde mean girl hop out of Lucas's truck. I wonder if she slept at his house or if he picked her up this morning.

"I have her panties in my backpack," I say, all monotone as I zone out watching my apparent arch nemesis shimmy down her barely existent corduroy skirt. I wait for them to kiss, ignoring my friend's elbow that has now nudged me twice. But from the moment they exit the truck it's as if they aren't even acquainted. Lucas peels off and joins the twins and this guy Cannon who came here junior year when I was gone. Abby is obsessed with him, but he never *ever* does anything social, or dates, or smiles. He clearly talks, because I'm watching that happen, but talking to Abby is another thing. I have the distinct feeling he is the reason I'm driving out to the creek Friday night.

"Panties. Spill it." She pushes me hard enough that I lose my balance and stumble a few steps to my right. I smirk, though, and bring my bag to the front of my chest, unzipping the top for her to peer inside. I don't expect her to reach in and grab them. Stupid of me.

"Get out!"

I blush a little because her volume draws attention, and she's unfurled a thong to display in front of us.

"Abs, those ain't washed," I warn, and she tosses them back in my bag, immediately digging in her purse for her orange-scented hand sanitizer.

"How did you end up with those?"

I'm not completely sure, but I have a pretty good idea. I tell my friend only the facts so I don't have to delve into the intricacies of me walking in on her and Lucas, which would undoubtedly lead to me doing our assignment on my own, and him taking advantage of me, and me pining . . .

"I found them on my car this morning." I meet her wide stare with a solid one of my own, my mouth a hard line touched with a hint of a smile that says, *"I can't make this shit up."*

Abby nods slowly and the first bell sounds from the school speakers.

"Guess that's better than dog shit," she says.

We kick off from her car and head toward the main doors, Lucas and the twins a few paces in front of us. This time, though, I don't bother walking slow. I let it all play out so my steps are only a few behind his, and when he glances back enough that I see his jaw and the flick of his lashes, I let a slow, deep grin take over my face.

When we arrive at the science building, I'm close enough behind Lucas that, if he were a gentleman, he'd hold the double doors open for me. I'm not surprised when they slam shut behind him; it only strengthens my resolve for how I'm going to handle this—*handle him.*

I slow my stride enough that he gets into our classroom and his seat before me. I want him sitting for this, and I want other people around to witness. His big frame is stuffed into the desk when I enter the classroom, his black bag on the floor next to one foot, his right leg stretched out into the aisle next to my seat. His notebook is out and he's slowly spinning a pen in his right hand, his eyes red from what I imagine was a late night. His focus on the whiteboard seems forced, reluctant. His concentration breaks only for a breath, and that's when his gaze flits to me. His pen never stops turning, but his eyes follow my movement, his expression almost hostile. He's wearing the same clothes I saw him in last night, and I force myself to soothe the burn and scorn eating at my insides with this newfound hatred that I've decided to nurture.

Pausing right in front of my seat, I dump my heavy bag on my chair, then unzip the top and look my former friend right in the face. His eyes move from my hands to my gaze in one blink. The blue is muddied by alcohol, lack of sleep, Ava—*whatever.* It's not as effective on me as it once was.

What was once so beautiful has become ugly. I wait for him to believe this is it, I'm just going to glare. Finally, he shakes his head and shrugs.

"What?"

My smile spreads a little wider. I reach in my bag and grab his girlfriend's panties, then toss them on his desk.

"Pretty sure these are yours," I say, waiting to capture a mental picture of his agape mouth, lost for words. His jaw works side to side while he stares at the undies, and a sharp laugh leaves his chest.

Satisfied, I take my seat and pull out my project and notes. I'm still undecided on dropping the fact that I did the project alone, not that it will matter to our teacher. There's an unwritten rule that football players get a free pass around here.

"Hey, June." Lucas's voice is steady and calm. I didn't think the bullet I fired would sting for long, but I know it stung. I saw it on his face, and that's enough.

I turn my head to the left enough that I can view him in my periphery. He leans forward and tugs lightly on my braid, an almost flirtatious tease that maybe would have sent my heart into butterfly Olympics before last night. Now, though, I see it for what it is. It's bait.

"Thanks," he says, his hand swallowing up Ava's panties in a slow sweeping movement along his desktop. He leans to his left and pushes the thin, lacey garment into his right pocket, his eyes never leaving mine. I can feel my body growing hot, but I don't let him see how affected I am.

"You're welcome," I manage to say. I'm stronger than I think I am. "Don't mention it," I add, then turn around, never letting my focus stray from the front of the room for the rest of the hour. And when our teacher collects our projects, I wait for most of the class—for Lucas—to clear out, and write a note on the top of my assignment.

Lucas Fuller had nothing to do with this project. If you want to know why, ask Ava Pryor.

I hand it in and leave without commenting out loud. It will be what it will be. And it is going to feel like forever.

CHAPTER EIGHT

I'd forgotten what Friday nights are like around here. For the last two years, I spent them watching back-to-back sit-coms while binge eating excessively-buttered popcorn and peanut M&Ms. Sophomore year, I was busy helping my mom care for my grandmother, and last year, I wasn't an Allensville Public Fighting Eagle so no need to expose myself to all of the rah-rah pep shit.

I'm in the thick of pompoms and shirtless teenage boys painted orange and blue now, though. Public is a decent team. Lucas is a more than decent quarterback. There's buzz about this season, but the entire school shows up for the first home game regardless. It's the perfect storm of panic-inducing high school chaos.

It's also easy to get caught up in.

I pick the girls up in my mom's van and we blare power-chick music all the way here. I almost forget how small I am by the time we walk through the gates to the field. Ava Pryor is sure to remind me.

"I'm pretty sure she gets in as a child," she shouts when I walk up to the ticket window with my five bucks and my ugly ID. As tough as I've trained my skin over the last week, her words still cut, almost as much as the laughter it spawns from people nearby. Even still, I walk on. But she catches up, shoving the blue jersey she's wearing in my face—Lucas's away jersey.

I've been staring at her back—the bold number 1 centered under his last name—and I can't shake how much mental space I am giving to such an awful person.

"She hates you, you know?" Lola rests her chin on my shoulder so she can talk into my ear above the sound of the drumline sitting a section to our right.

"I'm well aware," I say with a wry smile.

My new friend puts her arm around me and squeezes, an awkward hug, but mostly because I don't know how to do those kinds of things. I exhale and let my body accept her affection. Lola holds her popcorn bag out to the side, tipping it for me to grab a handful. Might as well have my favorite Friday-night food since I'm enduring being here. I scoop some kernels from the bag and lick at the salty bits one at a time, trying like hell to ignore the girl I hate as much as she hates me.

There's a camera crew on the field—a *real* one, not our student-run Internet show. They've positioned camera guys on either side of the banner being stretched out by a tower of cheerleaders. When the team trickles out, everyone in the student section—which has basically grown to be two-thirds of the stands—gets on their feet to scream. Abby is standing in front of me and she turns, catches me not doing my part, and points in that threatening way she has.

"Fine," I mouth, cupping my hands around my lips and shouting, "Go Eagles!" as loud as I can. The sheer volume of my own voice, the togetherness of this moment, all of it —it infects me. My smile quits being pretend, and I get caught up in my role. I have a part to play, albeit probably not as important as everyone thinks, but for the next three hours, I will be a superfan. For the next three hours, nothing matters more than winning this game and destroying some school from South Bend.

The young men on the field shout in unison, growling with testosterone and pounding into each other, smacking helmets to helmets and gripping at facemasks to amp up their game faces. They explode through the banner, confetti covering the corner of the field as it's fired from a few cannons held by some of our cheerleaders. Lucas is the first to break through, holding an American flag as he sprints straight down the center of the field, his co-captains running behind him with two Eagles flags.

My All-American boy.

He was so much younger the last time I saw him run like this. He was a leader that seemed too small to lead, but now —now he's the guy with the V that cuts down his abs and whose arms completely fill out the sleeves of his jersey; whose neck doesn't seem so pencil-thin anymore. His sweaty hair is swept to either side, and the black lines swiped under his eyes somehow make him seem like this superhero.

A hero who abandoned me when he got popular and when my life fell to shit, I remind myself.

The team captains are met by one of the coaches at the fifty-yard line. He takes their flags to fold them while the boys huddle up to pray. It's such a blatant disregard for the separation of church and state, yet it seems nothing could be more important than this bonding happening in front of us all. More than the quiet power of the moment, though, is that Lucas is the one leading the prayer. Arms over shoulders, circles standing within circles, these boys who I've seen do the most unchristian-like things give respect to his words. I wish I could hear him or be close enough to read his lips. Some of the boys look up to the sky, a few of them holding their helmets high while their heads lower. Lucas's eyes are closed, and there's an innocence in his features, that much I can see from here. They all start clapping and an echoing "Amen" accompanies their formation of a tighter circle until the clapping becomes thunder and soon . . . fuel.

Lucas is the last to walk away from this private spot on the field. His head down, I recognize the familiar invisible weight on his shoulders. Even as kids, he always felt so damn responsible for everything and everyone. Especially for me. He rode his bike through rain to sneak me my favorite candy bar when my parents were fighting downstairs. And he insisted we fall asleep still on our phone call to each other if I felt scared or off. He sensed things when I didn't share. He took burdens from me, whether I wanted him to or not, and shouldered them until he was sure my smile was real again.

I miss him. I miss him so fucking much.

I press my palms into my eyes while my friends aren't looking, and manage to stop myself from feeling all of this somewhere so public. In less than a minute, the game takes over and distracts me from anything other than the anticipation and hope that brews in my belly every time Lucas throws the ball. He's gotten better. I understand why his opportunity window is so big. There's an easiness to the way he moves, and it's more than instinct. He has plenty of that, though, after throwing the ball down our street to his dad every night—a million which ways and for hours on end. They haven't thrown since freshman year, but that's probably because Lucas has outgrown what his dad can give him. Either that, or his dad is too busy at his best friends' house.

It suddenly becomes impossible to turn off my thoughts. I wonder if Lucas knows. Maybe that's what changed him. I scan the crowd off to our left, to the sections where parents sit to gloat and brag which number their kid wears on the field. Lucas's dad is the only one standing the entire time, not giving a rat's ass about the dozens behind him who can't see. A week ago, I would have seen a proud father in this scene, but now, I see a man who wants the credit, a man who maybe wants to live through and off of his son's achievements. His expression after every amazing feat Lucas accomplishes is less one of pride and more one of validation. A check mark that moves him up a scale even though really . . . he hasn't done jack shit.

His wife sits next to him, her purse tucked close to her hip, her hands folded in her lap, knuckles near white as they squeeze in fear every time someone threatens to knock her son out. Still proud, she is also the exact opposite of the growing ego standing next to her.

I wonder if she knows where her husband goes during the day?

The more I study his parents, the more every inch Lucas fights for on the field is colored with resentment in my eyes. Balls are thrown with extra zip. I think the newspaper called him stronger than your normal high school senior, but maybe what they see is hatred playing out like a game. But his dad and him, they don't hate each other. They were just playing basketball together, laughing. *Until I kicked their ball into the weed oblivion of my yard.*

The truth about what I see and what this family really is muddies more every time I think I understand. I quit focusing so much on Lucas and pay attention to the other players, the ones I know even though I never thought I'd want to. Like the twins. Or that Cannon guy, who Abby has been straining her neck all night to stare at. I don't think she even knows the score of the game.

We're on our feet for most of the first half, and I can barely feel the bottoms of my feet by the time the buzzer calls halftime and our boys run to the locker rooms with a 14-0 lead. Lucas's mom joins his father, both standing to arch their backs and shake feeling back into their legs. I look away when Mrs. Fuller turns her attention in my direction. But I miscalculate and my gaze lands on Ava, who has turned around to stare straight up at me, despite every single minion around her facing the other way. Her eyes haze, so I jack up the right side of my mouth and lift my hand in a wave I'm sure makes her blood boil, then I get my friends' attention.

"Hey, did Abby tell you guys about Ava's underwear?" I'm not being quiet, but I'm not loud enough that anyone other than my friends hear. The way they all jerk their focus to me and then to Ava, though, makes her squirm.

"Why?" Naomi asks, turning to look at me again. Ava's glare grows heated, and my smile inches up into my eyes.

"Someone left them on my car. I'm guessing she did." I shrug and shift my gaze to my friend. Naomi busts out a hard laugh.

"Well, no shit. Girl hates you," she says, echoing the same thing Lola said when the game started.

"Why?" I shake my head, amused and a bit baffled at the concept. In terms of having your shit together, Ava's got me beat hands down—she has her hooks in Lucas, as far as I know her family isn't diced up by a nasty divorce, and, despite how much I like to poke fun of her glossy style, she's actually kind of pretty. *Really* pretty. Sexy for sure.

Naomi's cheek falls to her shoulder and Lola laughs at some inside joke I clearly don't get. The longer I don't laugh with them or nod or agree, the more amused they get until finally, Lola explains.

"You had him. Lucas! You guys were . . . " She twists her fingers together to show how tight Lucas and I once were. I nod like it all makes sense, but the part I hold on to is the moment her fingers pull apart and never come back to meet as they once did. I never really had him like she does. I can't imagine him looking at me the way he did her on the trampoline.

Hungry.

Despite wanting to break the rule I made for myself after the first half, I don't give Ava another ounce of my physical attention for the rest of the game. Mentally, though, she swims all over my insides. I replay walking in on them, measuring up her cruel glances over the years, the slight shoves against my shoulder when we pass in the hall, and how those things line up with Lucas and me, and our friendship. No matter how hard I try to see it, high-fives and late-night burger runs don't match up with the kind of relationship they have now.

H

I would trade twenty football games for one of these parties. Hell, I'd trade a dozen house parties for whatever the fuck this is that my friends and I are walking into.

I know my attitude is a little tainted from having to process more Ava business. Still, I don't think getting mud caked on the sides of my white Vans just to get pot smoke blown in my face is anywhere close to my recipe for the perfect night. On my way to the beer truck, I walk by some asshat carrying all the beer, which I won't drink. Maybe I'm the one with something wrong, though, because everyone else here seems happy—perfectly, miserably happy.

Almost everyone here is well on their way to becoming drunk. I've run into one other sober person, and I counted sixteen cars, which means a lot of these people better be camping here tonight. I'm sure they're not. I'd love to call every one of them out on it, but you don't win high school popularity points by stopping dumbasses from committing involuntary manslaughter.

"Miss Mabee!" The familiar D'Angelo lilt actually makes me smile.

"My second favorite D'Angelo twin," I tease back,

turning to find my unlikely friend sitting on the tailgate of someone's truck, covering his heart with both palms, feigning his untimely death by insult.

I nod to the rest of my friends to head to the beer truck without me and pull myself up to sit next to Tory. His hair is wet, combed straight back minus the stray section that squiggles over his left eye. He smells like men's body wash, and he's wearing his away jersey, his home one muddied from tonight's game.

"So tell me, you come to the party looking for me?" He winks over his crooked smile. I bat at him playfully.

"You know it," I say. His laugh in response is genuine.

"Abby dragged me here," I clear up, nodding toward my friend who has already found a spot near this mysterious Cannon guy.

"That's two parties, back-to-back weekends! Dare I say it, you're well on your way to a streak," Tory jokes.

I glance to my side with a tight-lipped smile, feeling a little prudish because he's right, I am a bit of a hermit. For good reason, though.

"I'm kidding with you. You know that, right?" His eyes soften and he dips his head, meeting my stare.

I nod. "I do."

Tory tilts his head back and takes a long swig from his bottle of beer. I take this moment to survey the rest of the crowd. I haven't seen Lucas's truck yet, or Ava, and I hate that I'm looking for them. Even more, though, I hate that Tory catches me in the act.

"He's always late to shit. Some things never change," he says, nudging my arm with his elbow as he scoots a little closer. I chuckle at his commentary, remembering all the things Lucas was late for with me.

"You know that jerk was late to our summer swim relay when we were eleven?" I say. "He showed up just in time to swim anchor." Tory laughs hard enough that he spits out some of his beer.

"Serious?" he questions.

I nod and hold up the scouts honor sign.

"He still a jerk?" he asks, laughing lightly through the words. His expression falls into a less spirited one though the longer it takes me to answer. I never do.

Jerk or not, he isn't late this time. He's right on time, pulling his truck up right next to the one Tory and I are sitting in. At least seven people are in the back, and four more lined up next to him in the cab. The scent of alcohol is strong, and bottles clank as people climb out of the truck. I kick my feet out and hop to the ground, dusting off the back of my jeans and twisting in place to find my friends, any of them. My attention comes screaming back to Tory after a second, when his hand grabs my fingers. At first, my eyes sear the place where he's holding my hand hostage, then my gaze flits up to Tory's cocky smirk.

"Don't let him run you off," he says, rushing the words out before Lucas rounds the back of his truck and stops a few feet away from us with a sour look on his face. The trapped feeling makes it hard to breathe.

"Hey, man. Can you help me with this keg?" Lucas's eyes bounce from where Tory's hand is on mine to Tory's eyes, and that little victory from seeing it bother him helps me slow my pulse and stay where I am a moment or two longer.

"Yeah, bro. Where we takin' it?" Tory runs his thumb over the top of my knuckles, and I react on auto, pulling my hand away and stuffing both of them in the front pocket of my hoodie. I don't leave yet, though. I'm not sure whether what Tory did there was for me, or for Lucas, but it was a weird line nonetheless.

"Uh, Jake's truck, I guess. Isn't that where the rest of the shit is?" Lucas shifts on his feet, glancing at me a few times, but never stopping to actually *look* at me. He's agitated and keeps pulling his black Public hat from his head to smooth out his long hair underneath before putting it back on backward.

Tory hops down from the truck, his feet crunching into the earth less than a foot from me. He leans in, the sweet scent from a wax pen on his breath. "Wait here. I'll be right back."

I'm not sure why I obey his request. I stay put, though, while he climbs into the back of Lucas's truck and the two of them haul the keg to the tailgate, then call Hayden over to help lift it out. I stick by the back of Tory's truck for several minutes while he lingers by the drinks, laughing and joking with his friends. Maybe he forgot about me. But before I give in to the urge to search out my friends, he jogs over from across the large open area we're all parked around.

He hands me a Coke, not fully letting go when I grip it, instead tapping the top a few times. "I ran with it. Don't want it to explode on you," he explains. I wonder if my face is as quizzical as it feels.

"You're being nice to me." I didn't mean that to come out with sound.

Tory stops tapping my drink as he shakes with a hard laugh and looks down at the ground, nodding and biting at his bottom lip that eventually slips into an amused smile. I pop the tab and take a long drink, thirstier than I realize.

"You were nice to me first, you know," he says, holding his beer up to toast against my can. I smile all crooked and tap my Coke into his Bud.

"Technically . . ." I nod my head side-to-side and look up to the right.

"Fine, I gave you a chair. *Oh, look what a gentleman I am,*" he mocks.

We both ease back into leaning against the tailgate and laugh together, maybe admitting we had each other a little wrong.

"So, tell me, Mabee I thought your parents were super strict. How did you get them to let you drive the mom van out here for such a sordid affair?" He eyes me over his bottle as he tilts it back for another long drink. He'll be drunk within the hour at this pace.

"Well," I begin, pausing as I shift my position, letting my free arm hug my waist. I don't talk about my family, but maybe that's another thing I should change. I lean my head to the side and let out a short nervous laugh. He reaches forward, lightly touching my arm.

"Go on," he urges.

I look up at him, a part of me maybe making sure he's earnestly interested. His eyes don't move from mine, so I take a deep breath. "It's just *parent,* really. They split up, freshman year."

He nods, and it's a little bit like he's familiar with this part, but maybe I'm just reading into that.

"And my mom, she would prefer me to be a little, no . . . *a lot* more social than I am." He snickers at that, taking yet one more drink. I let my arm fall free of my stomach and hold my Coke in both palms, swishing it a little to hear the fizz.

"She workin' tonight?" He cocks a brow, and I respond with a sideways look. If he's looking to take me home—*alone*—that's a hard no.

"Yes," I say tentatively. "But she knows I'm here. We switched cars so I could drive."

He licks his lips, the slightest appearance of his tongue, and my trust fortress rearms itself. He backs off though, shifting his posture and putting a little more distance between us. He holds his now-empty bottle up for me to salute again. He's getting buzzed, but I indulge him.

"Cheers to the designated drivers!" he says.

"Cheers!" a few people nearby echo, because he's getting kind of loud.

"You need another?" He taps on the top of my can. It's still half full.

"I'm good." I nod. He tips his head back and takes the last remaining droplets of his beer, then tosses the bottle into a pile forming at the center of this gathering.

"Well, I'm empty. I'll be back in a bit!" His stride has gotten looser, but for whatever reason, he's still a little engaged in talking to me. It's better than me wandering around lost. My girlfriends have all found circles to join, all of them drinking at about the same pace as Tory. I'm going to keep the windows down on the way home in case anybody vomits.

A heavy clunk to my right jerks my attention around.

Lucas is pushing the tailgate of his truck up, missing the catch the first few times and shoving it three more times before it holds. He claps his hands together to remove the dirt—his truck's been through some mud, it seems—but remains behind his vehicle for a few long seconds, his eyes focused on the ground. His jaw works back and forth in thought before his gaze finally lifts to meet mine. It doesn't stick. He and I, we can't seem to look at each other for long.

"Be smart with that," he says, signaling with a short wave to where Tory is talking with my friends. I stare at the scene for a beat to decipher his message. I glance back his way to find the top of his hat, the brim turned forward again so he can hide. Coward.

"You jealous or something?"

I can't believe that was out loud.

His shoulders quake with a quiet laugh and he shakes his head, eyes looking back at the ground. He lifts his head to meet my stare and to raise the right side of his mouth in a mocking laugh.

"Sure, June." His gaze lingers a little longer this time, a flatness to his eyes that insults me without words. That look is meant to call me stupid. But I know that look wouldn't be necessary if what I said didn't hurt him a little.

I had him. Once. In my own way. And that's why Ava hates me.

Lucas walks in the opposite direction from me, heading into a thick outcropping of trees that sinks down a ravine. It's where Ava is, and a few of the others I saw smoking joints by the beer. Maybe he'll get high and find some sort of peace. None of that will do anything to solve how he's going to feel when his parents' marriage falls apart. Of course, there's always the chance that his dad gets away with it forever.

Whatever.

I sit on the back of Tory's truck, waiting for him to come back, uneasy again when half an hour passes. I busy myself playing dumb games on my phone, eventually texting Abby to come rescue me. She doesn't show up for ten more minutes, and when she does, the other girls are with her. We all crawl into the bed of the truck and pull our knees up to gossip and talk shit about other people who are probably having the same conversations about us. For the first time since freshman year, I feel I belong. An hour of easy jokes passes, girl time and camaraderie. Tory and his brother eventually join us and we censor our jokes from including them, but the easiness continues.

Tory doesn't start next to me, but eventually he winds up there, sitting on the side of the truck bed, his leg against my shoulder, keeping me close. A few times, he even reaches down and squeezes my shoulders gently while telling a story. I look up at him, both nervous but kind of glad to be the object of anyone's anything. I should have known none of that would last.

"Careful there, Tory. Little virgin girl might just be a cock tease," Ava says, her voice carrying up and over our conversation from the end of the tailgate. It takes me a second to understand what's happening, how those words are meant to hurt me, but when I do, I scramble to my feet and walk to the edge of the truck. I might not have curves, but I do have muscle. And I have rage. I could pound Ava Pryor into the dirt if I wanted to.

"At least I'm not the one who throws her panties

around people's cars," I say, drawing exaggerated *ooo's* from my friends and a few who pretend they know what I'm talking about.

Ava lets out a short laugh and puts her hand on her hip, her makeup smudged from being drunk and her hair tangled from whatever it is she probably just did with Lucas. I hop down and land a few feet in front of her, my act tough enough to make her flinch back a step or two. Her reaction emboldens me. I step closer, but this time she holds her ground. Pretty soon, we're close enough to kiss.

"Mommy out working the streets tonight? That why they let you come out to play?" she says, her voice low but the words loud enough that the people around us hear.

My mouth waters with instant rage, and without thinking it through, I step back and fling my right open palm against her face hard enough that her body staggers a few steps to my left. Her squeal gets even more attention, and my hand throbs from the contact. *That fucking hurt!* She's totally going to have a black eye.

I'm glowing off this power trip, energized by the shouts from my friends behind me. Ava finds her balance and spits at the ground, then shifts her weight to come back at me. I lift my right arm again, figuring I might as well keep all the hurt in one place. Before I can take a good swing though, this time with a fist, a strong hand wraps around my wrist and pulls it to the side before another hand holds at the center of Ava's chest.

"You!" Lucas is staring Ava down, a warning in his wide eyes. She argues a few times but he talks over her, pointing to his truck. "Get your ass in there. That's enough!"

I've started to laugh, but Lucas's attention focuses on me next. His eyes lock on mine, a million words passing behind them all at once. Disappointment, regret . . . apology maybe?

"Just . . . fucking stop, June," he says, exasperation in his voice. My clenched muscles weaken, and my arm grows limp and falls from his hold. My eyes peer over his shoulder to Ava, slowly walking backward. *Why her?*

"Your mom's a fucking whore, you know!" she shouts, her words stunning me where I stand. Lucas took away my weapons. He left me defenseless.

"I said get your ass in my truck!" He points at her more forcefully, a redness coloring his neck, the lines showing how tense he is, how angry.

His eyes come back to me and the expression isn't soft. There is no pity in his gaze. He's holding back. There are things he wants to say, and I wish he just would. What else could be said that would hurt me now? He doesn't speak though, instead falling back a step or two as he shakes his head, a silent way to say "don't."

I shake my head in response, a shudder kicking my chest with a short cry that I wipe away in an instant with my forearm.

"Is she your girlfriend? That?" I let out a judgmental laugh and point at the cruel person crawling into his passenger side. I bite my lip through more sad laughter, then look into his eyes, the blue now roiling with fire. "Or is she just some girl you fuck? No matter what, you know she's part of your story now. That . . . that is what you are —*who you are.*"

Everything around us has become quiet. Lucas doesn't

flinch. The burn settles into my cheeks the longer he stares at me. I'm being foolish.

Foolish, foolish girl with some unrequited crush.

Goddamn, what have I done?

Lucas spits at the ground in front of him and looks to Tory who holds up two open palms, claiming his innocence. He is innocent. This scene, it's all me.

I remain still until Lucas walks completely away, rounding his truck and getting inside. His engine roars, but I don't move until Abby's hand gently runs down my shoulder and arm. She squeezes me to her side and I tremble a little, still coming down from the high of being so damn mad and letting it out.

"Can we be done now?" I ask, wondering how in the hell I'm going to calm down enough to drive.

"Yeah, we can be done," she says, moving her hand down my arm even more until her hand grasps a strong hold of mine. "I know it doesn't feel like it right now, but you did something good right there."

"It feels the exact opposite of good," I admit, nervous pulse-laden words falling from my numb lips.

"I know. Doesn't mean it's not, though," she says, guiding me to our van. I get in and wait while the others take their spot. They don't talk until I'm ready, and they never make me say anything more. They repeat the scenario over and over, praising me for being strong. All I can see, though, are those damn blue, disappointed eyes that went home with someone else.

For a while, I haven't come out here at night. Living next door to Lucas means our old shared hiding places are off limits. But eventually, I realize he doesn't care about the abandoned treehouse falling apart near the back of my yard, or the rusted-out shell of the Forty-eight Buick that my dad left behind for my mom to deal with when he decided he didn't love her anymore. I don't come out here often because I can still see Lucas's window, the view into his room all too clear when his light is on. He paces a lot when he's on the phone. He also likes to leave the lights on when he brings girls upstairs late at night. I've seen too much from this front seat of the tireless car that will never run. But the burn on my cheeks from the very public words said by his on-again, off-again girlfriend in front of virtually everyone in our senior class is too hot for me to care about any of that. I need a place to hide where even Abby can't find me for a while—a place to cry it out.

Goddamn him for deciding now, *of all the nows*, is the one he chooses to finally show up again in the dark corner where our yards meet. It's well after midnight, and I'd planned on staying here until sunrise, away from my phone that I'm sure Abby is blowing up, and away from my house where maybe my new friends might come knocking, worried. At least my mom isn't home; I'm not sure I could hide my state from her.

I close my eyes and sniffle hard while he's still a good four or five strides away from the passenger door. It creaks open, popping when the hinge catches, and I jerk my head to the right and open my eyes. He slides in next to me and yanks the door closed behind him. It's filthy in here, and his weight on the ripped fabric sends a poof of dust into the closed cabin.

"You didn't have to come check on me. I'll survive." I cough through my last few words and inwardly chide myself for liking that he showed up. He quickly dashes the fantasy that he came here because he cared.

He starts with a heavy sigh, his hands cupping his jean-covered knees and irritably scratching at them.

"I'm not here for you, June. I'm here to tell you—no, to *beg* you—to please keep your nosey ass out of my life."

My mouth falls open, and my chest is hammered with a mix of hurt and anger. Before I can react with words, Lucas shifts in his seat, bringing his right knee up to lean to the side and palm the rotted out dashboard. His large hand pats down, leaving a dustless print in its wake. I suddenly feel small.

His head shakes, and his face wears a soured expression.

"You judge—" he begins.

"No, I don't." I interrupt in protest, but his hand pats down again with his forced laugh.

"You do, and it's so . . . hypocritical. What I do with Ava, whether she's my girlfriend, whether we break up, whomever I decide to be with and however far that goes? None. Of. Your. Business." He leans back against the door and gives me the full heat of his stare. My pulse races to keep up with the arguments forming in my mind—all the things I know—that could devastate him. I was only defending myself. None of this was about him, not completely. And how can I be a hypocrite when I'm still a virgin?

"You missed most of everything I said, Lucas. I wasn't talking about you. That rant—it was about me." His face is stone cold and still. I don't know why I expect my childhood friend to break through this hard exterior that's swallowed him whole.

"I heard you. And you're right, every person you fuck becomes a part of your story."

I swallow at how bluntly he sums up my point.

"But people write themselves into our stories lots of ways, June." He shakes his head and lowers his gaze to his lap as his hand slides down the dash with a heavy exhale. The last evidence of his boyish youth is dusted along his cheeks and eyelashes in golden freckles and highlights picked up by the moonlight. Even those are seemingly disappearing before my eyes.

The crack of the door opening behind him breaks my hard stare, and in one smooth movement he steps from the passenger side and bends down to level me with his cerulean eyes. I wrote to Crayola once when we were younger because I wanted them to make a crayon I could use to do his eyes justice. What a foolish crush I've had.

"We've never fucked, but you sure are part of my story." I wince because that's not a compliment. "I can't delete you, but I sure don't need you taking up any more chapters. Stay the fuck out of my business, and go find yourself a boyfriend who can be all of these things you think are real."

He pauses for a brief moment, long enough to grin with half his mouth and puff out the smallest laugh at my expense. He slams the door as he backs away, and I don't bother to shift my position to watch where he goes. Like he said, he's none of my business.

Except as far as stories go, he's always been a major plot line in mine. Not sure life gets a rewrite the way fiction does. At the very least, I don't think I'll be hiding my feelings in the Buick again for a while.

CHAPTER NINE

I'm not sure I've slept since the party Friday night. Maybe my brain has shut down a little here and there, but I'm pretty sure my eyes focused on various points in my empty house for every single second of the last forty-eight hours. My head is pounding, deep dark circles look like charcoal under my eyes, and my mom should be home any minute.

I'm going to have to play sick.

I'm going to need my strength to get through Monday morning, sitting in front of Lucas without falling into the temptation to engage. Maybe it's delirium, but the more I think about everything he said, the harder it is to reconcile his arguments with his behavior. He pushes me as much as I push him. The fact we have to share proximity at home— At school? That's neither of our faults. But when he opens his mouth to speak to me, he makes a choice, and he chooses every word he says. I need to become the bigger person and ignore the temptation to participate in this tug-of-war we've entered into. Even if I have the power to win by dropping a bomb on his happy home life.

I hear the familiar whirl of my car engine in the driveway, so I get into position, wrapping myself in my favorite quilt and turning the TV low on the home improvement channel while I bundle myself on the couch for my mom to discover. It takes her a few minutes to get her things together and make her way through the side door, but when it opens, I call out to let her know where I am.

Time to perform.

"I'm on the couch," I yell, coughing at the end of my sentence. I saw a movie like this once where a kid faked sick so he could ditch school and run amuck all over Chicago. I only want to avoid prying questions over my emotional state.

"Hey!" She sounds beat, her bags banging into the wall as she rounds the corner to where I am. She stops just behind the couch, dropping her bags. "Oh, someone not feeling so hot?"

"Cold, I think. Started not feeling well after the party." This lie has to have some truth to it. I'm not good at lying to my mom. I don't do it, ever . . . much. Fuck, I'm doing it now.

"Fever?" She reaches over the back of the couch and presses her cool hand to my forehead. I don't have one, but that feels good. Lack of sleep might feel a lot like a fever.

I glance up as she pulls her hand away, and I must look rougher than I imagine because my mom flinches at the sight of me.

"I haven't slept very well," I say, adding to the hard sell.

Her gaze lingers on me for a few long seconds, and I

sense she's running her bullshit meter. I might not be passing.

We both startle when the front bell rings. I sit up and run my fingers through my tangled rest of hair while my mom rushes over to look through the side window. I've been wearing the same sweatpants and unicorn shirt since I left the Buick, but anyone who comes to our door wouldn't care, so I get to my feet in case it's something my mom needs help with.

"It's a . . . boy?" She says that as if she's not sure, so I move a little closer.

"Like, one we know?" My response sounds amused.

"Well, the only one I know lives next door, and this isn't him, but he looks like Lucas. Maybe one of his friends?"

Shit.

I glance down at my unicorn shirt with a new perspective. There's a chocolate ice cream stain right where the horn is, like magic popping out of the magic unicorn tip. I don't have to peek through the window to know, but I do anyway, just as Tory cups his eyes and peeks inside. He laughs when our eyes meet, then waves.

"Friend of yours?" My mom lifts a brow, teasingly. I don't get male visitors. I've had one boyfriend, and he was from my Montessori school and lived more than twenty miles away. We either met in the middle at the mall, or my mom dropped me off at his house.

"He's in my fifth hour," I say, moving past my mom to answer the door. "I'll get rid of him," I add, opening the door and hoping Tory didn't hear me dismiss him like that.

I'm not out to purposely hurt feelings—at least, not *everyone's* feelings.

Only a few people's feelings.

"Getting rid of me, huh?"

"Sorry." I wince. "I didn't want my mom to get all . . . nosy?"

He smirks at my response.

"No, no, I'm not flirting." I stop any ideas he might have about a me and him, expecting him to laugh it off with me. When he doesn't, I shrink my chin into my chest and back up toward the door, a little freaked out.

"Why would that be so bad?" He leans into the post of our front porch, thumbs hooked in his front pockets, hair combed to the side and one eyebrow raised. Basically, he's a character from Grease the way he stands in his letter jacket.

"Tory . . ." A nervous giggle is the only thing I can seem to get out after his name.

He stares at me long enough for my anxious laughter to subside, then moves down a step and sits, gesturing for me to sit with him. I do, resting with my back against the guardrail so I'm as far from him as I can be while sharing a step. He laughs at my invisible wall, mocking me a little by moving close enough to his side of the wooden stair to cling to the post. I relax a little when he does it and shrug off my overreaction.

"Look, I'm not saying date me. I don't date," he begins. I puff out a laugh.

"How romantic."

He glares at me with straight-lined lips.

"I can be very romantic. I promise you, romance is all

over this body," he says, running his hand around his chest. I laugh genuinely at his expense.

"Fuck off," he says, standing and walking down my walkway.

"Tory, I'm sorry," I say, feeling guilty. He stops and turns a few yards away, facing me as he exhales.

"I like your company. And honestly? I could use a friend who isn't . . . your jackass neighbor. Or my twin. Or some other jock who thinks and acts like I do."

I wait him out for a beat, surveying the nuances of his expression, but they never betray his words. I think he honestly just wants to spend time with me.

I look down at my shirt and pull the unicorn out from my chest. "Even if I decide to go somewhere with you while wearing this?"

His eyes dip down and his mouth hangs open.

"No, on second thought, forget it. I mean, I was digging your vibe and all, but then I noticed that little chocolate stain and—" He pauses, stepping closer and pointing at my shirt. I look down and he flicks his finger up at my nose, a joke my mom's brother, my uncle John, does every single freaking time he sees me. I roll my eyes and stand to face off with him.

"Come on, let's go get burgers. Drive-thru, clearly," he says, waving an arm up and down at my appearance. I laugh, but I also want to go. I want to get out of here, out of my funk.

"All right, let me get some shoes and tell my mom," I say, padding up the step and back to the door.

"Meet you in my car," Tory says over his shoulder.

I wave in acknowledgement as I step inside. My mom

is waiting right where I left her, probably overtly watching out the window.

"Don't stare like that," I say, walking by her and toward the sofa, where my flip flops have lived for two days. I'm doing my best to combat her gooey, mushy boy-crush eyes. My mom has long had hopes for some normalcy in my coming-of-age story. It's never been about being a busy-body, or a matchmaker, but more that she's afraid her story has changed the course of mine. I'd never tell her this, but I think maybe it has.

I toss my hoodie on over my makeshift pajamas, my phone and wallet tucked in the pocket, and slide back toward the door in my flipflops. My mom halts me with a stiff arm, though, before I get to the door.

"So, we're not feeling sick now, huh?" Her brow arches . . . again. It's been doing that a lot.

"I haven't been out of the house in two days, and someone wants to buy me a burger. It's a free burger," I say, shaking my head.

She turns her head just a fraction, side-eying me, and says "Uh huh." "Midnight," she adds, with a stern nod.

I nod back, though it is weird for her to give me a curfew. She's never given me one before, but that's prob-ably because I literally don't go anywhere. At least, I haven't gone anywhere during these risk-laden teenage years. My hunch is that Tory's slick look has something to do with this. He does put off a bit of an "I'm gonna head to some drag-races with your daughter in tow" kind of face.

The front door doesn't close behind me until I'm almost to Tory's car, and the only reason I know it finally does is because of the hysterical laughter Tory bursts into as he rolls down the passenger window of his Toyota.

"I'm sorry. My mom—"

"Is being a mom," he interrupts. "Mine is just as embarrassing."

I laugh lightly as I slide into the seat and buckle up, but when I turn my head away, I'm sure the scowl is harsh on my face. His mom. Lucas's dad. Best friends with this secret I know happening behind their backs. I swallow and turn back to nod that I'm ready while clutching my phone and wallet in my lap.

"Two-fers?" he asks, shifting into drive and flipping around in front of Lucas's house.

"Sounds good," I say, a little rush of nerves tickling my chest. Two-fers is pretty much *the* place for high schoolers in our community. They sponsor every Public football game. But they also have the best crinkle fries in the county, so having to sit in the D'Angelo car in my jammies in front of people who have always intimidated the hell out of me is maybe worth it. Plus, the drive is short.

I glance to Tory's phone screen, his cell sitting in the cup holder while it streams to his speakers. He's listening to old-school R&B, and I don't know why that surprises me, but it does.

"What? I don't strike you as a Wilson Pickett fan?" He turns the volume up and mouths the words along with the song. It takes me a few lines of the song to notice he's making his version up.

"You're such a bullshitter!" I take his phone into my palm and sift through the songs, all of them as choice as this one. Then I note the name on the playlist.

HAYDEN'S SHIT

I smack at Tory's leg and set his phone back in the cup holder.

"You like this stuff?"

I nod, singing along with the correct words. My voice, however, is terrible. This song in particular occupies space within me. Lucas and I sang this in a talent show at his parents' house, along with a few of his cousins and my parents and some other family friends. That was back when those backyard chairs that now collect dust had people in them.

We pull into the crowded Two-fer's parking lot and into a scene that looks a whole lot like the party I endured Friday night. Tory must sense my unease because he turns the music down and nudges my arm with his fist.

"We'll stay in the car, do the drive-thru and park out of the way," he says.

I smile and breathe a sigh of relief.

The drive-thru line is surprisingly short given the crowd around the joint, but most people go to the walk-up window then hang out. Two cop cars sit facing each other near the last two parking spaces. There tend to be a lot of fights at Two-fers, so the police have started filling out their reports here. I'm pretty sure they get free food.

"So, are you a dog or burger kinda girl?" Tory asks, leaning his arm out his window, waiting to give our order.

"Dog, all the way," I say, catching the instant snicker on his lips.

"Please don't make a dick joke," I sigh out.

"Doggy style?" He shoots me a crooked smile but quickly apologizes. He orders two double-dog deals with

Cokes and pulls around to the window. We're a few cars back from the front, and a new quiet has settled in.

"I'm not a prude," I say. Not sure why *that's* the word I choose, but I don't want him thinking I'm someone I'm not, or that I'm actually offended by his lame jokes. I just sometimes need a break from them.

"I'm not sure how to respond to that," he says through a nervous laugh.

I blush.

"I don't mean, like, well—" I stammer.

"I know what you mean. I talk a lot of shit and I'm loud and obnoxious, and fuck, can I get lit at a party!" Guilty laughter tumbles out of him. "I guess it's a little bit my crutch, if that makes sense? Like, that's my part that I play. I'm the douchebag." He swings his fist from right to left to accentuate his sarcasm.

"You're not a douchebag," I reassure as we move up another space.

He turns his head and tilts it to rest against his seat, a wry smile playing at his lips.

"Come on, be honest. You wouldn't have said that a week ago."

I fess up quickly and nod.

"Oh, absolutely not. You were a douchebag then, but that's only because I didn't really know the other identities of Salvatore D'Angelo." He cringes as I use his whole name.

"And what are those other identities?" he asks.

I twist my lips and look up, blowing at the loose hairs that have fallen loose from the messy bun I twisted my hair into while he was ordering.

"I think maybe . . . yeah . . . damn, I'm about to say this." I level him with a serious look. "You're part gentleman."

He stares at me, unflinching, dead serious—for about three seconds.

"Get outta here!" He shoves at me playfully and waves a hand, brushing off the compliment. I let it go there because that's his way of saying thanks. It was a rather back-handed way to say something nice to him anyhow, and that's because I'm uncomfortable. That trust thing with me, it's a tough nut to crack.

I flip through a few more songs on his brother's playlist until we get to the window for our food. I notice he gives me the box with more fries, and I almost point out how that's one of his gentlemanly qualities, but a black Nissan cuts off our path, pulling into one of the spaces to our right. It's Lucas.

And Ava.

"We can leave," Tory offers.

"No," I hum, my gaze stuck on Lucas's form as he maneuvers his truck in backward. Tory hovers near the exit for a second but lets me make this call, pulling his car into a spot almost directly across from them.

I do my best to focus on my fries after that, searching for the perfect one with slightly burnt tips and golden grooves. I lick the salt from my fingers and mumble out, "This is good" as I take a bite that clears out nearly a third of one of my dogs. I go in for a second bite, and Tory halts me, handing me a packet of ketchup. I look at it with my mouth agape and flit my eyes to him.

"Nobody, I mean *nobody,* puts ketchup on a hot dog," I

say, putting on the best raspy voice I've got. I play serious for a few more seconds, waiting for Tory to laugh, but he just shrugs and goes on drenching his food in that tomato shit.

Lucas would have gotten that joke. One summer, we watched every Dirty Harry movie Eastwood made. His dad had the collection on Blu-ray. He probably still does, last relevant Blu-ray collection in America, I bet. We liked the swearing and the violence—me, mostly because my parents didn't let me watch that stuff at home, and him, I think, because he was the one sneaking it for me. We couldn't eat hotdogs without laughing, but we never said the line out loud in front of our parents for fear they put it together.

That memory hangs heavy in my chest, and my eyes glance out the front window for the first time in a while. Across the way, Ava is talking out the passenger window to a few other girls, and Lucas is eating his fries one at a time, looking anywhere but at her.

I bet he's bored. That's me, wishing.

"Hey, don't you work at Eight Lanes?"

"Huh?" I stir out of my trance and turn to find Tory's eyes, his mouth full from his last bite. He glances out the window to Lucas then back at me with a muffled laugh from cheeks filled with bready bun bits.

"Sorry, I can't help it," I admit.

"You got a crush or something?" He takes another big bite, but stares at me through his chewing, as if that's an easy question to answer. Besides, I'm pretty sure he knows the history there. I've known him as long as I've known Lucas, longer maybe.

"It's complicated," I say.

"Yeah, I figured. He does this same weird shit you do when I'm with him," he says, finishing the last bite of his second dog. Meanwhile, I have one and a half left. He takes a long drink of his soda while I stare at him, waiting for him to elaborate.

"What?" he asks, when he finally looks at me again.

"What same weird shit?" I ask.

I'm jittery all of a sudden.

"You know, he stares at you to make sure you're not having too much fun over here while he's over there, pretending he's not *really* looking at you, or if he is then it's because you irritate him or whatever." He sours his mouth and rolls his eyes. "I don't get you guys."

"I was gone for a full year. I wasn't around to stare at." I brush him off. I pick at my hotdog, pretty sure I won't be able to eat the second one.

"Yeah, but like at your house on weekends, or if you were somewhere we were, his attention wandered off a little. He hated me calling him on it, which of course, ya know, means I basically watch him like a hawk so I can needle him about any glance he gives your way." He breathes out a laugh, lifting a shoulder in a braggart kind of way.

"What a friend," I deadpan.

"A real gentleman," he corrects, with a wink. He reaches toward my lap and points at the still-wrapped dog. "You gonna eat that?"

I lift both hands and puff out my cheeks. He grabs it and devours it in four bites.

"So, Eight Lanes," he says. "That's what I was asking

you about before, when you were off in your *la la fairy crush land.*"

I close my eyes and shake my head, dismissing that term.

"I know, I know . . . it's complicated," he says, reaching over to my box and stealing a few fries.

"Yes, I work at Eight Lanes," I say, pivoting the topic away from Lucas.

"Think you can get me a job there?" His hand creeps over to swipe a few more of my fries, but this time I swat his knuckles.

"Ow!" He plays it up a little, shaking his hand.

I try to imagine my work shift with Tory hanging around, and even though I think the bosses would hate him, he would be fun to have around, and we *are* hiring.

"I'll see what I can do," I say, not making promises.

Tory brushes salt from his hands and gathers up the trash into the Two-fers bag, tossing it out his window and into the trash about twenty feet away. I clutch my container of fries to my chest and continue to pick at them as he shifts gears and slowly pulls out. Always my own worst enemy, I spend these moments studying Lucas, half hoping to catch him in the act of looking back. I don't really expect to, but then, just before I look away, our eyes meet. I don't know why I care so much. And I can't believe he really does. But there's a visceral pain that comes with this brief exchange. I taste it. And for whatever reason, it hurts like hell.

CHAPTER TEN

Somehow, I manage to get through one Friday with no game and no party . My best friend has the flu. Even dog tired and burning up, she still tries to rally. But when she can't get through a sentence without hacking up a lung, her mom puts her foot down. Abby has a pretty big commercial to film in a couple weeks. Right now, she sounds like a chain smoker.

Lola and Naomi don't have the same pull over me that Abby does. Besides that, I picked up the Friday shift since I hadn't worked at the bowling alley during my first week of school. I need the cash. I'm going to need to save about two thousand dollars to pay for the first year at County College, which at this point is pretty much my dream school.

I thought I would enjoy my old routine—ear pods in, *Best of Bowie* on repeat, all the free popcorn I want. Yet, all I can think about is the score, where Lola and Naomi are sitting without me, and whether or not Lucas's dad is standing for the entire game. I give in about midway through my shift and follow the score on the high school sports app on my phone.

That's a lie. I don't care about the score. I care about Lucas's performance. I find myself rooting for him, waiting for small updates on passing yards and completions when we have the ball.

We win, and Lucas threw for almost three hundred fifty yards. I'm satisfied. I catch myself smiling as I wipe down the shoe rental counter at the end of my shift. I drive home in a roundabout way, finally giving in and driving by the damn field. The lights are still on, and the forty-two to ten score is still up on the board to show off our blowout. The stands are completely empty.

But not the parking lot.

One black Nissan truck. I turn off my lights and pull to the side of the road for a minute, maybe two. Lucas's lights are on, and his truck faces to the side, so I have a decent view of the cab. He's alone. No glow of a phone light, no Ava. He's merely a profile from this distance, but there are nuances to his movements.

He's slouched down enough that his head rests on his headrest, his eyes looking up, or maybe closed in thought. His palm runs down his face a few times, seconds apart. I leave just after he leans forward and presses his forehead to the steering wheel. I recognize when someone feels defeated and lost. Even as we stand now, I can't sit here and watch it. I think about it though, all the way until I can't keep my eyes open at 4 a.m.

I wake up this morning and pledge to clear my mind of all things Lucas. I blow that promise when all the seniors on the football team come barreling into the alley. I run to fix stray pins and clean the ball return gears, a job I really don't need to do; I run back there to hide. And now . . . I'm stuck.

It's amazing the clout people give to seventeen and eighteen-year-old dudes simply because they can throw balls and run into people while wearing pads. Morty, the guy who owns this joint, just brought their table a pitcher of beer and a full pizza. I bet he doesn't bring that when the marching band kids come in for the midnight bowl.

Hypocrite.

It's a bit of a tight squeeze back here, so I find a spot between lanes five and six, wedged between the pinsetters. A few of us eat our lunches back here because the Wi-Fi is pretty good in this area and you can stream Netflix on your phone without buffering. I finished the first season of *The Office* back here during my first month on the job.

I'm not streaming anything now, though. I'm too caught up in the show happening at the other end of the lanes. They're loud, typical jockheads making crass jokes and picking each other up just to prove they can. We're a little slow this morning, but a few of the families have moved to lanes on the other end just to gain some space. Morty should probably turn the music up, too.

While most of the guys pace around racks looking for balls, Lucas and Tory enter names on the screen. Lucas is wearing his hoodie pulled over his head, his mouth a hard line and face full of shadows. I wonder if it's leftover frustration from whatever feelings he was trying to process last night after the game. I read the highlights when I got home, thinking maybe I missed something when I was following on my phone, but no—his game was impeccable. Maybe his father didn't think so.

His father.

I keep coming back to it.

My phone buzzes in my back pocket, so I stand to pull it out, balancing carefully in the small space so I don't bump into any of the machinery. It's a text from a number I don't recognize.

We can see you, FYI

I scrunch my face and glance to either side. Nobody is back here, which means whoever is texting me is out there.

Tory?

It takes less than a breath for my phone to buzz in my palm.

No shit.

I laugh silently and lean out to peek through the back of the pinsetter to where the boys are, about three alleys over. I hold my palm out close to my body when I spot him standing behind Lucas, who is still focused on the screen. He holds his hand out the same way then looks at his phone and begins typing again.

There's a mirror.

Brow drawn in, I blink at his text a few times, now settled back in my safe spot. My eyes scan to both sides again while I mentally draw the schematics of this place and think about the sound pads on the walls, the bright lights and disco colors. And then it hits me. I lean my head back slowly, lifting my chin until my gaze finds itself reflected right back at me, upside down.

Motherfuck.

I punch out a laugh and contemplate how many times I've sat back here, oblivious to the fact anyone with a little curiosity could watch the flip-side version of me doing lord knows what. I'm pretty sure I've picked my nose once or twice, just a little. I *know* I've pulled out a wedgie or adjusted bras. The more I study my reflection, the more I realize all of the details you can see—like the way even a modest shirt like my Eight Lanes uniform is unbuttoned just enough for a view. I think about the senior league made up of mostly sixty-five-plus men who comes in on Sundays and always tries to "tip" me, and cringe.

Are you hiding or on break?

I consider going with the harmless little lie, then I fall into my usual pattern.

I'm hiding. Don't laugh.

It's too late, though, because I already hear him bellowing. I twist to look around the pinsetter again and this time, I'm met with four sets of eyes—both D'Angelo twins, some big guy who I think is named Kade, and Lucas. Three smiles and one mouth that is completely void of being human.

My body is hot, and I'm pretty sure a bead of sweat just dripped down my spine. My neck is hot; even with my hair pulled back into a knot, I'm cooking. They keep this place freezing, so I know it's just me.

Tory invites me to join them with a huge gesture, as if I'm somewhere on the other side of a field. I swallow and

Lucas turns to look at his friend; his shoulders visibly slumping. I type a quick message to Tory.

Pretty sure I'm only half invited.

I stare at him while he reads, noting the way his body shakes in amusement. He doesn't bother to text back this time, instead cupping his mouth with one hand. I brace myself for it about a half-second before the sound comes out.

"Maybe Mabee would like to come say hi to her friends!" His hand slowly falls away, and a smug-ass grin covers his face. My joints turn to Jell-O.

Friends.

I'm pretty sure I only have one friend over there. I definitely have one enemy.

I can't stay here, though. Even faking work on one of the ball returns would look like an excuse. Plus, now that I know everyone can see me, I might not ever break back here again. I shove my phone into the back pocket of my jeans and relent, ducking under one of the frames and stepping onto the space between the far lanes. I know better than to look away from my feet, but my ego gets the best of me and I glance up, just for a second, to see whether Lucas is watching me. That's when I fall.

Bowling lane wax is not to be trifled with. One misstep sends my left foot two feet to the left, my arms flailing to find balance while my right foot struggles to hold on. It's useless to fight it, but I decide to give in too late. My legs jut out too far in front of my body and I'm airborne for what feels like a full minute, though I'm sure it's only a blink. The wind leaves my lungs as soon as I slam to the wood, but that's not what hurts the most. My head falls back onto the sharp corner of the gutter, and actual stars form around my vision like bright fireworks flashing in front of my face.

"June!"

My name sounds as if it's being shouted through a tunnel. I'm not sure whether the echo is in my head or in the room. The gasping sounds coming from my own mouth seem so foreign, and my head is ringing. The thunderous sound of running feet rushes my way, and in my daze, I expect to see ten guys rushing to my aid. My head falls to the right and my eyes struggle to stay open.

I have a fucking concussion. I know I do.

My vision is super fuzzy, and fading in and out. What appears to be three pair of legs sliding my direction settles into one pair by the time the person they belong to is at my side.

"June, careful. Don't move."

Ignoring the advice, I roll to my side, but only because I think I might vomit.

"You can't carry her on that. You'll slip, too!"

That voice is distinct. It's Morty, worried about all of the damn accident claim forms he'll have to fill out. Whomever he's yelling at doesn't seem to be listening because hands slide under my ribs and my right hip . On instinct, I reach up with my right arm and grab on to the shoulder of my life raft. It's only when my face is flat against the soft cotton of the hoodie that I recognize who is lifting me against his chest.

I breathe in Lucas's scent, the mix of his mom's lavender fabric softener and the wood and cinnamon of his cologne. He shifts his arms as he moves his legs under his body to stand, and I cling harder, not wanting to fall again. We rise easily, his arms and chest muscles flexing to maintain balance and hold me up.

"I can walk," I utter.

"Shhh," he responds quickly.

My view is of his jawline, the tendon on his neck defined from stress. His feet give way with his tiny steps, and he pauses.

"This shit is slippery," he shouts to his friends.

We have a carpet we roll out when things like this happen, not that they happen often. It's happened twice since I've worked here, and both times were drunk league bowlers who rushed the lane, pissed off about the ten pin not falling. I'm sure Morty is rushing to get the rug now, but Lucas keeps moving us forward.

I stare at his chin, not wanting to look because things around the room are spinning. His chin is my true north. It's the only thing not fucking moving.

"Almost there," he says, reassuring me.

I flinch when his body lunges forward with two massive steps. His balance steadies, though. He tucks his chin to look down, and our gazes meet for a second. That void expression I've seen lately has been replaced with a more stoic one, and his eyes have a concerned tilt to them.

"Tory, someone needs to drive her home, man. Get your car."

Lucas bends down and sets me in one of the plastic seats by the computer and ball return. My hand grips his sweatshirt as he slides me from his hold, and I end up tugging on the material at his waist. I think maybe he's going to step away, put some distance between us. But when I tug, he crouches down next to me and keeps his hand at the base of my neck.

"She's your neighbor, Lucas. Get over yourself and drive her home," Tory says. Lucas twists his head to look up at his friend, but I keep my focus on his chin and jaw. It's firm, and I sense he's not thrilled about getting a lecture.

While their stare-off stretches into long seconds, a new wave of vertigo tackles my brain and I have to close my eyes to will it away. With his attention divided, Lucas's help with my balance slips and as the stomach acid crawls up my throat, I lurch toward the floor. I fall from his grip and catch myself with my palms on the floor, but not before I throw up a little on my Eight Lanes shirt.

Keys jingle as they soar through the air over my head, and Tory takes off in a sprint. Finn, the college dude who's my assistant manager, has already rushed over with a bucket and mop, and the scent of Pine Sol assaults my nose. I cup my face as Lucas sweeps me back into his cradled arms and carries me through the front area and out the doors. I'd be mortified by all of this but I am in so much pain and so sick and dizzy that I don't have room to consider anything else.

Lucas's truck rumbles to the curb, and we pause as Tory rushes from the driver's side and opens the door so Lucas can set me inside. I fumble with the seat belt once he gets me into a sitting position, but his hand covers mine to stop me.

"You're not even close," he says, taking over until I hear the click.

He gently closes the passenger door, and I rest my

head on the window as soon as it's secure. I'm not totally sure when Lucas gets into the driver's side, or when he pulls away from the bowling alley, but we're suddenly about halfway between my work and my home, and I'm kinda freaked because I missed some stuff.

"Hey, the tracks are coming up. I'll try to take them slow, but you might wanna pull your head from the window," he says. His voice is soft. I guess all our relationship required was a freaking traumatic brain injury for us to not be dicks to one another.

I sit up just before his tires crawl over the rough road, but the slow rocking sensation makes my world spin again and I moan.

"I think we need to get you looked at," Lucas says, reaching across the seats and palming my shoulder to help center me. I roll my head and look at him with sleepy eyes. When he pulls up to the last stop sign before my house, he glances to his right and studies my gaze for a few long seconds. For the slightest moment, I feel fine.

"You wait in the truck. I'll run in and get your mom," he says, gaze turning back to the road as he moves through the intersection. I reach up and press my palm against my own head, trying to work the thought inside to my mouth.

"She's not home." I finally get the basics out for him.

"Okay, well, I need your phone then so I can call her."

I nod slowly and reach around my body, feeling for my phone. My grip on it is poor when I get it out of my pocket, and I end up flinging it onto the floor in front of me.

"I'm so sorry," I say. I start to bend forward to get it, but Lucas pulls to the side of the road and touches my shoulder again to get me to stop. Once near the curb a few houses away from where we live, he scoots to the center of the seat and bends down, his body basically covering my entire lap. Despite my whirling environment, I'm acutely aware of his nearness and touch. Somehow, I don't fall over his back in a desperate hug. I want to, though, so my head must not be that far gone.

He lifts himself upright with my phone in his palm, and taps my screen to bring up the keypad. I open my mouth, prepared to utter my password. but he just types it in—04080901. I stare at him until he presses the phone to his ear and looks my way.

"Your birthday and your mom's birthday, same as the garage," he says, blinking once. I can't look away, even when he drops his gaze to his lap as he waits through a few rings before my mom answers.

"Mrs. Mabee, it's Lucas . . . Fuller," he says.

My mom's voice is muted, but her concern comes through in her tone and pitch.

"It's all right, but June slipped at work. I was there with some of the guys, and I didn't want her driving. Yeah . . . of course." He leans forward on his fist, resting his weight on his steering wheel like he did in the parking lot after the game last night.

"Sure, I can wait here. I kinda think she needs to go to the ER though?" He rolls his head to give me a sideways glance. I lift the right side of my mouth in a half grimace. I don't love doctors. Since my grandmother stayed with us and passed away, I've become a little wary of medical stuff.

"Yeah, she threw up once." He keeps his gaze on me but his focus roams around my face, his expression a little scientific, as though he's playing doctor and trying to diagnose something.

"I can do that. Yes. No, not a problem." There's a pause while she talks and he shifts the truck into drive and glances up into the rearview mirror. "I will call you the second we're there."

The call ends and Lucas sets my phone in the small cubbyhole above his stereo buttons. He isn't pulling forward; instead, he makes a wide U-turn, so I know we're not going home. We're going to the hospital. I'm a little panicked about it.

"Your mom said she's at the market or something? Is she like a cashier?" I can barely focus on his question, and my answer comes to me slowly.

"What? No, ummm," I stammer, scowling while I try to organize my thoughts. We are going to the ER but he also asked a question, two things. "She's selling her photography. She's shooting on her own now, and it's a farmer's market up north. Good for business."

He nods.

"Am I going to die?"

Lucas spits out a laugh and turns to see whether I'm joking. I'm not joking. Even though I know I'm not going to die, I'm not joking. This is how my brain works when hospitals get involved.

"No, June," he assures, looking back to the road. He reaches over and pats my knee, almost a fatherly gesture. I'm not sure how I feel about it, but I do feel less like I'm going to die.

My phone rings so I reach for it at the same time Lucas does.

"You're driving," I chastise.

He chuckles. "Yeah, well, you thought you were dying so I thought I should maybe answer."

I'd roll my eyes but I'm pretty sure that would send me tumbling out of the truck, so I look at my phone screen and palm the device between both hands. The caller ID says my mom, so I answer and put her on speaker.

"Mom?" I do a lousy job of hiding my panic.

"June? It's gonna be fine. We just want to make sure it's only a concussion, okay? Lucas? Are you there?" My mom has flipped into management mode. She's good in a crisis, which is probably a good thing because I seem to find a lot of those.

"Yes, ma'am," he says, moving into the left turn lane for the main road out of our neighborhood.

"I called the advanced urgent care on Seventy-Fifth. She's on the waiting list so hopefully you can walk right in and get through. They have my card and insurance on file. If you don't mind taking her home after? I would never make it there in time." I think she feels like a bad parent for leaving my care in the hands of a seventeen-year-old boy who bullied me only a week ago. She doesn't know that last part though, so maybe she just feels bad about the first thing.

"Got it. I'll make sure I call you when we get out of the doc," he says.

"Thanks," my mom says, pausing on the line. I pull the phone into my lap and take her off speaker, lifting the phone to my ear.

"I'm a little freaked out," I admit to her.

She expects this from me. I can tell because she has a

speech prepared; I'm sure they're all the right words. It turns out I don't need any of those right now, though, because while I listen to her, Lucas reaches over and grabs my left hand. I don't think he's letting go, either.

I know I'm not.

CHAPTER ELEVEN

My head will be just fine. That was the consensus after an MRI.

My heart, however—it's fucked.

We wait for almost two hours before they call me in, which means it's dark by the time Lucas brings me home. We didn't talk much in the waiting room, mostly because my head was killing me and the TV mounted to the wall was playing *Friends* reruns so it was pretty easy to space out. It was never awkward, though. The quiet? It was natural, as were the few times he leaned forward to make sure my eyes were open as I sat slumped in the chair next to him, or when he made sure the air wasn't hitting me too hard during the drive home.

I start to think—hope—that maybe we're turning some kind of corner, that my clumsy fall and head injury might result in a little bit of good. Then Lucas turns his headlights off about four houses from ours and slows his truck as he leans close to the windshield, searching for something mysterious up ahead.

I ask if he sees something, like an animal or a person. My heart jumps, imagining maybe there's a burglar at my house.

"Get out." His voice is quiet but urgent. I sit up, attentive, and cling to the seat.

"Is something wrong?" My skin tingles with the rush of adrenaline.

"June, just fucking get out!"

I listen. I goddamn listen and obey and get out of the truck, medical papers in my hand along with a list of concussion symptoms to watch out for. I barely get the passenger door closed and he turns around and speeds off, leaving me under a canopy of trees casting creepy-ass shadows on the road, about four hundred yards from my house. When my mom asks a half-dozen times on Sunday to call Lucas for her so she can thank him—walk next door and ring their bell, buy him stupid cookies—I lie and say Tory ended up bringing me home.

"Lucas had somewhere he needed to go," I say. "He basically handed me off. He said he wouldn't be home all day."

She knows I'm lying by about 3 p.m. when the thump of that blasted basketball pounds on the driveway next door. She quits asking after that.

Thing is, not once do I think about that my car is still parked at Eight Lanes. Not when my mom took off early this morning for some school photo sessions she booked at the elementary school. Not a single time when she and I discuss that I'm not allowed to drive for twenty-four to forty-eight hours. And not when I talk to my best friend over breakfast, swapping stories about our weekends and how much shittier mine was than hers.

I don't think about it until right now as I look out upon my very empty driveway.

"Shit."

I pull my phone from my back pocket and redial Abby, hoping to catch her before she gets to school. I have a glint of hope when she answers right away.

"Dude, I need a ride!" I'm pacing while I talk, and as I move up the driveway, the Fuller garage opening clanks behind me. I shade my eyes from the morning sun as I glance over my shoulder to see whose car it is. It's Lucas's mom, and his dad's car is already gone.

"I'm at school. I have to meet with my counsellor about taking off most of November for that short film I was telling you about." Damn. I forgot.

"It's okay," I say, feeling very much *not* okay. I'm going to be late, and to me, being late is maybe one of the most painful things in life. I'd rather go through another MRI.

"Maybe you can get the bus?" She knows better, but I let her off the hook with a casual "Yeah, good idea" before I let her go. The bus left several minutes ago. I'd be better off running to school, but I'm not a runner. Two-plus miles might get me there by lunch. Fine, by second hour.

I'm staring at Lucas's truck. He's definitely leaving soon. It only makes sense for me to ask him for a ride, yet I still mull over the idea of a taxi or an Uber. He rounds the back of his house before I have a chance to duck out of sight, and stops about ten feet away from me, our eyes locked in a state of awkward panic. He's slowly chewing a bite from a protein bar, and his hand is frozen, holding it near his lips.

"I need a ride." I blurt out my request fast and loud. I wish I could write it off as a side-effect of my injury but no, that was just nerves playing out.

"Why?" he asks through a full mouth. He finishes chewing his bite and swallows hard while glancing over my shoulder as if there's some invisible van ready to take me to school.

"My car is still at work and my mom had a job," I say. I swallow, though not because I'm eating a protein bar. I'm choking down pride.

Lucas shifts his feet and glances to his truck, then to the closed garage behind him.

"Your mom just left," I say, filling in what I suspect he's trying to discern. Maybe he's hiding me from her. It stings a little.

His teeth grip his bottom lip and his jaw tightens as his eyes flit a few times between me and his truck. I start to feel really uncomfortable. I'm also dwelling on the dark walk home I had Saturday night, when he told me to get the fuck out of his truck.

I walk toward his passenger door without permission, and when he utters the word "Wait," I cut him off.

"You fucking owe me," I say, turning and pointing at him harshly.

His tongue pushes at the inside of his cheek but I hold my position, my glare full of fire and determination. He exhales and looks down, his expression frustrated but also yielding. I tug open the door the second he pushes the key fob and releases the lock, and I'm buckled and ready with my bag nestled between my knees before he even opens his door.

He drops his bag in the back of the truck then sighs, staring at the open space between us. He climbs in and reaches for the folding console on his way inside, knocking it down so we have a barrier. It's childish, and I don't care that he helped me after my accident; he's treating me as though I have the plague.

I wait until he gets in, his stupid letterman jacket sleeves crinkling as his arms bend, and I slam the center console back up to create a bench seat, leaving the path between us wide open. His head falls to the side and he stares at the space, an annoyed smile playing at his lips. Eventually, he shakes his head and turns on the truck, looking up to adjust his mirror.

"You and Tory friends now?" He slides through his phone and starts a playlist, some rap song playing loud enough to drown out my reply, so I decide I just won't answer.

A short laugh passes through my lips before I can trap it, but it's masked by the vibrations rattling the truck so Lucas doesn't notice. I lean my head on the passenger window but the buzzing is too much to take. My head still hurts a little, but thankfully my vision has been fine.

We zip backward down the driveway and Lucas jerks the wheel, taking off with enough force that my body jostles and my head slams into the headrest. A momentary heartbeat must fool him into caring because he glances to his right to check on me, and I happen to look just in time to see his widened eyes. The concern quickly switches off, though, and he's back to staring straight ahead, rolling through the various stop signs out of our neighborhood.

I'm sick of this hot and cold thing he does. I know I'm guilty of sometimes provoking it a little. Honestly, I'm not sure what drives me to needle him so much, other than no matter how hard I will this feeling away, there's a constant broadcast running through my head, telling me that the Lucas and me from a few years ago is still salvageable.

"Why did you make me walk?" I speak that loud enough that there is no doubt he heard. His eyes flinch a little, his lashes quaking at the sound of my voice. He pretends he didn't hear a word, and maybe it's because he doesn't want to answer. Or maybe he doesn't know the answer. Or maybe he's continuing this push-pull routine because he's as desperate as I am to cling to some sort of connection between us.

I let my glare burn into the side of his face until the heat of it is so intense that he has to deal with it.

"June, just drop it," he says.

Damn it. I'm going to engage. I punch the power button on his stereo system with my thumb, stuffing the cab with silence while we still have at least a mile or more in our trip to school. When he reaches forward, I slap his hand away, my fingertips stinging his wrist. He bunches his face and turns to give me an angry stare, but in the midst our childish feud, a car turns into our lane, nearly side-swiping his truck right outside my door. Lucas swerves and his arm juts out to hold me in place, a stiff arm across my chest that I grab like a child on their first roller coaster. The entire incident lasts maybe three seconds, but in its wake, Lucas is protecting me and I'm holding on for dear life. I unfurl my fingers and release my hold when our eyes meet, and he retracts his arm, putting his hand back on the wheel. His expression goes blank, and I hate how practiced he's become at erasing moments.

My breathing is hard, the in and out keeping pace with the pounding in my chest. Meanwhile, Mr. Stoic-faced letterman-jacket wearer rushes through the last light before school, clearing the intersection on yellow.

"You trying to get into another near accident?" I scold. The look on his face remains impressively unfazed.

We're running a few minutes behind, but the twins are still waiting around their parking spot, the space next to them open and waiting for Lucas to pull in. No Ava around, or Abby, or my new group of friends. Nobody to witness the shocking display of the two of us pulling into the school lot in the same vehicle. But having to face Tory and Hayden with me in tow must be enough to make Lucas overreact because he cruises right past his usual spot, opting instead for one in the far corner, near the football field. We'll have to haul ass to make it to class on time from here, and my ankle isn't in sprinting shape.

I pull my bag to my chest and get out before Lucas fully shifts into park, and manage to get a few yards ahead of him before he reaches into the back of his truck for his things. I notice when glancing over my shoulder that he's ditched his jacket, leaving it in his truck. He's wearing all black, a thin long-sleeved T-shirt that hugs his body and black jeans that ride low on his hips. I hate how attracted I am to him, even still.

It takes every ounce of determination in my body to maintain my speed to make sure Lucas doesn't somehow sprint past me, and when I find my legs working into a near jog, I laugh inwardly at how ridiculous all of this is. But that doesn't stop me from taking things up one more notch.

"And yeah, Tory and I are friends now. *For now.* I mean, who knows," I say as he moves into the space next to me just outside our first period doorway. I glide into the room first, taking my seat a breath before he falls into his, the now familiar kick of his foot against the leg of my chair jostling me. In my unreasonable state, I dig my feet into the floor and push back in my chair with just as much force, my seat back clanking into his desktop with a snap. Momentarily, I actually wanted his fingers to be caught in there, like a trap. My emotions are cooled by the puzzled look on our teacher's face, so I lift a hand and apologize, making an excuse.

"Sorry, bag strap was caught on something," I say, fussing with my backpack at the side of my chair.

Lucas's heavy foot hammers at the leg again, but this time I'm level-headed enough to ignore it. And as the pattern continues for the next hour, I grow smug, because I pissed him off with that Tory thing, and more than that, that I've stopped playing along.

Game. Set. Match.

CHAPTER TWELVE

Abby is able to drive me to Eight Lanes after school. A lot of good that does, though; my car refuses to start. The sweet girl gave me her last rev over the weekend. I wish I had known, maybe I would have savored the sound. I call my mom while Abby drives me home and tell her the bad news; she arranges for a tow truck to haul my car home. My Uncle John knows his way around an engine, and he promises to come up from Fort Wayne to give it a look next weekend. In the meantime, my trips to school are going to be pieced together with rides from Abby, Lola, and Naomi, because my mom's photography venture is taking off and she's looking to rent studio space for portraits. It's good news, and I'm willing to wake up early and walk to school just to keep her busy and our bills paid.

"Do you think your mom would be down with doing my new headshots?" Abby's been posing in front of the mirror on the back of my closet door for about ten minutes.

"For sure," I answer, tugging out my laptop and logging in to my student portal. My friend flops down on my bed next to me and pushes my laptop closed.

"I was working on that, you know," I groan. She pulls it from my reach.

"You work too hard on that. Senior year, remember the plan? Coast a little." She lays back and tugs at the back of my T-shirt, coaxing me to rest next to her.

"I'm pretty sure the plan has been blown." I blow out hard enough to move the few stray hairs that fall across my lips.

"Nah, plan is in full motion," my friend says, pulling her phone from her back pocket and holding it above her face. She scrolls through a few social media apps in search of something and stops on some comment left by a person tagged RedTedFred.

June and Tory totally dating.

My eyes blink quickly and I push the phone away from my face. I'd call it meaningless, but even a wallflower like me knows that high school gossip carries a little bit of weight.

"We're not dating," I clarify.

"I know. You'd tell me." There's a lilt in her tone that tells me she's not one-hundred percent sure that I would. And since I'm sitting on so many things I haven't told her, I can't honestly agree and say "Of course I would," so I say nothing.

"Rumors are stupid. And I'm not dating Tory D'Angelo." Of course, I totally used that very same suspicion to piss off the boy next door and let him wonder what's up between Tory and me. I'm such a fucking hypocrite.

"The fact you've stirred curiosity is a good thing," Abby says. She rolls to her side to face me and begins twisting pieces of my hair.

"How is that?" I don't know why I'm asking. I guess maybe there's a little part of me that's hooked on the drama. That's painful to admit to myself, so I tuck that thought somewhere deep and pretend I never had it.

"People like a good story." She shrugs her top shoulder and lets go of the twist of my hair she's been holding. It unravels like silk.

"I don't like being the story." I glance at her sideways and she gives me a crooked smile.

"Yeah, you do. Just a little." My friend tucks in her knees and rocks herself back to a sitting position. I stay where I'm at, pondering her words and feeling a little guilty about the dash of truth to them.

"I miss Lucas," I admit. It's strange how light my chest feels after saying that out loud.

My friend swings her backpack over her arms and stands from my bed.

"You should try really talking to him, and then tell him that," she says with her back to me.

"Probably," I agree. I do a sit up on the center of my bed, then scoot my feet to the floor to hug my friend goodbye at the waist. Maybe next time I'll tell her about the affair I witnessed and she can help me figure out how that secret fits in with me and Lucas having a real conversation.

I follow Abby downstairs, answering a call from my mom as I wave bye to my friend.

"The tow should be there in an hour. Can you hang

around the house to sign for it? They have my card on file." There's chatter in the background.

"Sure. Where are you?" My eyes tail my friend's car as it rolls down the street, switching focus to an unfamiliar red sports car that passes her on the way and slows at Lucas's driveway. There's a blonde woman driving, her hair cropped bluntly at her shoulders and oversized black sunglasses shading her eyes.

"I think I found a space!" My mom's excitement draws me back in, but from the side door of our house I spy on the stranger pulling slowly up the Fuller driveway. The garage opens, unveiling Lucas's mom's car, and his mother guides the red car into the space where her husband usually parks.

Divorce attorney? This is how rumors start.

"That's awesome, Mom. Are you gonna get it?" My attention is split in half.

"Negotiating now," my mom says. She mentions a few other things, and I hear the words dinner and order, but I don't retain much else. I end the call with her and close the side door most of the way so I can spy the proper way.

My mind spins with these clues, rearranging them to make sense, and then the roar of Lucas's truck grinds up the driveway. I slam the door closed, eliminating the slight crack I was peeking through and move to the kitchen window, slitting the shutters enough to hide my profile.

Lucas should be at practice right now. He pulls his truck in close to the house, slipping out the driver's side and rushing around the back of the house as if he forgot something. He's wearing his gray practice shirt and his football pants, halfway dressed out for a practice, so I wonder if he did forget something at home. The longer he remains inside, though, the less likely that theory holds.

Almost thirty minutes pass with me staring at Lucas's truck and the closed garage door hiding some strange visitor's car. I have to pee, but I'm so afraid I'll miss something and waste this time I've invested. My persistence pays off a few minutes later when the garage door opens and the red car's reverse lights glow bright. Lucas walks out through the open garage along with his mom, and they both wave to the blonde woman backing out. I'm too far away to discern whether they're scowling or smiling, but they don't linger. Lucas jogs backward to his truck and his mom gets in her own vehicle, and they both disappear in less than a minute.

An hour of my life is gone.

It's almost seven at night by the time the tow truck driver rings our bell. My mom's words are starting to make more sense now, since it's dinner time and she isn't home. I ordered a pizza from Rudy's twenty minutes ago, and the delivery man shows up while I'm guiding the tow up my driveway. I pay for the pizza and hold the box at my hip while the tow driver disconnects my car from his bed.

As the tow truck leaves, I plop a seat on the trunk of my car and open up the piping hot box of pizza next to me to let it cool. I should call Abby or text the other girls to see if they want to come over and share. I pull out my phone to do just that, but stop short when Tory pulls up at the end of my driveway. I tuck my phone in my pocket and lean back against my rear window while he walks up my driveway.

I'm fanning the rumors.

"What's up, Mabee?" His gray shirt is drenched with

sweat and his hair is damp and twisted in various directions from wearing his helmet.

"To what do I owe the honor?" I gesture to the pizza at my side, offering him a slice. He doesn't hesitate, pulling a piece free, the stringy cheese threading through the air.

"I'm starving, thanks," he says, blowing on the end for a few seconds before taking an impatient bite. He waves his hand at his mouth and chews with it open.

"It just got here. Might be hot," I say, wincing with guilt.

"Ya think?" He laughs while he chews, but goes in for more, not deterred by the burn I'm sure that left on the roof of his mouth.

"You waiting on Lucas?" I glance to my right, to the driveway still empty after all the activity it held earlier.

"I came to check on you," he says, moving the pizza box closer to me and taking a seat on the back of my car. It dips with his weight.

"Really?" There's a twist in my chest from his answer. I'm not sure I want him checking on me because that lends credibility to the rumor, and we aren't dating. It makes me think maybe he thinks we are, though.

He leans back on the rear window and holds the slice at an angle, guiding the rest of it in his mouth.

"You ate that in three bites," I observe.

He chortles with his cheeks puffed out, full of crust.

"Like I said"—he muffles out the words—"I'm starving."

He pulls out another slice and hands it to me. I test the temperature with my palm. It's cool enough to nibble. Tory doesn't waste time with small bites, devouring a second piece in the time it takes me to get through an eighth of my first one.

"So. Abby . . ."

I'm chewing when he hits me with the awkward transition. That's probably for the best because the little pause I'm forced to make helps me put things together. He has a thing for my friend.

"What about her?" I smirk to myself.

"You think she really hates me?" he asks.

We're both leaning back on the car window, staring up at the dimming sky and eating pizza. I can tell he's trying to keep this casual, to not assign it too much meaning. Somehow, in the first two weeks of school, this obnoxious twin has become one of my best friends. I breathe out a little laugh at that thought.

"Sometimes it seems she hates all of us," I say, rolling my head to the side and squinting at him with one eye.

He pulls out another slice, this time folding it in half and biting from the crust end. He nods slowly and glances at me sideways while chewing.

"Sometimes isn't *all* the time, so that means there's a shot." He winks and his coyness sparks a warm feeling in my chest, making me grin.

"There is always a shot," I say.

He turns his head to face upward and nods, smiling through another bite.

"Speaking of . . ."

The rumble of a truck breaks up our quiet. I will myself to not glance to the right, even as the driver's side door opens and slams shut.

"Hey, Princess!" Tory teases, holding up his hand in a

wave as he lies next to me. I eye him from the side and notice he's not looking Lucas's way. He's taunting him, maybe for sport . . . maybe for me.

I let him.

There's no immediate response from Lucas, only the slow shuffling of his feet drawing closer. Nerves make me want to fill the silence, but I'll only say something I'll regret, or something that will push this game between us to a new level. I can't judge Lucas for being hurtful and taunting if I do the exact same things.

"You got your car back," he says.

Yeah, guess you don't have to worry about me begging for rides anymore. I let that thought pass through, discarding it. It's not the right thing to say.

"I did." I pat my hand against the metal and roll my head to the side until my gaze lands on him. He's trying not to say the wrong things, too. I can tell by the tightness in his neck, the way his shoulders are high despite the bag of gear dangling from his right arm and heavy backpack pulling down the left.

"That's good." He takes a few steps closer, stopping just short of the place where his driveway blends into the shared grass between our yards. My gaze flits down to his feet, his socks rolled down to expose the difference between the clean skin on his legs and the dirty. He's wearing the same Nike slides he's had since junior high.

"Your feet never grew after that big burst, huh?" I nod toward his shoes and he lifts his right toes. This natural conversation feels so strange but so nice. I'm a little sad Tory is here to witness it, because his presence keeps things from getting too deep.

"Yeah, well, it took me a few years to grow into my size thirteens." His laugh is raspy. It's real. I trace his body up to his face, catching a glimpse of his mouth before he raises his head to look at me. He's biting his lip like a child, amused by his own giant feet. When his eyes meet mine, there's a softness there that's been so fleeting. It's the same face he wore in the truck on the way to the hospital and when he sat next to me in the ER.

Such sweetness ruined in a blink by the sound of his father's truck pulling in the driveway behind him. Lucas looks down and to the side, his muscles automatically growing harder and his attention shifting. He takes a few steps back as his dad stops just short of pulling into the garage.

"Lucas?" He slams the door closed behind him and takes a few long strides in our direction. I swear Lucas swallows hard.

"I was just talking with Tory," he says, leaving me out of the picture. Tory's elbow moves into my side in acknowledgement and I swallow down the hurt feelings.

"Mind telling me why Coach called me tonight?" His dad couldn't care less that Tory and I are feet away from them.

"Well, I wasn't on that call, you were, so . . ." There's an edge to Lucas's voice.

Sucking in my lips, I make myself quietly invisible as I look to my left and meet Tory's heavy stare. He shakes his head slightly, a hardness to his jaw and sadness in his eyes. This is something we aren't supposed to see, a moment Lucas would rather keep from my view.

"Tory, do you know why my son skipped out on an hour of practice today?"

Tory's eyes don't immediately shift from mine, and I keep my head turned to face him, not wanting to be questioned next or see the look on Mr. Fuller's face that matches his tone. Tory blinks his gaze up a notch and casually shrugs his shoulder.

The quiet brews thicker, so much so that there's almost a smell to it—a choking thickness with the scent of iron.

"Thanks, Tor. You're a real fuckin' help," Mr. Fuller says.

Tory's eyes dim and a heavy grimace glues his lips shut.

"Let's just go inside," Lucas says, his shoes rubbing along the pavement with belabored steps that scratch and pull, as though he's trying to drag every ounce of this topic and conversation somewhere private along with him.

"This a joke to you, Luc?" The sound of his steps halts with his dad's accusation.

I shouldn't get involved.

"Maybe Mrs. D'Angelo knows." The words come out without a plan or a filter. My voice is loud, and my eyes scan the stars above my head in an effort to seem indifferent. Tory snorts a laugh at my side, because he thinks I'm saying random snarky shit to help Lucas out. There's nothing random about the words I chose.

With a deep inhale, I sit up and slide from the back of my car, my stare finding the one I knew would be waiting for me. Todd Fuller has always had a heavy brow. It's a little gray, a peppering that matches his short, well-trimmed beard. He wears a suit well—the look of a boss with expensive ties, his gold watch exposed when he raises his arm. His glare is purposeful, meant to intimidate me, but it also hides some major fucking fear. I shot close to home, and he knows there's no coincidence in anything I said.

A menacing grin flashes across his face, wicked like his eyes, and then he resumes his act, shaking his head and waving his hand at me, dismissing my words as garbage.

"Get inside," he finally huffs, marching past his only child, his golden boy who I'm starting to think only ever played football to make his old man happy. Pity they're both so miserable.

Lucas stays put until his dad climbs back into his truck and hits the button to raise the garage door. His mom's car is already parked inside, and I can't help but believe Mr. Fuller is taking this inside because he doesn't want her overhearing.

"I gotta go, Mabee." Tory squeezes my shoulder from behind, then leans to grab one more slice of pizza as he heads back to his car. "Call if you need me, Luc." He holds up a peace sign and Lucas does the same. His gaze follows his friend's path until he pulls away in his car, then it flits back to me, a deep crease cut between his brows.

A few wordless seconds pass, and my need to fill silence gets the best of me.

"I'm sorry," I croak out. I feel a heavy coat of shame, and I don't know whether it's my empathy for Lucas or for what I know but don't fully disclose.

"Don't be," he says, no bite or warning in his tone. His mouth forms a tight line. a forced smile meant to cover serious hurt and pain. He glances to the side of me and nods. "Glad you got your car back."

I nod, keeping the details of the blown engine and my lack of transportation to myself for now. This isn't the time for favors, and my ride is covered. Plus, I can tell Lucas wants to get whatever is waiting for him in the garage over with; I'd rather not have to look him in the eye.

This is a good place to leave things.

CHAPTER THIRTEEN

I t was an impulsive decision. Almost as knee-jerk as
when I blurted out Mrs. D'Angelo's name in front of
Lucas's dad. Whatever it was that made me go through
with it, when I walked into school on Tuesday morning
after Abby drove me in, I went straight to the office and
begged my counselor to put me in an independent study
for my physics credit. As much as I want to have forced
interactions with Lucas every day, I haven't wanted them
for the right reasons. Starting every morning like that, so
negative and contentious, won't get either of us anywhere
healthy. I might not see much of him anymore, but I'd
rather have rare, meaningful interactions that he chooses to
be present for than ones where we show up for attendance.

I easily got my mom to buy off on the plan. I'm good at
physics, and I did most of the work my junior year in other
ways. I just need the official credit. I took advantage of my
mom being busy and distracted, trying to get out of the
house with arms full of gear and her phone on speaker

while she spoke with her broker about the studio space she's renting in Old Town.

I miss our angsty morning battles—little pushes and shoves and biting comments—but the void is the kind a druggie has when going through withdrawal. Maybe that's why I agreed to the game tonight—a little taste of Lucas from a safe distance.

Controlled abuse.

As the fourth quarter ticks down, I don't feel any giddiness at all over the sight of him. We're down by two touchdowns. I'm not much of an optimist, but the small fraction of me that is knows that even the great Lucas Fuller can't close that gap against Pinewood Crest in less than two minutes. Their defense is rabid, borderline on sportsmanship, and twice the size of our offensive line. Lucas has been sacked three times this half, two the first half. His dad left at the end of the third, forcing his mom to leave her spot in the away stands so he could drive them home. He didn't even stand during the game like he normally does. He was disappointed, and he wanted to make sure anyone looking knew he was not proud of his son's performance.

As if anyone gives two shits what middle-aged Todd Fuller thinks.

"Hey guys, the party got moved to Sammy's garage. I'm still in if you are," Abby says, glancing over her shoulder at me with puppy eyes. I sigh and picture my evening, sitting on some metal chair in a garage while people drink and play beer pong.

"I'm down."

"Me, too."

Lola and Naomi sell me out quickly. I laugh under my breath and close my eyes as I lift my shoulders.

"Fine," I say in one long breath.

"You don't have to," Abby says, and I open my gaze on her, expecting to see the opposite message in her expression. She seems genuine.

"Are you sure?" I tilt my head, waiting for her to smack my leg and tell me to get my ass to the party.

"Yeah, I mean it's Sammy's garage. It's not an epic moment." I'm not sure whether she classifies it that way to let me off the hook or she's strategically saving up my party attendance requirements for better, bigger blowouts ahead. Regardless, I'm thankful for the break.

"Ohhhh!" The collective moan in the small crowd left on our side sends my attention back to the field, just in time to catch Lucas pulling himself to his knees.

"Line isn't doing their job tonight," some old man commentates behind me.

"Bullshit. QB's head isn't in this one. Sucks to lose to them, too. We might not make playoffs because of this." I recognize the second voice as Mr. D'Angelo. He doesn't make it to many games because his work puts him out of the state a lot. Tory mentioned something about him getting home for this one, though. At least his son looked good tonight, as good as anyone can look losing twenty-one to seven.

The girls stand, straightening their jeans on their hips and putting on their mini backpacks to leave before the rest of the home crowd. I kinda want to see this game to the very end, though. Not because of optimism, but because nobody here is in Lucas's corner. I feel . . . obligated, I guess?

"June, you ready?" Abby is already a few steps down the bleachers. I haven't even stood.

"Can I meet you guys at the car? I want to see the end."

My friend scrunches her face as if I just told her I'd like to eat a cup of ass soup.

"I told Tory I'd stay," I say, playing guilty.

Her eyes narrow.

"That thing still just a rumor, June?" She's only half teasing, I can tell by the slight slant of her head.

"Yes, Abby." My response is stern enough for her to stop prying, and over her shoulder she tells me to hurry while she and the girls leave the sparse away stands.

Lucas won't even get in the game again. The clock is under a minute, and the other team is just burning the seconds. He's alone on the opposite end of the action, helmet off and dangling from a weary right arm, a towel tucked in the back of his pants on the left side. He's staring at the clock instead of his defense, just hoping it all ends. None of this is fun for him; I can tell. I'm starting to wonder if I'm the only one who can.

Both teams crowd the field before all the seconds tick down, and Lucas is last to walk through the Eagles line and shake hands with the other squad. Even his coaches are ahead of him, avoiding him rather than getting angry. Not that the outcome of this game rests squarely on his shoulders, or that the failures were completely his fault. Maybe everyone here has just gotten used to him carrying them. When talent runs thin, Lucas plays harder to make up the difference. He's always been that way. Always can be exhausting.

I wait until our line of players filters toward the end zone before I climb from the stands. I'm the lone person on this side, a standout. I walk around the track on the outside of the fence while the team crosses the field on their way to the bus. When I reach the gate, I have to wait for them to exit, not wanting to dart through the horde of pissed off teenaged boys and grown men who act like them. I catch Tory's eye and he lifts his chin in acknowledgement, the strap of his mouthpiece dangling from his lips as he chews on it. Most of the guys wear the same expression, defeat haunting their eyes, fear draining the color from their cheeks. They're going to get their asses chewed in that bus for the thirty-minute drive home, and that lecture . . . it matters to a lot of them. Not all of them, though.

Clearly not *one* of them.

Lucas wears his helmet balanced atop his head, the face mask not pulled down but resting against his forehead. He's chewing at his plastic mouthpiece with such a vice grip that it's become malformed, the gnawed remnants hanging from his mouth. We're close enough to touch as he approaches the gate.

I form fists with the long sleeves of my Eagles hoodie and hold my breath, hoping it's okay that I'm even here. His gaze flits toward me for a beat as he passes, just long enough for the muddied blue to reach inside my heart and spear it just a little.

I wait for the field crew to zip through with their cart, mostly to buy time and distance between the team and me —between Lucas and me. I spot Abby's car near the exit, pulled up close to the curb, and I jog toward her before she honks and draws attention to me. I lost the front seat to Naomi, so I round the car and climb into the seat behind Abby. I catch her eyes on mine in her rearview mirror while I buckle up, and there's an understanding in them that I should have known would be there. She knows why I stayed, same way she knows why I would never date Tory D'Angelo. My heart is still loyal to Lucas Fuller, no matter how much of an asshole he can be.

Our exchange is wordless, and I'm strategically quiet for the ride home, making sure to sing along with the radio and give my opinion on things when it's easy. I speak up just enough to not make anyone question where my mind is, but my mind is long gone. It's at home, in the front seat of a rusted-out Buick, while I stare up at the window of the boy I once knew so well.

When Abby drops me off at my house, I make her promise to call me for a ride home from the party. My mom is home, which means the van is mine. It would have been the perfect night for me to play designated driver, but I *really* don't want to be at a party. I want to be right here, sitting in this dirty seat that I swore I'd never get in again the last time Lucas found me here.

Maybe I knew deep down he would come. A part of me surely hoped for it. I've been sitting out here for about an hour. I expected it to take time for the team to make the trip home, for him to shower and change, and to get out of going to a party he doesn't want to be at either.

His hair is damp and falling over his eyes as he weaves through the tall weeds and the abandoned tires that will never hold air. Nicolas Mabee's Junkyard, that's what this place is. Fitting that I'm out here, too, among my dad's left-over, forgotten treasures.

The door pops when he opens it, the palm print from the last time he sat here waiting to greet him. He leaves the door open but sits with both legs inside. I roll down the window on my side as far as it will go, which is only inches, but it lets a cross breeze flow through the cab, clearing out some of the mustiness.

I'm stuck on the faintness of his freckles across the bridge of his nose. I get lost in them, admiring quietly while he stares straight ahead into whatever picture his mind is conjuring. We sit like this for long minutes, hiding from expectations, from our past, from our futures—from our parents. I'd be content if this quiet lasted for hours, for it to be all he needs before he leaves the car and goes back to his life inside that house. But the outside world doesn't want anything I do.

His phone blares out the Kanye song he was listening to the night I walked in on him with Ava. He leans to the side to pull his phone from his pocket, checks the screen, and quickly dismisses the call. The alert sounds again the second he tucks his phone away, so this time he powers it off and tosses it on the filthy dashboard. He leans forward and rubs both palms over his face, then into his hair.

Through it all, I don't talk. I'll wait as long as he needs to find his words, and if he never finds them, I'll be his companion for this soothing bit of silence.

His hands clasp in front of him as he leans forward and rests his weight on the dash. His body inflates with a deep breath, spilling out through his nose.

"I want to go to MIT." He nods, acknowledging his wishes out loud.

"That's amazing." I hope that's the answer he wants to hear. His head falls forward, resting on his hands, and he rolls it side to side as he kicks at the ripped-up flooring beneath his feet.

"It is, isn't it?" He rolls his head to the side until our eyes meet. A smile flashes on his lips, a defeated remnant of pride.

His palms flatten and he shifts his weight so his cheek rests on his folded hands and arms, his eyes blinking slowly as he stares at me. I feel this overwhelming pressure to give him some sort of solution.

"I got an offer from Tennessee," he continues.

I nod, remembering the conversation I overheard him have with Mr. Newsome.

"That's awesome, too." This time, my response makes him laugh. He leans back and balls his fists to his eyes, a semi-maniacal laugh slipping into a more desperate one.

"You're right. It is." His hands fall into his lap, and I'm caught on the dirt and tape that still mar his fingers.

"What do you want?" My gaze moves back up to his, and everything behind it is so lost. He shakes his head while he turns to the side, twisting so his body faces me.

"Does that matter?" he says, a quick lift of his shoulders.

"It should," I answer. Another laugh punches through his chest.

I look down to the shifter between us, the marble ball on top of the stick the one thing my dad put new in this car before he took off. I wonder if it's even worth anything. I grab it in my palm and twist until it gives, unscrewing it until it's finally just a stone ball with a screw-hole in it. I toss it in my hand a few times, testing the weight, then I hold it out for Lucas to take.

He squints a little, leaning closer before taking it from me. Our fingers touch slightly, and it's everything to me. Somehow, I steady myself enough to take in the way his lashes shadow his eyes, blinking as he studies my stupid gift.

"Thanks. I always wanted this thing," he says.

"I know," I say, chuckling.

My dad used to yell at him for taking this ornament off the car and throwing it around the yard. Lucas even tossed it in his pool once and made me dive in to get it back.

"It's yours now," I say, though my worst self is waiting in the wings to bite me. "Or you could give it to Ava."

He doesn't glance up at my comment, and I'm glad. I wish I could take it back. I hate that I said it. I know it was her who called. She's probably burning up his phone while it's powered down, leaving angry messages and threats for me. I'm probably giving her dislike for me too much credit; I doubt I take up that much of her headspace.

"Why'd you leave physics?" He still hasn't looked up, instead keeping his focus on the shiny ball in his palm. Oh, how I wish I could look away from him.

"Seemed it was for the best." I give him the truth, and I don't really have to dive into the details. He knows how we've been behaving. We haven't been very good to each other, not for a very long time.

"Yeah," he breathes out.

He tosses the ball in his palm a few times, then lines it

up with the screw sticking out of the top of the shifter. He turns it, tightening it back into place.

"I don't really want it," he says, finally glancing in my direction. An amused curve plays at one side of his lips. "I just liked that it pissed your dad off."

We both laugh.

"It did," I recall.

His gaze lingers, but rather than turning mine away, I spend it on his every facial feature—the permanent crease that's etched into the corners of his mouth from his smile, the tiny scar that splits his right eyebrow from where he hit his head on the monkey bars and needed stitches, and the way his right ear sticks out a little more than his left.

"Ava's not my girlfriend, just so you know."

His words slam into my chest, but I mask my reaction, drawing in a long breath through my nose to keep my heart at bay.

"She seems like your girlfriend," I say, not even sure why. Maybe I just need to be sure of some things.

"She's not," he answers quick. "She's just . . ." His chest fills with a heavy breath and guilt taints his eyes, pulling the corners down along with the edges of his mouth. "She's just this mistake I make sometimes."

I shake my head, and his face puzzles.

"She's not a mistake," I say.

"Okay," he says. He doesn't understand, and I don't entirely either, but there's something behind that word that needs fixing.

"I might not like her very much, but no girl deserves to be labeled a mistake. She's a lot of things, but mistake isn't one of them. Your moments with her had purpose, even if they were brief and not love. Your actions can be a mistake, but not the person." My eyes tear at my own words. I don't know that I've ever been this vulnerable, not even with Lucas. I run my arm over my face and sniffle.

"Okay," he says, a gentle laugh seeping through.

"Okay," I repeat.

Every light in his back yard flicks on at once, and we both turn our heads, startled by it. His dad's figure moves from one end of the patio to the other.

"He's probably looking for me," he says.

"Let him," I say, my bravado amusing him.

"I wish I could, but—"

"But he's the reason you can't go to MIT?" I kinda knew in my gut, and when his gaze shifts to mine, he confirms it.

"He went to Tennessee, and me and football—"

"You're living his dream," I fill in. He nods, every bit of joy slipping from his eyes and the lift in his cheeks. His dad is an anchor that is drowning him. I should tell him the truth, set him free. If only there were a way it wouldn't destroy his family like it did mine.

"He'll come around," I say, my words the push he needs to exit the car and abandon our conversation.

"Doubtful," he says, both palms on the roof of the car as he dips his head into my view. I can feel the part of him that wants to stay here screaming from behind his eyes. Those damn expectations, though—the pull is strong.

"Thanks, June." He raps on the top of the car once then backs away, closing the door. I wait until he disappears through the thick brush and weeds, then I roll the window up and leave the driver's side. I can hear his father's voice through the night air. He isn't shouting, but he's also not being a father. He's lecturing, reprograming, willing Lucas to love all the things he wants him to. People don't work like that, though.

If they did, I would have willed Lucas to love me a long time ago.

By the time I get inside, my mom isn't around; she probably went upstairs. I shut off the lights downstairs, and gather up the documents she left scattered on the counter. There are a few printout photos of a storefront, so I carry them over to the faint night light glowing near the stove and picture her space being there. It's the perfect size, with an old-fashioned awning over a huge window and green door. The inside is empty except for the black and white checkered tiles and a single barber's chair in the middle. I'm sure she'll have to redo the inside, but I kind of hope that chair sticks around.

I leave the photos on the stack of forms and round the corner, racing up the stairs two at a time because I don't like the dark. My mom is asleep sideways on her bed, still wearing her jeans and the business blazer she says makes her look professional. I don't want to disturb her, so I turn her light off and close her door so she has quiet. I'll make sure she's up when I leave for work in the morning.

My room glows from the small mood lamp that is never off in the corner of my room. The blue light is just enough to see by, and it calms my active imagination whenever I'm alone. I pull my phone, cash and school ID from my back pocket and toss it on my bed, kicking my shoes off and rolling my socks from my feet with my toes. I move to my window to close my shutters, but I tilt them enough to look into Lucas's yard before I shut them completely.

The lights are off now. I push the slats closed, but a ticking sound rattles against the other side of the glass. I hold my breath to hear it more clearly, and just when I think maybe my mind is playing tricks on me, I hear it again. This time, it's more of a scattering sound—pebbles. I open the slats and look down, my pulse racing. I manage to catch a view of Lucas's next throw. This time, it's a dozen tiny rocks clinking against my metal frame, the vinyl siding, and the glass.

I pull both sides of my shutters open and lift the window open so I can hear him.

"What are you doing? You can't run away to here. I mean, he'll find you," I joke.

"You were never a mistake," he says, not even reacting to my words.

I stare at him with my mouth agape, not sure what to make of this gesture or this big revelation that's so important he has to throw rocks at my window at eleven-thirty at night.

"Okay," I say, grinning with a thumbs up.

"No, June . . ." He holds up a finger then rushes forward. Lucas used to climb up the eaves on our porch to tap on my window all the time. He was like Spiderman, his hands sticky and feet stickier. His body is a lot bulkier now, and the sounds of his shoes on the lower angles of the roof are clunky, but his height makes up for his lack of agility. His hands grip my window ledge within seconds, and he lifts his body up easily as I back away.

The racing in my chest is nonstop, and it's no longer

fear of a boogeyman or the dark. I'm afraid of this not being what I think it is—what I hope it is. Lucas pulls his body through my window a leg at a time until he's literally the air I'm breathing. He looks almost lost, standing right inside my window, his hands not sure whether they should relax or move to illustrate his point. His eyes blink rapidly at first, then his gaze locks on mine and his teeth hold the tip of his tongue as he breathes out a nervous laugh.

"When you said those things, about how no girl wants to be a mistake." He shakes his head but his eyes never leave mine. "You meant you. You weren't talking about Ava."

He steps toward me and my hands ball into fists at my hips. I bang them against my skin anxiously as I glance to the side, to my mirror that still has pictures of me and Lucas taped to it.

"I'm sorry, June," he says, and even though I feel him stepping closer, I don't look. I can't look. If my eyes meet his right now, I'll sob, and I don't want to break down in front of Lucas Fuller. That's not how this goes.

"You are not a mistake," he repeats, his body close enough that heat radiates from his chest, blocking the cool breeze streaming in through my open window.

"Got it. Thanks," I say, belittling his honesty. I thought this is what I want, but now that it's happening, it's too hard. There's too much attention on me, too many things stripped away.

His fingertips tickle against my chin and with slight pressure, he coaxes my gaze toward him. Fighting it would be childish, but looking him in the eyes feels deeply impossible. I'm not sure I'll survive it.

He takes away that choice.

With both of his hands cupping my cheeks, Lucas erases the few inches left between us, tilting my chin up so I'm forced to meet his eyes. They're even bluer in my light, blue like the midnight sky.

"You are not a mistake," he says, his eyes holding mine hostage to make sure they see every word formed on his lips.

I nod, a shaky movement on the verge of falling apart in a breath.

"Okay," he says through a crooked smile. I'm too close to see the dimple it forms, but I don't need to, I've memorized it.

His thumb sweeps away the moisture forming under my right eye and I croak out, "Thanks."

"Don't mention it," he says, repeating the touch on my left cheek.

I've held my breath so long, through my words and his, that the sensation makes my head float and my chest burn. I'm afraid of the sound I'll make, but if I don't get air, I'll die here. This would be a good death.

My lips part with a quaver, and the light gasp is the last thing I remember before Lucas's eyes dart to the slight movement. His right thumb traces along my cheek, over my top lip and onto my bottom one, stroking along it slowly until my eyes have no choice but to close. I sense his body moving before his lips touch mine, a feather-light brush of both of his lips along the plumpness of my bottom one.

Another tear is forming, and I have no choice but to accept it. My hands relax at my sides and move forward until I find the softness of his shirt. I grip it, bunching it tightly against his chest.

Lucas's nose brushes the side of mine as he cocks his head the other way, his mouth taking a gentle taste of my upper lip this time. My mouth on autopilot, my lips beg to move with his. I'm not sure whether I'm the one who deepens the kiss or he is, but as my hands let go of his shirt and snake their way up his chest and around his neck, his palms move to the back of my head and draw me close to taste me fully. His tongue teases against mine, the softness meeting the sharp edges of my teeth. I nibble at his top lip as he sucks in my bottom one, running his tongue along the delicate skin. I wait for him to walk me backward, for him to lift me up and force my legs to wrap around him. All of my fantasies over the last two years rush my senses at once, but I let him be the guide. I'm still not certain this is real.

Only when he's out of breath does he release his mouth's hold on mine. I chance opening my eyes when his forehead rests against mine, and I look up to see his eyelids closed tightly as he rocks us back and forth where we stand.

"That was not a mistake," he whispers, his body sending me zero signs that he plans to move from this position any time soon.

"Okay," I whisper back, stepping up on my toes and chastely pressing my lips to his. This time, his are the ones to break and tremble. I hold our kiss still, my teeth grazing against his bottom lip when I finally let go.

"Okay," I repeat the words against him. I say them again, hoping maybe, after enough times, we'll both believe this. "Okay."

CHAPTER FOURTEEN

"You can't tell anyone."

That's the last thing Lucas said to me before he fled out my window, leaping from the eave to rush across the lawn toward his house.

He didn't say why, but his eyes expressed how important it is that this thing, whatever it is, stay between us and nobody else. I think maybe he's worried about Ava or his dad saying something to interrupt whatever we have.

What do we have?

Besides secrets.

I'm going to drown in secrets.

Something has to give, and having my best friend spend her Saturday afternoon with me at work while I dole out shoes for league bowlers is making it incredibly hard not to break my promise to Lucas. There are so many things I haven't told Abby, and she and I don't keep secrets. We don't lie. I'm not supposed to lie to anyone—my mom,

Lucas, Abby. I may as well add Tory to that list because I don't like lying to him.

I don't want to stop kissing Lucas, or do something that might risk him ever kissing me again. I can't tell Abby about last night, not yet. Not the kiss. But I can maybe tell her about some things. I need someone to tell.

"I caught Lucas fighting with his dad last night," I spill out while I refill my friend's Dr. Pepper. I swear the only reason she comes to visit me at work is for free sugar.

"Tell me something new," she says, her eyes fluttering with sarcasm. I slide the full cup of soda over to her and she puts her lid back on. Her straw is pink on the end from her lipstick.

"Yeah, I know, but I mean, I heard *a lot* of their argument. I guess Lucas wants to go to MIT?" Her eyes blink wide as her lips let go of her straw.

"Lucas Fuller is smart?" She coughs out a laugh.

I chuckle.

"Yeah, I know, it's a surprise. He's like, maybe fourth or fifth in our class?" I don't know why I'm being vague with details. He's fourth. I know because I checked.

"Huh. Who knew?" she says.

I did.

"That must drive you wild. Your hottie crush also has a brain!" she cackles out and leans back, spinning once on her stool.

"You have no idea," I say, more truth to those words than she realizes.

"So, what's the big deal? The Fuller kid is smart and wants to build rockets or some shit, and they, like . . . don't want him to do that?" She goes back to taking a long suck on her straw. She's already gulped down a third of her refill.

"He got an offer from Tennessee," I add.

This time, she puts the drink down. Abby was a cheerleader our freshman and sophomore years, and she knows football. She quit cheering after she broke her wrist, but she's still a diehard for the game. Notre Dame football used to be a holiday in her house, every Saturday. Her dad played. Her mom cheered. And now that they're divorced, Abby has to sneak-watch the games because her mom can't stand the sight of the blue and gold. All of this to say, she gets how big an offer is to play at Tennessee. She also knows that's where Lucas's dad played—until one game knocked him out of the sport forever.

"Damn!" She shakes her head as her gaze drifts off with thought.

"Yup." I nod.

A few league teams wrap up their games and deliver their shoes to the counter. I hate getting backed up with racking shoes, so I set them all on the floor to spray the insides, coughing from the cloud of fumes. When I stand again, it's no longer my best friend sitting on the other side of the counter from me—it's my best friend, and Lucas Fuller, and both D'Angelo twins.

Shit.

"Maybe Mabee, what's up?" Tory leans over the counter with an arm stretched out to give me a sideways hug. I walk forward, stiff and unsure how to navigate this, reach around and pat him on the back while his arm encircles me. I look to Lucas mid-embrace, and his gaze traps mine, not letting go until Tory's hand is no longer touching my skin. His look is possessive, and if anyone else were looking at him, our secret would be blown.

I'd be fine with that.

"Nice game Friday, Luc." Abby gives me a sideways glance and a short wink, and the moment she starts, I regret not giving her every single detail of every secret I hold. As far as she believes, Lucas still treats me like shit and feels pressure about football from his dad. It's the perfect storm for my best friend to enact a little vengeance on my behalf.

"Fuck off, Abby," Lucas fires back. He takes a seat on the stool farthest from the rest of us and shifts his gaze to me. His face is full of indifference, and it hurts a little to see. I can't tell whether he's acting or changed his mind.

"Can I get a water?" He nods toward the tap.

I saunter toward the ice machine, grab a cup and scoop ice while my eyes hazily study him.

"It's a buck for the cup," I say.

Abby titters and takes a long drink through her straw until her cup is empty enough for her to make the slurping sound.

"Ahh," she says, tapping her cup on the counter. "Some of us get freebies."

A short laugh escapes my nose, and my cheeks burn a little with guilt. From this new perspective, it's funny to watch my friend stick up for me.

Lucas cocks his head to the side and shifts his eyes to glance harshly at my friend, but leans to pull his wallet from the back pocket of his jeans. He mostly wears all black, black jeans, black hoodie, and his black End Zone ball cap pulled low and shading his eyes. It makes his glare more ominous, especially when light finds a way in to illuminate his blue eyes from the shadow. I can't stop staring at his mouth. He's wearing a hard expression, so his lips don't stretch with the fullness of his smile, but it doesn't stop me from imagining it. That smile played out against mine only hours ago. I kissed that smile until I was raw.

Wallet in hand, he slips out his debit card and tosses it so it slides toward me on the counter. I slap my palm down to stop it, and pick it up, checking the name against the person who sent it to me.

"Lucas *A.* Fuller," I accentuate his middle initial, knowing it stands for Andrew. I set the card back on the counter and flick it back toward him with my index finger. He catches it in his lap. "I'm afraid I can only take cash."

I shrug and give him a wry smile, pulling the lid from the cup I just filled so I can threaten to pour out his water. I'm partly playing along and half sincere in pushing him, and the mix of it all makes me drunk on feelings. Why can't we tell people that we've found our way back? Why can't I kiss him again here and now?

His mouth ticks up on one side as the water trickles from the cup. I think he doesn't think I'll go through with this. A cup of water isn't a very big deal, but it's the only deal I've got. If we're playing the part of hate-mates, I'm going to make it convincing.

"Ah ah," he says, lifting his palm slightly. He tucks his card back in his wallet and leaves his grinning eyes on me as he feels around for something else. He pulls a folded receipt from one of the compartments, then digs into the next slot to slide out a folded up dollar bill. When it falls on the counter, though, a golden wrapped condom packet slips out with it. My eyes flit to that first, as do his.

I stop pouring, my gaze on the condom that fell out, the condom that is probably tucked in there for those "mistake" times he mentioned in the car last night. I top off his cup and refasten the lid, pulling a wrapped straw from the box under the register.

"Here," I say, walking it over to stand right in front of him, the bar top between us. With my tongue wedged between my back teeth and cheek, I breathe out a snort laugh and smile on the right side of my mouth as I slide my palm across the counter, collecting both the dollar and the condom.

I unfold the bill and slip it in the register, shutting the drawer with my hip. I then pinch the condom packet between my thumb and index finger and hold it up for everyone to see. The twins are holding fists to their mouths to contain their laughter, and Abby is twisting in her seat with nervous excitement. I examine the print on it closely, my stomach swimming with jealousy.

"Ribbed for her pleasure," I read, punctuating the short sentence with a click of the tongue. "Well . . ." I lean forward, resting my elbow on the surface between us, and hold out the package for him to put back where it belongs.

He pinches the other side and we both hold on for a second, his eyes hazing in a warning that I'm taking this too far. I can't help the green monster that beats in my chest, though.

"I hope she enjoys it," I say, finally letting go.

He lets out a breathy laugh and chews at the inside of his cheek as he tucks the condom back in the tight fit of his wallet. He stands to put his wallet back in his pocket, then pulls the water cup in his grip, holding it up to toast me before biting the end of his straw with his teeth.

"She better," he says, a flash to his eyes that sends an electric jolt through my veins that makes me want to crawl over this counter and both choke him and kiss him at the same time.

"Gentlemen?" He turns his focus to his friends and they shake their heads, I'm guessing in awe of how big of an ass he can be. They follow him toward the pool tables anyhow, leaving me with Abby to pick apart the scene I just lived, but with her missing half the story.

"That was intense," she says, holding her lid down on her drink when I reach for it. "I'm good. I think three Dr. Peppers in an hour is my max."

"You want some water?" I want to give her more free shit, and to brag about it loudly.

She shakes her head and stands from her seat, pulling her keys from her purse. I still have two hours on my shift. I guess it's not fair to expect her to hang out here the entire time.

"Think you can manage to not get in any throw-downs before I pick you up at five?" Without warning, she spins around, lifts her phone and snaps a photo of the both of us. I'm sure I look like a raging lunatic or a cross-eyed loser.

"Why? When are you going to stop doing that?" I whine.

"Oh, June." She leans forward and blows a kiss at me over the counter. "You know the answer to that." She winks and I flip her off.

"Have a good day at work, honey," she says, her heels

clicking along the polished concrete floor on her way out. I stare over to the pool tables and catch both D'Angelo twins angling their necks to watch every sway of my friend's hips as she leaves. Heels aren't part of her normal wardrobe; she has a shoot in them in a few days and has been wearing them nonstop this weekend to get used to balancing in them. When paired with her short-shorts and tight sweater, though, she looks like a fucking natural.

Rather than take my break under the mirror again, I decide to skip it altogether and just pick at the sandwich I packed. I slip it out of the plastic lunch bag under the counter and unwrap some of the plastic wrap to tear off a piece of the crust covered in peanut butter. We were out of jelly, so I loaded it up thick. Just one bite has my mouth fighting for moisture, so I fill a cup with ice and water.

"Employees don't have to follow that dollar rule I guess, huh?" Lucas walks over alone, the twins still battling over a new game of nine-ball several yards behind him.

"You just missed it. I donated a condom to the register," I say, my tone flat and eyes focused on nothing but the edge of my sandwich.

"June, don't be like that," he says, and I laugh at his pathetic apology.

I tear off another bite and pop it in my mouth, flitting my gaze up to meet his while I chew. I lean my hip into the counter and smirk through my bite, licking peanut butter from my teeth before taking another drink.

"Be like what? Like your dirty little secret?" I narrow one eye and tilt my head as I stare at him.

He props himself up on one of the stools and runs his palms over his face.

"It's complicated, June." He pulls his hat away and weaves a hand through his hair as he glares at me.

Your dad is having an affair.

With your best friend's mom.

The hard truth runs through my brain on a mental teleprompter, over and over. I take another bite and chase it with more water.

"Excuse me," I say, haphazardly wrapping my sandwich and tucking it back in the plastic bag. I wipe my hands on a damp towel and step around the other end of the bar, around the counter to the hallway that leads to the child care room and the bathrooms. I dip inside the women's room and walk into the last stall. Before I can latch the door closed, someone pushes from the other side.

"June, don't do this," Lucas pleads.

I laugh, nervously, because *what the fuck*, we're in the ladies room!

"You need to get out of here," I say in a loud whisper. I push back, my feet sliding with my effort. It's the stupid Vans; these aren't nonstick shoes. Morty is right to lecture me about it every time I'm up for review.

When I realize I can't overpower him, I relent and step back; he falls into my body in the tight space, his hand clutching the top of the stall. Stepping in even closer, he closes the door and locks it.

"What, because the two pair of legs won't be a giveaway?" I grimace then glance down, but he doesn't laugh at my attempt at humor, and just sighs.

"Where should I begin?" His left hand slides down the wall until his forearm rests to the right of my head. I should probably feel trapped but I somehow don't.

"You said I'm not a mistake," I begin. The burn is already crawling up my throat and I won't be able to handle this conversation without getting a little ugly.

Lucas lets out a soft breath that tickles my face. I try to look away and avoid his eyes, but his other hand finds my cheek and he turns me toward him.

"I did, and I meant it," he says, this Lucas so very different from the one who gave that little performance at the bar. I suppose I'm a different June, too. Here, I'm vulnerable. I hid it better before.

Our eyes tangle with near apology, our lips twitching with almost words.

"Out there," I finally muster the beginning, only to be stopped by the hard breath that leaves my chest. I shudder and Lucas's eyes drop just below my gaze. It gives me the excuse to cry, so I do. I blink out a single tear that stops at the corner of my mouth. "I felt like a pretty big mistake out there. And every single second that passed just made me feel more and more like I . . . like me and you? We don't belong."

My breath hitches on the last few words, and I hate how weak my voice sounds. I sniffle and straighten my posture, standing taller with my back flat against the fiberglass wall I'm leaning on. Lucas blinks a few times, his gaze still a fraction below mine, eventually closing his eyes completely and letting his head fall forward to rest against mine. Both of his hands draw in until his thumbs are on my cheeks, not sweeping the damp emotions away but rather feeling that my tears happened and he's to blame.

"June, nobody can know," he hums, and the words

come out as if they're covered in razors, cutting him from the inside.

"Is it Ava? So you can still sleep with her?"

"No, June. Fuck Ava," he growls, stepping back, shaking his head and finally meeting my stare.

"Exactly," I laugh out.

His glare dims, and his jaw tightens.

"I ended things with Ava. Completely."

"Mmm." I nod, feeling the last vestiges of my tears cut down my hot cheeks. "That what you held on to the condom for?"

His head falls to the side as he exhales, his mouth a frustrated line and a sag to his shoulders.

"I didn't even know that was in there, June." He swallows and looks to the side, to the tiles on the back wall that are scrawled with insults about girls from now and long ago, and proclamations of love for boys who will probably never know some girl loved them.

I'm being unfair.

I'm overreacting.

We had one kiss, and maybe it doesn't mean anything.

He's keeping me a secret.

So many secrets.

"Your dad is having an affair," I blurt out. I cup my mouth quickly, wishing I could swallow the words before their sound meets his ears.

His eyes flare.

I wait for him to counter my accusation, to explain it away or deny it. He does none of it, though. All he does . . . is leave.

CHAPTER FIFTEEN

That's not how I wanted any of this to happen. I never wanted to hurt Lucas with the things I came to know, but that's exactly what I did. I hurt him. And that hurt us.

There's no more keeping a lid on things when Abby picks me up. I held myself together through the rest of my shift and then fell apart in her car to the point she had to pull over and just stare at me. We've been squatting in this sketchy abandoned convenience store parking lot for the last hour while I blubber through the whole story over and over again. No matter how many times I tell it, the end is always the same.

"Are you sure you saw what you saw?" She's asked me this once already. I wish my answer was different. I could even argue that I didn't get a good look at Mr. Fuller's face pulling out of the D'Angelo garage, but the truck was undeniably his.

"It was him, Abs. And I just ruined Lucas's life." I feel

sick because I told him the truth out of spite. Because I was jealous.

"Well then, you should talk," she says, turning to put her seat belt back on and shift her car into drive. I do the same, fumbling with the buckle because my hands are jittery all of a sudden.

"What, like . . . now?" I say.

"No, I was thinking maybe you could wait another two years, then show up at his dorm at MIT or Tennessee or wherever the fuck he ends up going." She's gotten too good at sarcasm.

"That's not fair," I protest.

"Look, I'm driving you home. If you decide to go inside and hide in your room until school on Monday, that's on you. But if you want to see a change, well . . . to quote the inspirational sign in our principal's office—'you must be the change you want to see.'" She's proud of that speech. She lifts her detox juice drink from her center console and puckers her lips on the straw as she sucks up the last few drops.

"One day, you'll need my advice, and I'll be right about something you won't want to do. It's going to feel really good." I slump in the passenger seat and cross my arms, pouting out the window.

"Probably not, but okay," my friend says. I try to hold in the laugh, but I end up spitting it out despite myself. Damn her, so self-assured.

The closer we get to my house, the tighter my chest becomes, my lungs squeezed by the invisible elephant rocking into me. By the time we're a block away, I realize that even avoiding Lucas won't get rid of the massive anxiety knot caught in my throat and making me sick. The only thing that can get you to the other side of the circle of fire is walking through the flames.

Abby pulls into my driveway, stopping near the end. I figure she does it so I have to walk the extra distance and really consider my options, but when I look up, I see that's not why at all.

Lucas is sitting in the bed of his truck with the tailgate down, his back resting against the cab, ankles crossed. He's wearing a cut-off pair of sweats, the ones he usually wears when he goes out for a run, and the same black hoodie he had on earlier. His hair is tousled and sweaty and his cheeks are red from the cool air. He runs when he needs to think. He's been doing that since junior high. I could never keep up.

"I guess that makes my decision easier," I groan, lowering myself in my friend's seat just a little.

Her lights shine on him, but he doesn't bother to shade his eyes. He draws one knee up and pulls a water bottle into his hand, twists the cap off, and gulps most of it down.

"He doesn't really look like he wants to talk," I say. More excuses.

My friend turns her head and I feel her heated stare on my face seconds before I let my head fall to the side to meet the reckoning of her gaze.

"I know," I say, unhooking my seat belt to let the strap slide up and over my shoulder.

"It's not like things between you can get any worse." Damn her for being so on point tonight.

I nod and get out of the car, untucking my Eight Lanes shirt from my skinny jeans as I drag my zipper jacket along the ground at my side. I feel as if I'm in trouble. My heart drums to the rhythm of a death metal band, and to kick things up a notch, my friend beeps her horn as she pulls out of my driveway.

"Shit!" I jump and clutch my chest, glaring at her as she drives away, and hoping like hell Lucas is laughing at me when I turn back around.

He's not.

"What's up, Maybe Mabee?" He uses the nickname Tory has for me on purpose. I guess he gets jealous over things, too.

"I'm sorry." I ran through a dozen different methods for getting into this conversation with him during my trip home. Now that I'm staring into his sad eyes, the light completely dim behind them, I decide direct is best.

He nods. "Okay. Thanks," he says, drawing the bottle to his lips and tipping his head back to drink it dry. He screws the cap on and throws the empty plastic container into the middle of his driveway. I shuffle over in its direction to pick it up.

"Let my dad pick it up. Maybe I'll throw the rest of his shit out here too."

I stop where I stand and evaluate his face, the lethargy of his limbs and the crushed spirit emanating from behind his eyes. I've been that disappointed in someone before, too. Ignoring his wish, I pick up the bottle and walk it over to the recycling bin my mom put near the curb this morning.

His eyes meet mine when I turn around again, and as tempting as making a break for my house is right now, it's less of an option than it was a few minutes ago.

"Can I climb in there with you?"

His eyes remain blank at my question, but when I lean into my steps, attempting to move toward him, he stiffens.

"Can't." His back teeth clamp down hard. "This"—he pauses, pointing at me and then himself—"does not happen in front of people."

Undeterred, I move forward anyhow, because who's going to see besides his dad pulling in late from who knows where? Or his mom, who never leaves the house after she's home. Before my palms touch the back of his truck, he gets to his feet and vaults over the edge to the ground.

"Just get in," he huffs. His keys jingle on their way out of his pocket.

I push up the tailgate and do as he asks, climbing in and buckling up, then studying his every tick and nuanced motion as he revs his engine and backs us away from our homes. We get a comfortable six or seven blocks away, near one of the preserves and out of view of streetlights or passing cars. He pulls to the side of the road and flips on his hazards.

"Tell me how you know," he demands, his hands rolling against the steering wheel with a strong enough grip that his skin squeals against the rubber.

I'm speechless for a few long seconds, working out what order to say things in. There really isn't a way to protect everyone involved, which means Tory will be hurt by this too. I'm instantly thrown back into my own parents' divorce, the way my mom hung up the phone and just stared at my father, knowing that whatever the person on the other end of the line told her was true.

"I hate that I'm the one who knows this, Lucas," I begin.

"I understand." He's strangely calm, and I wonder if he had his suspicions. Drawing in a long breath, I steady myself and simply talk, like a well-rehearsed witness on the stand.

"There are details that are hard—"

He cuts me off mid-breath.

"It's all hard. I know. Just . . . just tell me," he begs, his voice a mix of frustration and maybe suspicion, as if on some level he knows what I'm about to say.

"I was dropping something off at Tory's house while you all were at practice. I'd just put my car in park when I saw their garage open and a truck pull out."

Again, when I pause for a breath, he interjects his own reasoning. "Lots of people have trucks," he says.

"They do," I respond. His body is fully relaxed, but his hands still cling to the steering wheel. "Not ones with license plates framed in gold with *Tennessee Forever* etched on the top and bottom."

His throat moves with the harsh swallow of truth. I twist in my seat to face him more directly as I continue.

"I saw them kiss, Lucas. Your dad and—"

"Don't," he interrupts, shaking his head. There's a coldness in his tone, and a definitive essence to his request. I don't know if I expected him to get angry, to cry, or what, but his reaction is almost robotic.

His eyes are still fixed on the empty roadway ahead.

"I don't want to know too much. Details have a way of becoming nightmares and they poison everything." His eyes glance downward, and his hands fall to the sides of the wheel.

I suspect he doesn't want this to become a permanent wedge in his friendship with the twins, Tory especially.

"Just promise me that you are sure."

I let the request linger in the quiet of the cab, my concentration on the perfect syncopation of his clicking hazards and the on and off of the red glow that comes with them.

"I wouldn't have ever said it if I wasn't one-hundred percent sure, Luc." My hand makes a move toward him, but he's still closed off so I leave my palm flat on the seat between us.

Squinting, he leans forward and looks up through the windshield.

"There's supposed to be a meteor shower tonight. They said on the news that the best views are after midnight." His profile glows from the moon and the lights of the car. The quiet on the surface of his face covers a lot of other junk, but peeling masks off takes time. I still wear mine a lot. It took Abby and her push for me to actually enjoy my senior year for me to even try wearing different ones. I still don't think I've found my own yet.

"I don't have anywhere to be," I say, my voice devoid of the unease from a moment ago.

"We need full dark," he says, leaning back and turning his head to face me slowly. Our eyes meet in the glowing red moments of the flashing lights.

"We should keep driving then." My gaze is met with a slow blink before he turns to face the road again, shifting the truck into drive and killing the hazards as he pulls us back onto the roadway.

I count the mile markers on the roadside, though both of us are familiar with the route. We rode our bikes out this way one summer. My tire blew, so Lucas let me sit on his handlebars for the rest of the way. From the thick trees, there's an open field where the abandoned drive-in theater used to stand. One day, it will be bulldozed and turned into fancy houses. That hasn't happened yet, though, and the only question that I'm pretty sure nags in each of our minds is whether the radio boxes are still standing on their posts.

I count five miles before I stop keeping track and dare to push the power on his stereo. I brace myself to be assaulted with heavy bass, but the volume is surprisingly low. The familiar riff of Mustang Sally pushes my smile into my cheeks. What are the odds that I hear the same Wilson Pickett song twice in the same month. I mouth the words out of habit, but when Lucas's voice utters the lyrics along with me, I let my terrible voice go and sing at the top of my lungs. We're both grinning by the time he pulls onto the dirt road and through the unintimidating trespassing warning signs covered in graffiti.

"I heard this song last week with Tory," I say. Lucas drops off from the chorus and glances at me as we rock along with the tires on the rough terrain.

"Oh, yeah?" There's a tinge of jealousy in his voice, and I quickly try to fix it.

"He didn't know the words," I add in, laughing. He just nods, and when he looks away I squeeze my eyes shut, feeling daft because the song has nothing to do with his reaction. It's that I was sharing one of our songs with Tory.

Lucas flips his high beams on so we can tell where we're at and whether we're going to run into remnants of the old screen and the sound box posts. The landscape looks almost exactly the same as it did after that long bike ride, only more of the wood has rotted away and vandals have taken care of other bits. The radios, though, still seem intact.

"They're still here," I say, the delighted voice of a ten-year-old coming out of my mouth. "Stop the car. Let's see if any work," I say, unbuckling quickly.

Lucas skids to a stop and we both jump out, searching with the help of his truck's brights. The first three boxes I find are missing cords, and even though Lucas finds a few that are connected, he can't get power to any of them. Stubborn and unwilling to quit, he and I scour the lot until we're out of the shelter of his truck beams and are now fumbling in the moonlight. When I find one that lights up when my thumb presses the button, I squeal.

"Oh, my God!"

I can barely see Lucas's form, but I hear his steps along the ground nearby.

"Don't let go. I'll find one, too," he says, rummaging through a few more boxes before reaching the final row, closest to where the screen used to be.

The dark surroundings close in on me, and I consider giving up or asking Lucas to pull his truck closer so we have some light. My fears dissolve the second I hear Lucas's voice pipe through the radio in my hand.

"Breaker niner-niner," he jokes. It's the only trucker lingo we know and it's probably not even accurate.

"I cannot believe we found two that work!" We laugh with a mixture of nostalgia and exhaustion.

The twins taught Lucas this trick when we were younger, and he's the one who talked me into riding our bikes all the way out here one day to try it out. For whatever reason, the old radios have a setting that turns them into makeshift walkie talkies. It's more of a channel, like what the police use, my dad explained when we told him. We didn't care what it was. For us, it was like having a cellphone when our parents said we weren't old enough. Of course, we could only talk to each other. And we had to ride our bikes out into the boonies to make the calls.

"It's so dark, I can barely see you," I say into the intercom.

"Mwahaha." He drags out a devilish laugh that crackles through the microphone.

"Don't be a jerk. You know I don't like the dark." I squat down and pull an abandoned crate close enough to sit while we talk.

"I wish someone would reopen this place," I lament.

"Maybe I do that instead of go to MIT or Tennessee. Look, problem solved." A bitter laugh slips out.

"I think you really want to go to MIT," I say.

There's a long pause before he breathes out a "Yeah."

"Your dad has even less of a right dictating now."

He coughs, and I can tell it's forced.

"We can talk about other things." I'm not sure what else there is, so I wait for him to lead.

"I'm sorry I was a jerk," he finally says.

I was one, too, but I'm not ready to admit that to him quite yet.

"I miss us, Lucas." I cup the radio in my palms and stare at it, willing him to say the same words through the microphone.

"What happened?" I wipe away a quick tear and wait again. The only sounds I hear are his occasional breaths from yards away over a barely functioning line. I don't know why it's easier to talk like this. It always was. The first time my parents had a blow-out argument that ended in my dad storming out and staying at a hotel for a week, I confessed it here and only to Lucas. And when he threw all our best glasses to the floor and told my mother she was a tramp . . . we talked about that here too.

"Do you think you could help me with something?" His ask feels heavy, partly because of his tone but also because he purposely avoided the things I asked. I kind of want to force a trade, a favor from me for a truth from him.

"One date," I say.

His silence tells me it's either a *no* or he's confused.

"With me, I mean. I want to go out on a real date, in front of people." I grip my bottom lip with my teeth and brace myself for rejection. I expect it, and if he does say no then at least I'll know what this is and where I stand. I'll know that our kiss was a moment of weakness on his part, and I'll quit trying to break inside his toughest parts.

"One date," he repeats, and I sit up straight, muscles tight at the thought that he's actually considering it.

"Yes. That's my offer. Take it or leave it."

The quiet lasts a little longer this time, and the dead space is filled with the occasional crackling sound of our connection. After a few final pops, the small green light on my device flickers off. Whatever residual electricity I was drawing on is gone.

"Went dead!" I shout, waving my hand.

Lucas drops his box, and it swings from the cord, banging into the post. I wait for him to come back, but he hasn't moved. I can tell he's standing, and his hands are either rubbing at his neck or on his face. The lack of response to my offer is starting to make me feel desperate, and the more seconds that pass without him moving or speaking, the less I want a yes at all.

I'm about to shout "never mind" when his voice cuts through the cool air.

"I get to pick the place," he yells.

His body shifts, the shadow of hands falls to his sides.

"So you can pick somewhere nobody will see you with me?" I let out a guttural laugh after my fair question. I don't want to be a secret. And I refuse to believe that kiss was anything other than real and honest. Whatever he's afraid of in this world, it can't be me. It can't be *us*.

I can tell his head is bending down as he moves closer. He's still too far to hear the crunch of his feet on the dirt, but with every stride he takes, I'm given a new detail. His right thumb is hooked in the pocket of his torn-up sweats. His brow is heavy and his focus is on the ground before him. His mouth is closed, but the usual tightness is gone.

Soon, I hear him. I smell him.

"You ashamed of me, Lucas Fuller? Is that what all of this is about?" I hold out my open palms, the harsh realization that I've been pushing aside for two years finally boiling to the surface.

He lifts his chin and his eyes soften with the slight tilt of his head.

"It's nothing like that, June." He shakes his head as if I'm supposed to understand, but I don't.

"What's it like then, Lucas? Because here's what it's like to me. We're best friends, then we're not. We live a hundred feet apart, and for two years, I see you only in passing, through open shutters and truck windows. I come back to school, and we're enemies. I resent you, but only because you resent me, and I have no idea why. None of it —no clue. But then there are these few tiny moments when I see you. When I *really* see you. My Lucas shows up to take care of me, and he talks and he shares for one night. We kiss, then just . . . like . . . that." I snap my fingers and his eyes flit to my hand. I hold my turned-up palm, thumb against fingers, in front of my eyes.

"You can't tell anyone." I throw his words back at him, the ones he said after the breathtaking night that left my lips raw and my heart even rawer.

His lips shut tight and he draws in a long breath through his nose, slowly shaking his head. I think it means he understands me, but at this point, who knows? Maybe it means he's about to tap out and ditch me here. Wouldn't be the first time in the last month he made me walk home in the dark. Though this is a hell of a lot farther than a block.

"You're right." His scratchy voice breaks through the quiet.

I blink.

"I'm sorry, could you repeat that please?" I say into my broken speaker. He glances up from the ground and wears a brief crooked smile. His gaze holds on, and after a beat, his head falls to the side.

"You . . . are right," he says again.

I'm skeptical, so I turn my head and glance at him sideways.

"So, is that a yes? To the—"

"It's a yes to the date. And a yes that it won't be in a cave. I will take you somewhere that has actual living, breathing humans nearby. There might be food, and there will probably be a movie because this is Indiana and our options are slim."

I let out a short laugh.

"Come here," he says, finger calling me to my feet. He drops both hands in his pockets and cocks his head to the side.

He can make me so damn mad, and then he looks at me like that. My stubborn side stays put because I hate that all it takes is a look.

"Please," he adds, and his sweetness—his attention— pushes me over the edge. I stand and brush off the back of my jeans, then stuff my hands in my pockets, swishing side-to-side while I scoot my feet closer to his. He takes the final few steps toward me and gently grabs my wrists, pulling my hands from their hiding spots. His fingers find the spaces between mine until we're holding hands palm-to-palm like a mirror image of each other.

His bottom lip is heavy with unsaid words, and his eyes dip below my gaze as he struggles to speak.

"I don't want—" He stops short, knitting his brows. Eventually his eyes close. "I don't want my family to fuck it up. I want to keep this ours for a little while."

His eyes reopen on mine and there is a hardness to them, a brewing anger that I want to ask about but somehow know that now is not the time. His father holds him to his own set of expectations yet doesn't live up to them himself.

I step close, bring our elbows together until we stand like extras doing some ballroom dance in a period drama. I lift myself up on my toes so I'm closer to his face, staring hard into his eyes.

The crickets from the surrounding trees are singing, and if I were rich—I mean *really* rich—I would buy this lot of land and build a home for me and Lucas right here. It's a fantasy kind of future, but I haven't indulged in fantasies in a very long time. What's the harm in giving in to one right now?

"What's the favor?" A faint smile paints my lips. We're standing so close that Lucas can only focus on one of my eyes at a time. I shift my gaze in harmony with his until the curves in our mouths match exactly.

"I'm going to interview for MIT. And Coach and my dad . . . they can't know." Uneasiness pulls the corners of his eyes down, and his breathing stills.

"They won't," I assure him, knowing that I can't—and shouldn't—make that promise. But more than that, I can't let him not try for this. It's what's in his heart. He wouldn't have told me about it if it didn't weigh on him so heavily.

"I have a plan. You'll need to take my truck."

I grin and he shakes my hands in his, laughing lightly with his head tilted back.

"I'm gonna want it back in one piece," he says.

I shake my head. "No promises."

He smiles with puckered lips and looks down at me with narrowed eyes.

"Do you need help getting ready for the interview? Is it at school? Or do you go to an office?" I rattle out a few more questions, but stop, letting my voice trail off with breathy whispered words when I realize he's more than just amused by me.

"What?" My cheeks are burning and I'm so grateful that it's dark outside.

Lucas pulls my hands up around his neck, then delicately traces his fingertips down my arms to my waist until we stand like we're dancing without music. I fall back down on my heels and he removes the last few inches between us so he can tower over me. My eyes flit up to his hair, mussy from his run but now dry. I push the locks dipping over his right eye out of the way, the soft curl that the strands form tempting my fingers to stick around and play.

"June?"

It's hard to look him in the eyes right now. He's looking at me with want, which is something I never fully prepared for. I look up briefly but dip my gaze when the pounding in my chest feels unbearable.

I have zero control over my mouth right now. My lips are vibrating, and if he forces me to use words, they will be a scrambled, blubbering mess. Lucas eases my nerves with a soft stroke of his thumb across my bottom lip. Then a tender touch from the back of his fingers along the line of my jaw and my cheek. He lifts my chin until it's hard to not let my gaze follow, meeting his. Wordlessly, he asks for permission, eyes falling to my mouth briefly, then returning to my stare.

I melt quickly, wanting badly to relive the kiss we had in my bedroom. I'm still so full of questions, though. I feel this pull that comes from somewhere else entirely, and I think it's my past self. I owe it to the girl I was a year ago—two years ago—to get answers before I give in to the lure of kissing Lucas Fuller. I spent too many nights wondering what I did to cause my best friend to abandon our relationship. He was too cruel for it to be meaningless hormones, and too committed for it to be high school politics or a dare. My feelings war inside my head until it becomes impossible to hide the trepidation that drags down every last bit of happiness finally blooming on my face. My body stiffens in warning and Lucas steps back just enough to study me, and the reciprocal weight of doom that tugs at his light gives us enough space for me to once again ask the hardest question of my life. This time, I can't give in without getting an answer.

"What happened?" I'm shaking where I stand, terrified of the answer.

Lucas shakes his head, and I think he's begging me not to ask. The mystery is too much, though. I need to know. I need it for there to ever be an *us* again.

"Why did you pull away? Lucas . . . I need to know."

His hands fidget at my sides, his fingers squeezing at my hips with light pressure, as if he's afraid I might run.

"Please don't make me tell you, June. Don't make me say it."

A wave of nausea makes me dizzy, and a light sweat covers my neck. He has to know I'm too far in to go back now. I can't kiss him with this cloud threatening us. I could never accept it as real; it would always be a distraction, his way of once again getting out of the hard truth. He is my weakness, but he used to be my strength. I need to know where that part of him went and why.

He shakes his head harder, like a man trying to banish a bad dream, troublesome thoughts or voices in his head. Through it all, his hands stay on my hips, threatening to slip away but never quite fully letting go.

"June," he pleads, squeezing his eyes shut. He finally breaks his touch on me and grips at his hair, and I am truly scared.

I wait through his labored, heavy breaths and force myself to maintain my hold on his red, tortured eyes. When the fight is finally choked from his body, his hands go limp at his sides. He offers one last breath, one last chance to touch my hand to his mouth and stop the onslaught of words that will change everything.

I don't.

"This isn't my father's first affair."

We're both breathless. I ignore all other sounds; no more crickets or faraway hum of traffic. The darkness has eaten any light that's left, and I hold on as Lucas drags me down a rabbit hole that will change me forever.

"My dad was seeing your mom."

Those were the nights I made my own dinner.

"My mom caught them together."

That's when my dad said she was a hypocrite.

"He begged my mom not to leave."

My dad took advantage of an easy out.

"My mom wanted him to make you and your mom move, but she settled for us never talking to you again."

Us. Lucas. Me.

"She said she would tell everyone how your mom and my dad met."

My mouth waters with anger and all I can muster is a strong shake to my head.

"He hired her, June. She needed money to get away from your dad and still be able to afford . . . things. And my father paid. He paid over and over. And he said he wasn't the only one."

Over and over.

I am numb.

"I didn't want you to know. I didn't want anyone to ever know. I didn't . . ."

My mom slept with Lucas's dad so I could fucking go to college. Those are the *things* she wanted to afford. Me. She wanted to be able to afford me.

Lucas didn't want me to know.

And now I do.

And nothing.

Is.

The same.

CHAPTER SIXTEEN

"We haven't seen the meteors yet," I say, lying back on the roof of Lucas's truck. He's still standing on the ground next to the driver's side door.

About an hour ago, Lucas asked if I wanted him to take me home. That's when I climbed up here. I'm not even sure what home is anymore. I have too many questions, and every single one I ask doesn't seem to have an answer.

None of this makes sense.

Mrs. Fuller caught my mom and her husband together late one night at my mother's photo studio. She hired a private investigator who traced the money, about ten thousand dollars, and who followed my mom for two weeks, documenting a dozen late-night meet-ups with her husband at the photo studio as well as twice at his office downtown. It was all suspicion until she read the six months of text messages between them. Six months is how long my parents were in therapy. When she confronted her husband, phone records in hand, he caved. I keep asking Lucas for details, but he says he doesn't really know. It's more likely he doesn't want to tell me.

What did the messages say?

Did she tell him she loved him?

Did anyone say they were sorry?

"The clouds are rolling in," Lucas says. I think he's said it twice. I'm only half here; the other half is still mining theories and picking apart scant information while feeling incredibly betrayed.

"Sit with me?" I roll my head to the side and stare at him sideways. He wants to take it back. How do I tell him I don't believe it? Am I being naïve?

Lucas exhales, his hands tucked in the pocket of his hoodie, which is now pulled up over his head, weighing down his wild hair in the breeze. It's getting colder out, and he's still wearing shorts.

"You can grab my jacket from the floor of your truck. Use it to cover up?" I offer.

His mouth ticks up in a slight smile before he glances down and nods to himself.

"Okay, June," he says, giving in to my request.

He opens the passenger side to grab my jacket, also flipping off the headlights to save the battery. A second later, music plays from the radio. I flatten the side of my head so my ear is pressed against the roof. The song is familiar, but I can't quite place it. When the truck rocks from the weight of Lucas hoisting himself up on the roof, I turn the other way.

"Here," he says, handing me my jacket as he slides his legs up to sit beside me. I push the jacket back to him.

"You're in shorts. I thought you could use it to cover up," I say.

He shakes his head with a soft laugh.

"I don't get cold." His eyes seem so damn sorry.

"That's not true," I say, wincing at my words. That was unfair.

"I didn't mean it like that," I add.

His head falls to the side.

"Yes, you did," he says, his voice breathy and full of regret.

"I'm sorry."

"Don't be." His eyes move down my body to where my hands are balled up in the bottom of my shirt to stay warm. He unzips my jacket and spreads it over my torso.

"Your mom is probably worried about you," he says out of the side of his mouth. He leans back, palms against the roof of the truck while his long legs drape down the windshield. My legs are falling asleep from being bent in front of me, but I don't want to stop looking at the stars. I haven't seen a single meteor yet. I want to. I want something to make a wish on.

Without asking, I lift myself on my arms enough to shift my body to the side, lying my head in Lucas's lap. I roll so I'm looking up again, and his eyes are waiting for me.

"I'm probably not very soft," he says through a breathy laugh.

"You're softer than you think," I say, one eye squinting a little. Lucas's body shakes with his amusement.

"Okay then," he says, tilting his chin to the sky. The moment he looks up, a flicker of light streaks across the sky, ducking behind one of the thin clouds and reflecting little flickers of light as the meteor burns up.

"Oh, my God!" My grin stretches into my tight cheeks. Joy is such a foreign feeling.

"Wow," Lucas says, his eyes still trained on the space above where a piece of star just died. I should probably close my eyes to make a wish, but I've shut my eyes enough lately. I want to keep them wide open. I want to take the things I want.

I pull my hands free from the cover of my jacket, slide my left palm up Lucas's chest, and lift myself just as his chin drops to look down. My hand travels up his neck and jaw, ducking underneath the cover of his hoodie into the cool thickness of his hair. Without giving myself a chance to think twice, I press my lips to his.

His body hesitates in reaction, a flinch that nips at my lips. There's a sudden stiffness in his chest as it sucks in a quick breath and his muscles become defensive on reflex. I get it. After what he told me—with confusion taking over my head and the mess that is us—kissing is probably not the way to work through any of it. But kissing Lucas Fuller is the only thing that makes sense right now. I let my lips dance along his like a ghost, light tickles of skin on skin until he breaks and brings his hands up to cradle my body and head. I push his hood from his head as both my hands dive into his hair, his mouth now working mine with urgency. His kiss feels desperate, as if he wants to get as much as he can before this all disappears. The sensation spurs me to do the same.

My face cradled in his hands, I slide my palms forward to do the same to him, shifting my body until I'm on my knees. Lucas leans back a little and I slide my right leg over his lap so I'm straddling him. The sensation of my body sitting on the hardness of his reaction causes his breath to hitch against my mouth. His hands break free of my face, falling back to catch his weight on the roof of the truck.

I sit up but leave my hands on him, raking my fingers down the front of his hoodie like claws. His hooded eyes stare at me and his lips are pink from where my teeth held on just a breath ago. He's panting, trying to be good, but his eyes betray his wants as they dip and lower, guiding his thoughts to my mouth, my neck, my breasts. I roll my hips against him and he swallows, biting his fat bottom lip and letting go with a "Fuuuck."

I'm out of my element, guided only by what my body feels and wants. I've kissed boys, made out in dark corners or, when teachers weren't looking, behind the trees surrounding the basketball court at my tiny Montessori school. I don't want to chastely kiss Lucas like a child right now. I want to touch him, taste him, leave my mark on him so anyone who questions us knows we had this—a moment for us.

For me.

My hands wander to the bottom of his hoodie and I lift it until he helps me remove it completely, tossing it over his shoulder and into the back of the truck. He's so very much not the boy I first met when my fingers roam along his bare skin to discover hard muscles that curve and dip. I flatten my palms against his sides and trace the proof that despite what he wants, he is disciplined in the gym and on the field. I paint my fingertips back down toward the light dusting of golden hairs that begin at his belly button and disappear under the band of his cut-off sweats.

I tug at the knotted string, easily sliding it free, but before I can touch inside, Lucas's hands cover mine. He pulls them to his mouth, tethering them together and grazing his teeth against the inside of my left wrist with a gentle bite. He lifts my arms high then glides his hands down the length of my arms over the hard peaks of my breasts to the bottom of my work shirt, quickly rolling it up in his palms and raising it up my midriff and chest. I tilt my head up as he pulls it over my face, then take over and toss it into the truck bed where his sweatshirt now lies.

My arms fall to his shoulders, fingers musing in the soft tufts of hair that curl from his scalp at the base of his neck. I bend my head down enough that our noses touch, my gaze locked on his. His lashes fall shut with the heavy weight of want, and his mouth moves to the right side of my neck. I lean to give him access, his hand sliding the strap of my bra down my shoulder. His mouth follows the trail of his fingertips as they drag the satin, then the lace lower until the hard pink peak of my breast is exposed. His tongue circles it just before his lips leave a soft wet kiss that he dries with his cooling breath. I pucker under his control.

I lean back to expose more of my neck, my body angled so he can easily slide the rest of my bra away. Virgin white lace that has only ever been seen by me loosens around my skin as his hands deftly unclasp the hook in the back. Lucas discards the garment to the side, covering my right breast with his palm while his mouth covers the left. He sucks me to a hard peak, painful pleasure igniting a pool between my legs. I push into his erection to ease my need and he groans against my body.

My hair is twisted in a loose bun at the base of my neck. Lucas hooks a finger in the band and pulls it free, letting my hair blow wildly until he can gather it in his palm. He wraps it around his hand once and tugs it back, coaxing my back to arch so my breasts are high enough for his tongue to taste them raw. I push into him when his teeth graze against the hardened peak of one. I'm begging him to bite, and I know he wants to.

My hands push down the back of his neck to his shoulder blades, and I pull myself into him as I right my head. I need to kiss him. My mouth is hungry. His hands clear the blowing strands of hair from my face as our mouths connect again in a kiss that means to strip us both of oxygen. Our tongues tangle as I pull his lip into my mouth a moment before he does the same to me. Heat boils in my body and I grind into his lap, needing the friction—needing to feel how hard he is for me against how wet I am for him.

The moment I press into him, his hands let go of my face and rush to my hips, tugging me close, fingers gripping at the back pocket of my jeans and rocking me back and forth on his lap. I ride the sensation, knowing I'm going to have an orgasm still in my panties and jeans, but I want more from him—more *for* him. Even if our past fucks up our future, I want to have this moment. I want Lucas to be my first.

I always have.

I feel between us, finding the strings I was forced to abandon a moment ago, once again tugging his pants loose, this time without him slowing me. My fingertips feel along the band of his waist and I pull toward me, making room for my hand to slip inside. Lucas isn't wearing anything underneath, and my hand immediately brushes the searing hot hardness of his cock.

"June." He croaks out my name.

I sit back to make room and lean forward, pressing my forehead into his, both of us breathing as our lips touch with many tiny kisses.

"I want to touch you," I say. He's weak under my spell, nodding and shifting his hips; I lower his shorts enough to completely free his erection.

"Am I doing this right?" I ask, my fingers slowly wrapping around the warm shaft. I squeeze with light pressure and I feel him flex in my hold.

He nods, grabbing the back of my head and bringing my mouth to his.

"Yeah," he pants.

I move my hand up and down in a slow rhythm, letting the soft skin slide under my touch. I pull myself up as tall as I can on my knees. While my head rests on his, I lower my chin to see how he reacts under my touch. It's both exactly and nothing as I imagined this part of him to be. I'd never admit to anyone, not even Abby, but I've fantasized about this too. Along with the romance and kisses and sweetness, I also lay in bed some nights and pretend my hands are on him, and his are on me.

His palms grip the back of my thighs as I stroke him, sliding up centimeters at a time until he finally cups my ass. I grip him harder at the sensation of his fingers clawing into my back pockets, his fingertips rough against the denim of my jeans.

Impatient, I put my hand over his right one, threading my fingers between his knuckles to guide his grip forward and to the front of my jeans. He's more than willing, his hands tugging on the button of my jeans and unfastening it deftly, followed by the zipper. His thumbs hook inside the band of my panties, plain white and cotton that I wish were sexier than they are. I hadn't planned on any of this.

As he tugs my pants down my hips, I shift from above him, helping to pull them down completely. His hands grip my sides and he encourages me to lie on my back. I kick my shoes from my feet and wriggle my legs free, parting my knees as he moves to kneel between my legs. His gaze begins at my breasts then rises until his eyes meet mine. I nod and whisper "Yes." It's just enough for him to reach in his front pocket and pull out his wallet.

I hold my bottom lip between my teeth in anticipation, and giggle when he holds the small black packet up in presentation. It's not the same one I teased him about the other day, which means he got this new, in hopes that maybe he and I would take this step.

I flatten my sweating palms on the surface of the truck, tucking them under my hips to hide my nerves as Lucas rolls the condom on himself. He's somehow bigger in his own hand, though it's probably my perspective. I'm nervous, and a little afraid of the pain.

Lucas lowers himself so he hovers over me, his weight held by his forearms as I lie caged between them. His nose brushes against mine lightly and his lips brush against mine, parting just enough to suckle on my top lip. I lift my chin to give him more of my mouth, shutting my eyes to be brave.

His right arm moves to the space between us so he can guide himself inside me. I feel the tip at my entrance and clench, sucking in air and arching my back so my hips reflexively pull away.

"Okay?" he whispers, his mouth ticking against my ear. A rush of shivers trails down the right side of my body, leaving tiny bumps in its wake.

"Yes," I nod, squeezing my eyes tighter.

I try to breathe and force my body to relax as he pushes himself in more, pausing to let me adapt to the feel of having him there. He rocks his hips in short strokes, never fully leaving me and not fully pushing inside. His tongue traces a cool line from my chin down to the nape of my neck where his mouth sucks at the tender part of my skin. He kisses the spot.

"I left a tiny bruise there so you'll see it in the morning and know this was real." His voice is husky and a little dominant, but not overbearing. It's perfect, and it turns me on.

"Ready?" he asks. I nod again, this time moving my hips lower so his access is straighter. He rests his weight on me, holding himself up on his arms so his hands can brush the sweat-dampened hairs from my face. His thumbs run along my cheeks just under my eyes, luring them open to witness his devilish smile. The faint curl on his lips is proof of how satisfied he is with this, how much he wanted it, too.

His head tilts enough for him to kiss me hard, and with my cries muffled by his mouth, he pushes in deep, breaking any remaining threads of my youth with his thrust. I whimper against his mouth but kiss back harder, holding on to his bottom lip with my teeth, biting through the pain so hard that I may have drawn a little blood.

Lucas pulls back, the slide of his hard-on slow and slick. I feel wet and swollen despite the pain, which lessens with every plunge he takes into me. For minutes, he's methodical and gentle, though his cock sinks in deep. The feel of the tip against my insides teases a sensitive spot that drowns my head in endorphins every single time his hips rock. Soon, I'm meeting his thrusts with pressure of my own, my hands no longer sitting by idle on the roof of the car, but gripping at the material of his sweat shorts that are pulled so low on his hips that his ass is exposed. I pull him into me by the band of his pants, eventually wrapping my legs around him to hold him deep inside while his lower body pumps rhythmically, keeping up with our panting breaths. We chase the sensation and my insides constrict and pulse uncontrollably, forcing a moaning cry from my mouth. I muffle it against the bare skin of his shoulder as he grows tight inside me, filling the condom.

Pulses carry through our cores and he pushes into me a few more times before rolling to the side and pulling out, leaving our sex-covered sweat-strewn bodies exposed to the open air, now fully dark of stars as a thickness of clouds shrouds the sky.

I always imagined this is when I would be shy or embarrassed, when I realize what I did and everything that can be seen, and feel suddenly inadequate. I don't feel any of that. I've pushed aside every part of our story that doesn't fit and that I don't want to yet accept so I can label this moment as purely mine, a greedy piece of our story that I will come back to always.

No longer the girl playing the part of a woman, I roll to my side and trail my fingers down Lucas's chest and stomach, moving lower until I reach the still pulsing tip of his swollen cock. I glance up to catch his eyes shaded by his long, dark lashes as he stares at me with both suspicion and need. My body still teeming with electricity from every firing nerve, I hold his gaze hostage and roll to my knees, once again straddling him. I pleasure myself by pressing his erection into his abdomen, writhing and teasing myself against its length until I come again . . . and again.

CHAPTER SEVENTEEN

The sun is up, barely, as we pull into Lucas's driveway. I'm sure my mom is livid that I didn't reply to any of her calls or texts. I also didn't answer my phone when Abby started calling. I'm a little surprised there isn't a police car in our driveway. I started feeling guilty when we decided it was time to head home. It was selfish to ignore everyone, but I couldn't handle all of the extra noise. My head isn't right to talk with my mom, and I don't know where to begin in explaining all of this to my best friend.

But now, the reality is playing out. I have to let it, and I have no choice but to be present for it. The empty driveways, the quiet homes, the light glowing from my kitchen window where I know my mom is sitting, phone in hand, waiting. I have to face it all. I'm all she has left, besides her brother who we see maybe three times a year. How do I untangle all of the questions I have for her? My gut says one thing, but then Lucas is so resolute about his version of the story. Even if none of it's true, having the theory live in this universe has changed how I see things, how I see people.

How I see her.

I knew we wouldn't be alone in this driveway for long. Lucas's truck lights up the first floor of our house, so it's inevitable that my mom sees it and comes outside, hoping it's me. She looks manic, her hair wild in all directions as she pads out clutching her phone as she tightly hugs her body. She's wearing the same T-shirt and jeans I saw her in yesterday morning.

"How come boys have it so easy? It's so hypocritical," I say. "You're rolling in at the crack of dawn too, but I don't see your mother out in the driveway waiting to rip your head off after she finishes hugging you." I make no attempt to leave this quiet bubble I'm in with Lucas. The moment I open this passenger door, our moment will be over.

"I guess it's a matter of conditioning. My parents are kind of used to me not coming home on weekends." He stretches his hand out on the seat between us and rolls his palm over. I put my hand inside and he squeezes tightly.

"I don't want to do this," I say.

"That's why I never said anything before," he says, his voice full of sorry.

I grimace in the other direction because I wish he had. We could be well past this point if I'd only known. Waiting to get a shot at the doctor is always so much worse than when they put on the Band-Aid.

My mom has stopped about halfway between our house and Lucas's truck, but her face is easy to read from here.

Where the fuck have you been and why didn't you call or text like you always *do?* That's what that expression says.

"Wish me luck," I say, leaning into him, turning his chin to face me and pressing my lips on his one last time. I slide across the seat and pop open my door, but the moment I step outside, I catch his mom's waiting stare, and her expression . . . it's nothing like the worried one my mom wears.

"I'm sorry," I say to my mom, my eyes bouncing between her and Lucas's mom, who stands just inside her side door. She's holding a coffee mug and casually leaning into the frame as she blows on the steam rising from her cup. Her stance suggests she's not amused. Maybe it's the information I'm now privy to, but I can see the subtleties—the disapproving glare and tight grip on the mug. I turn around, mostly out of loyalty to the boy I just gave my most important first to, but he's already backing out of the driveway. I'd fault him for running away, but I had the same idea. He just had the keys.

"I was worried sick." My mom's words come out with vibrato, the result of wanting to cry and being too tired to give in to the urge.

"We lost track of time," I say, taking urgent steps past her, heading inside our house. I don't want to put on a show for Shannon Fuller, especially when I'm not convinced she has her story right.

"Lost track of time? June, it's another entire day!" My mom slams the side door closed behind her. I'd turn to face her but I'm too busy taking in the various open drawers dumped onto the counters and the contents of my backpack spilled out on the kitchen table.

"Were we robbed?" I know we weren't but I can't quite figure out what this mess is all about.

"I was trying to find clues about where you were. Phone numbers, information in your school planner, a ticket stub . . . I don't know!" I turn to catch her hands in the air, phone still clutched in one of them. I wonder who she's dialed. I don't have many friends, and she doesn't know Naomi or Lola.

"I'm sorry. I really am," I say, because—right now—I am. I didn't mean to make my mom worry, but I would spend my night exactly the same way every time I'm given the chance. I move toward the refrigerator, pausing to rummage through a few of the things on the counter from the drawers. I lift up a pizza menu and laugh out a breath, holding it up for my mom to see.

"You checked with the pizza guy?" I'm making a joke of something she doesn't think is funny. It's not funny. I'm just not ready to tell her how unfunny all of it is.

"June, I called every phone number I could find in the goddamn house. You never just disappear. We—me and you—we don't do that to each other!" Her eyes are glossy, and I should probably drop my edge and step into her with a hug right now, but what she just said sticks a little. I cock my head slightly and narrow my eyes on her.

"You sure?" I'm slipping into one of those conversations I can't take back, and I don't like that I am. Nevertheless, I can't stop.

"I'm sorry?" Her voice has elevated into yelling. This is the voice she used with my dad when he came home late.

"I'm just saying, me and you . . . we don't hold things back from each other. Is that what you're saying?"

An intense quiet builds between us for a few seconds before she answers with a booming "Yes!"

I slowly nod and turn to the fridge, pulling out a bottle of water. I'm so thirsty. I pull the lid off and drink nearly half of it before recapping it and holding it to my side as I let the fridge door close and turn back to face my mom.

"Okay, then," I say. "I was out with Lucas. We had sex. I'm going to bed." I march past her, knowing she's stunned by that little bomb, and I take the time it bought me all the way upstairs, where I proceed to lock my bedroom door, set my water on my night stand, close my shutters, and crawl under my velvet blue blanket with my phone.

I don't want to talk to anyone except Lucas, so I shoot my bestie a short text so she knows I'm alive and epic shit went down, but I can't tell her until tomorrow. She responds instantly with about four lines of exclamation points, but she follows it up with two hearts, so I know Abby and I are good.

I toss my phone to the side and pull my blanket up over my head, and for the next two hours I remember every single spot that Lucas touched me. Somewhere in my best daydreams, I fall asleep and don't crack a lid open until early evening, when my phone buzzes at my side with a text from Lucas.

Hi.

CHAPTER EIGHTEEN

I n many ways, it's another typical Monday morning. Abby is waiting in my driveway blasting some song she texted me was super hype and dropped late last night. I rush around my room searching for a T-shirt that's not too wrinkled to wear because I traded time to shower and prep a normal look for the day for thirty extra minutes of sleep. I've lived this morning before. It's my normal mode. My Groundhog Day. I'm always a bit disheveled, not great with sticking to a morning routine, and my haphazard style makes my supermodel best friend mental. But this dose of chaos, it works for me. Usually.

Today, my mom is waiting downstairs in the kitchen and there is an invisible brick wall between us that she'll expect me to climb over before I leave. I don't feel much for climbing. At least, not *that* wall. Lucas always made the trip up my porch roof look easy. I'm nowhere near as strong as he is, but down has to be easier than up. The thought struck me before I fell asleep again at about four this morning, mid-text with Lucas as we went over the plan for today. I juggled between messaging him and Face-Timing Abby so I could give her a full deposition of all things drama that is my life. Not surprisingly, most of her questions weren't about the gossip about my mother but instead were centered around my first time and details of Lucas's, umm, parts. I learned two key things from our talk. One, my best friend has seen way more penises than I have. Seven to my one, to be exact. Also, apparently, Lucas stacks up pretty well in terms of size. The entire conversation made me want to die, especially because I was texting him while having it.

I maybe should have taken Lucas up on his offer to drive me to school—he could have helped me scale down the side of my house—but I didn't want to risk running into his mom again. I don't like the way she looks at me, as though I'm guilty. And even though Lucas said he no longer cares what his parents think, deep down he does. He cares that his dad doesn't like his choices, and he cares that his mom has been hurt.

My mom has been hurt, too. And I care about that, which is the reason I don't want to face her just yet, or at least that's what I rationalize. I'm not ready to be civilized, and I don't know how to word my questions. I need to be prepared for her answers, as well—whether my suspicions are right, that she's done nothing wrong, or Lucas's version is true and she's as much to blame as my father. I need to be mentally prepared to embrace and move forward on either path. Right now, I only want to floor it in reverse.

This brings me to where I stand right now, literally, two feet planted on the tacky surface of the A-frame that covers my porch. I've taken myself to the brink of reason, avoiding my mom by roof leaping. The slide down the wall was a longer drop than I thought, and it's left me a bit frozen here. The drop down from the spot where the A-frame ends, where the gutter drips rainwater into my mom's flower garden, is about the same distance. My pocket buzzes from my phone so I lean flat against the wall, my backpack strap wrapped tightly around my right wrist, and pull my phone out with my left hand. It's Abby calling, so I glance up to see her hunched over her steering wheel and staring out her windshield with her mouth agape.

I answer.

"I didn't think this through," I say through nervous giggling.

"What the fuck, June!" It's kinda funny how her mouth moves just a hair before I hear the words in my ear.

"I'm avoiding my mom." I shrug, the movement making me a little off balance for a blip and I bend my knees, gripping to the surface beneath my feet.

"Yeah, well, you're probably gonna have to deal with her when you fall and break something and she has to haul your ass to the emergency room." She leans back in her seat but just a little. My friend is looking from side to side, maybe searching for help. I don't want any, except for hers. The last thing I need is assistance from the problems I'm hiding from.

"I'm coming down," I say, my voice quavering as I cautiously lower myself until I'm on my ass, sitting with legs pointing down the slope. God, how I wish this were really a slide.

"I'm coming out," Abby says.

"No!" I stop her fast. "Don't. If you come out, my mom will see you and then she'll come out, and then—"

"And then your ass climbed out a window for nothing. Yeah, I got it. This is fucked up."

I sigh.

"I know. Just give me a minute. I'm going to scoot." I drag my butt along the grainy shingles about six inches before stretching my legs out like an inch worm to do it again.

"You look ridiculous," my friend says.

"You better not be filming me," I fire back.

"I'm not, but I took a picture. You know, for my collection of June in her moods." She's amused by this, but all I can focus on is not dying. I end our call and slip my phone back into my pocket.

In reality, I'm not that high, but maybe I have a fear of heights I was never fully aware of. Being up here has my heart racing and sweat pouring from every part of my body. I scoot and work my feet in a rhythm, quickening my pace until I finally reach the edge of the eave and am able to slide forward enough that my legs dangle. Our living room windows are just to my right. This is the corner where we usually put our Christmas tree. There's a lamp there now, which helps to mask the view of me. My mom was in the kitchen before I left. I snuck a quick view down the stairs to see her sitting on one of the stools by the counter closest to the side door. If I can be silent with this, I might just make it out without her hearing.

I pull my backpack to my chest and ready my hands on either side to heave it into the middle of the lawn. The grass needs to be mowed, but it's also dry from the cooler weather, which makes it kind of like hay. I count on my decent aim as I shove my bag through the air. It lands on a thicker spot in the lawn and rolls a few times until coming to rest about a dozen feet from my friend's car. I'm next, but there is no hay beneath me, only damp soil and my mother's petunias. That isn't much to break a fall.

Feeling all kinds of ridiculous, I push myself up so my feet are under me, balanced on the edge of the eave, toes on the curve of the gutter. I rock forward and hold on to the edge with my hands, leaning out just enough to spot my landing before gravity takes over and I tumble to the ground. I land with my knees and palms deep in my mom's garden, muddy water squishing up from the ground and staining my jeans and covering my hands. Amped from adrenaline, I bolt to my feet and sprint to my bag, grabbing it and rushing to my friend's car. I shut the door on the strap of my backpack but leave it there, the strap dragging along the ground and my bag locked to the area near my feet.

"Go, go!" I wave my arms emphatically. In my own mind, I just made so much noise. I nervously stare out the windshield as my friend pulls out of my driveway; my house remains still, and the side door stays closed. In about twenty minutes, my mom will discover the open window from my room and skyrocket to a new level of pissed. She'll probably think I'm on drugs. I'm going to have to deal with everything today one way or another. I can't live like this, and if I don't come home for another night, my mom will think I've run away. That's not even on the table. I'd miss her too much, even if the things Lucas told me are true.

Abby finishes poking fun of my lame-ass sneaking-out skills for the first few minutes of our drive, but she becomes quiet as we get closer to school. I haven't asked her point-blank what she thinks the truth is, and I know why I haven't. Abby cuts through bullshit. She's rarely wrong, even if the way she gives advice comes off harsh. She was right when she said I had to break out of my shell and quit worrying what people thought of me. As crazy as all of this shit I'm going through is, at least I'm living. I'm experiencing, growing, falling and picking myself up. I've rebuilt myself into something stronger, into the kind of girl who is on the verge of being an adult and who might be capable of handling the cruel things this world throws at people. Before this, I was balancing on eggshells and sheltering my feelings. Abby was right, I needed to move forward.

Just like I need to now.

"Do you think—"

I stop there, bracing myself for her honest answer before finishing the question. I don't even have to, though, because my friend is so in sync with me that she knows where my words are going.

"I think it doesn't matter," she says. I glance at her to assess her expression. Her face is matter-of-fact as she lifts herself high enough in her seat to check the line of red on her lips.

"How can it not?" I ask.

She shrugs and sits back down as we cross the final intersection before school.

"Well, either your mom did what she had to because she didn't have a choice, or Mr. Fuller is a big fucking liar. And frankly, he's already proven he's the least to be trusted in this cast of characters. I'm pretty sure no matter how this plays out, your mom is the good guy." Abby eases into her favorite spot right by the front of school and turns her car off before facing me with her signature *you-know-I'm-right* smile.

"How come you get to be smart and confident, *and* look like that?" I'm only half joking. For real, it isn't fair.

She purses her lips with sarcasm and leans her head to the side.

"June, honey. Looks and brains are not mutually exclusive."

Her lips briefly curve up on the ends to punctuate her brilliant response just before she opens her door and gets out of her car, leaving me there in wonder. Sometimes I wonder whether she and I would have become such good friends if Lucas and I never had our falling out. Maybe things do happen the way they're supposed to.

Lucas is waiting for me in his truck, the twins hanging out on the bench near where they park. Abby and I walk over to get Lucas's key and go over the plan for the day with him. Tory pops up from the bench to offer her his seat, and I chuckle lightly as I hop into the passenger side to talk to Lucas.

"What's funny?" he asks.

"Tory thinks being a gentleman is going to win Abby over," I say.

"Huh," Lucas responds, leaning back with his wrists balanced on the steering wheel as we both stare at the odd little love triangle forming in front of us. Last night, Abby told me she was thinking about making a move on Hayden, already moving on from the new guy, Cannon. "He's too moody," she said.

I haven't mentioned anything to Abby about Tory because I don't know how serious he is about the little crush he eluded to, and I've got enough balls in the air. I don't need to stir up new drama.

"So, the key?" I bring Lucas's attention back to our mission.

"Oh, yeah. Here," he says, pulling his key from the ignition and handing it to me. The only truck I've ever driven was my uncle's, and it was a piece of shit stick-shift with zero power steering. Lucas's truck is a four-by-four and the engine rumbles in the driveway. There may be more car geek in my genes than I ever realized.

"I see that twinkle in your eyes. Don't get crazy," he jokes. His hand covers mine, which now holds his key. My eyes dip to where we touch. I wonder if he'll hold my hand when the bell rings and we walk into the building.

"Let me go over things one more time, just to make sure I have it down. At lunch, we both slip out the gate and you get in the car with the MIT lady while I go to your truck and drive it to Two-fers."

He nods, but I can tell he's anxious.

"You'll do great," I reassure him.

He quakes with a breathy laugh and turns to the side, resting his head on his seat back as his blue eyes settle on me. There's a trust in his gaze that I've missed so much, but there's a new fondness—a deep tenderness—in his expression now too. I know in my heart that he has never, not once, looked at Ava this way.

"I'm not really worried about the interview," he says.

I twist to face him, mimicking his position. I tuck his keys in my bag by my feet and lean forward, taking his hand in both of mine. His fingers are callused from falls and summers spent taking snaps and gripping the football. These same rough hands felt so soft on my skin. His palm opens and I weave my fingers through his, and his thumb strokes the side of my hand, tracing a line from knuckle to knuckle.

"Lucas, there is no way your dad can't be proud of his son getting into MIT," I say.

He nods half-heartedly. He doesn't believe that's true, and maybe I don't fully either. I'm starting to think his dad might not actually *have* a heart, but rather a cold stone in his chest that serves as a greedy magnet, driving him to take and take with little or no regard for the people he hurts along the way.

The bell sounds, forcing us to break from this quiet moment inside his cab. Still not sure how things stand about Lucas and me in public, I squeeze his hand just before letting go. I reach for my bag to bring it to my lap, but before I fully open the passenger door, Lucas leans across the short distance between us, gliding his hand along my cheek and into my messy twist of hair. He kisses me hard, with a deep sense of urgency as if my kiss will somehow be his lucky charm to survive the day. Any thought that's the case, though, dwindles the moment our lips part and my gaze lands on a steaming Ava Pryor standing a dozen feet away.

"Fuuck," Lucas breathes out, sinking his gaze to his lap, then out his window.

"She'd find out eventually," I say, ignoring the

hammering in my chest that warns me bad shit is coming my way.

"Yeah," Lucas hums. His already tight face is now tighter.

"Does she know about MIT?" I ask, and he quickly shakes his head.

"She doesn't know shit," he says, flashing his gaze to mine quickly for reassurance.

I spare a quick glance in her direction to see if she's still lingering, but she already moved on. Her tiny form punches harsh steps into the ground as she marches down the main walkway into school.

"I'll see you at lunch," I say over my shoulder before opening his truck and sliding to the ground. I hoist my bag over my shoulder, giving Lucas one last glance.

"I wish you were still in my first hour," he says before I shut the door, and even though I do, too, I'm also glad he misses me being there.

I smile and ponder how much I want this day to go smoothly for him as I head on my way to the independent study room. Even though he said Ava Pryor doesn't know shit, I can't help but constantly scan my landscape on the lookout for her. That bitch is a sniper, I swear.

The lunch bell blares, and I practically leap from my seat, my legs having primed themselves with nervous bouncing for the last twenty minutes. My stride is so long that I get to the gate at the front of the school well before Lucas shows up, so I walk near the office and check a few texts on my phone to avoid eye contact with any of the teachers or administrators. There's a single text from my mom that I can't get myself to open. I've only seen the preview, and the beginning words make me feel pretty terrible.

June, I am worried sick. Please just tell me . . .

I assume it goes on to say "that you're all right." I am all right. *Ish.* I'm also a lot wrong. And a whole lot confused and angry.

"*Psst,*" a hushed voice sounds from behind me. I turn to see Lucas walking up, his tall, muscular body looking like an elite work of art in black pants and a crisp white shirt with rolled-up sleeves. The gray tie that I can tell he made a few attempts at hangs loose around his neck. He lifts his chin as he approaches, so I drop my bag at my feet and reach up to grab the satin ends.

"These things are tricky," I say through a wide smile. He's so handsome right now, my mind has become complete goo. I'm not sure whether I want to straighten his tie, or lick him.

"I fucking hate ties. They choke me," he complains, swallowing hard and stretching out his collar with the movement of his neck.

"You're a big man," I say, blushing at my words, my focus on the work my hands are doing with the tie. I catch the smirk playing on his lips, so I playfully bat at his chest.

"Shush, or I won't help you," I say.

A gravelly laugh leaves his chest.

I get the knot just right on the first try, which is impressive since I haven't tied one of these since my father left. I tug a few times to get the line of it straight, tucking the back tail into the loop on the back of the front one. I fold his collar down and brush away a tiny bit of lint. He smells like soap and vanilla. I'm almost certain his mom pressed this shirt for him this morning. Her towels always smelled just like this; I remember from the times I went over to swim.

"There," I say, bashfully glancing up at him. He looks down at me with a coy smile, and for the first time maybe ever, I believe in my gut that this boy is truly smitten with me, as much as I am with him.

"Wish me luck," he says.

I shake my head.

"You don't need it. Break a leg," I offer instead. He laughs with a short eye roll and then grabs the open gate as one of the late-start seniors walks through.

"Ready?" he asks. I hold his keys in my palm and jingle them.

"Let's do this," I say. I let him walk out first, his strides long and purposeful toward the middle of the lot, the same direction he went the last time I saw him do this. The red car sticks out, though I think only to me, and because I'm looking for it. I pieced it together when he told me he already met with the representative a few times.

Today's interview is at a nearby restaurant, with two other admissions deans. Our principal knows he's leaving for it, and Lucas said he understands the sensitivity of keeping this a secret from his coach. I'm not sure he knows about me, though, so I don't dawdle. I jog toward Lucas's truck in an effort to get there unnoticed. But I don't make it without at least one person seeing me. I don't see her coming at all, or the fist she sends into my nose like a rocket.

Ava fucking Pryor just punched me, and I'm pretty sure she spit on me too. I'm in a fit of rage, and all I want to do is drive every ounce of my body right through hers, flattening her ass on the pavement. But that would make a scene. Teachers would come running, and people would spot me out here at Lucas's truck, with his keys, while he's on a covert mission to live his best life without interference from the people who want to run it for him. Goddamn, my face hurts, and my pride hurts a shit-ton more, but I have loved Lucas Fuller longer than I've hated Ava Pryor. So for him, I wipe my bloody nose along the sleeve of my sweatshirt and get in his truck, firing it up and peeling out to head to Two-fers, where I hope they have a lot of fucking napkins.

CHAPTER NINETEEN

There really isn't an easy way to mask a black eye. There's also a chance my nose is broken. I'm honestly kind of impressed with Ava's form. She hit me good, a nice shot, square up on the bone, causing my right eye to swell shut.

I spend my entire lunch hour in the Two-fer's bathroom. I know I'm supposed to go through the drive-thru so nobody can tell for sure who's driving, but I'm such a mess. And now, I'm the proud owner of a Two-fers long-sleeve T-shirt. I bought the red one because I might as well be prepared for the next bloody nose.

There isn't a way for me to hide this from Lucas. I have to give him his keys, but the plan is to be super discreet on his way into the locker room. Maybe he'll be in such a hurry he won't have time to ask questions. What I don't count on is Tory.

"Maybe Mabee, wonder what you're hanging around here for," Tory teases as he jogs up the ramp to the locker room entrance. I'm sitting on the middle of the steps that rise up the opposite side, my right eye facing away from view.

Tory isn't shy with me. He moves up the steps and sits with his back resting on the opposite wall, our feet practically touching. He stretches his toes forward, tapping the sole of his shoe into mine. I do my best to look at him sideways, but when he mocks my weird posture and side-eyes, I give in and get it over with.

"Damn! You get in a fight, Mabee?"

I shrug it off, but his eyes linger on the puffy side of my face, and I can only bluff that it's no big deal for so long. When his eyes narrow, I glean that he's probably piecing it together. I don't have more than one enemy. Hell, I only have a handful of friends.

"Ava do that shit to you?" He knows; I can tell by his tone.

I tip my chin just a little.

"Hope you fucked her shit up right back," he says, leaning forward and moving to the step above me to inspect my eye more closely. "You need to get a cold compress on that. I can get something in the training room."

"It's fine," I say, not wanting the attention. Besides, the last thing I need is Lucas seeing this.

"It's not fine. I'll be, like, two minutes, tops. Just sit tight," he says, rushing in the door and cutting off a few guys heading in for practice.

My pulse is jittery, and I keep feeling as if my heart is missing beats. I just want to get Lucas his key and be on my way. But if anyone sees me handing it to him, they'll know I had his truck, and then maybe he wasn't at Two-fers, and instead . . .

"Here," Tory says, making better time than I expect. He hands me a small plastic bag filled with ice, and one of the white towels they use at practices. I put the ice on my face first without wrapping it, but Tory stops me before I press it on my skin too hard. "No, here."

He's wrapping the towel around the bag when a shadow moves over both of us where we're sitting.

"What the fuck happened?" Lucas kneels down next to me, his eyes glaring at Tory as if he had something to do with my face.

"I'm fine," I say, clutching his key in my right palm, wanting to slip it to him and run away.

"Your ex had a field day with her face," Tory says, a hint of accusation in his tone. There's a short standoff between them as they hover on either side of me, the cold ice bag still clutched in Tory's hands.

There was a time when the thought of two varsity foot-ball players fighting over my honor seemed like a dream, but now, in the middle of it, I just want them to get over themselves—get over me!

"Gentlemen?" Coach Loma has a very distinct voice. It's effective on a field with a hundred teenaged boys all vying to be hotshots. He barks and they listen. One word brings Tory and Lucas to instant attention, eyes widening before their necks snap up to look him in the eye.

"I had an accident, Coach, and they happened to catch me before I fell all the way. I went end-over-end," I lie, laughing nervously as I rip the ice and towel from Tory's grip and hold it to the side of my face.

Lucas understands why I'm lying, but Tory's reaction is a little less believable, which causes Coach Loma to question things more than I want him to.

"Lemme see what you've got going here," he says, pushing Lucas out of the way. Stress knots my stomach and chest as Lucas hops down a few steps, now too far to pass him his keys. I'm so focused on the mission that I barely respond to Coach as he peels the towel from my face and tips my chin up to have a good look at my shiner.

"You said you got this falling down the stairs?" he asks.

I nod, but it's painfully obvious that didn't happen. This is going horribly wrong.

"Mind if I get our trainer to come give you a look? Just a little concussion protocol, and since it happened on campus, we'll need to fill out an incident form," he says, standing and pulling his khaki pants up by his belt loops.

Shit. An incident report.

"Okay," I croak. As everyone stands, I flutter my eyes closed, wishing like hell I could go back and tell him I got in a fight. I'd still probably be dealing with a trainer and an incident report, though. Goddamn, Ava Pryor!

Lucas's bag is about an arm's length from me, but my aim is shit so I can't toss his keys with certainty that I'll make the shot. I can discern from the heavy silent glares Coach is giving both of the boys that he's dismissing them from my aid and telling them to get their asses to practice. My last chance is to somehow stall Lucas. As he reaches for one strap of his backpack, I reach for the other, pulling hard enough to yank it from his hand and slide it closer to me.

"Oh, dang, sorry. I thought this was mine," I lie. My

bag is bright pink. Lucas's is black. I'm so lame it's painful. While everyone puzzles at me, I manage to slip his key into the side pocket before Lucas lifts the bag up and over his shoulder.

"It's fine," he says, brow heavy as he stares down at me. I'm pretty sure he knows I put the key in there. That's not what his frown is about. He's worried about my face, and maybe he feels a little responsible. He doesn't own Ava, though. She's a bitch all on her own.

"Maybe call your mom or dad, Miss . . ."

"June," I finish for Coach. "June Mabee." I add my last name. He has no reason to remember who I am. I am one of hundreds of students he had freshman year for health class.

"Right, okay. Well, call your parents, June," he says.

"It's just my mom," I respond. Not sure why he would care about that detail, but I've become accustomed to making the correction. I don't like my dad getting parental credit. Of course, I'm not exactly thrilled to call my mom right now.

Tory and Lucas reluctantly head in the locker room, and I pull my legs in to make room for the dozens of players now rushing down the steps to go change. Coach Loma is on the phone with who I assume is probably the trainer, and he nods toward my bag and mouths the words, "Call your mom."

I don't want to in the worst way, but explaining would make things so much worse. I'm already neck deep in fibs. I nod and pull my phone from my bag, noting the text message from my mom that I still haven't fully read. I swipe right by it and hit call on my phone to dial her. She answers before I even hear a ring.

"June?" She's frantic, and her voice is raw with exhaustion. I'm an asshole. And a coward. I don't even know for sure if she's a liar, or worse.

"I'm at school, and I fell. They're going to fill out an incident report, but I'm by the gymnasium, and Coach saw me. He thinks maybe I have a concussion?" I'm trying to keep my voice quiet and calm, but I can hear her rapid breathing on the other end quickening with worry.

"I'll be right there," she says.

"Mom, I'm fine. Abby is giving me a ride home anyway."

"June," she interjects. Her voice is stern.

I swallow.

"Okay," I say.

"Tell the coach I will come in through the office. Should I meet you by the gym?" I can already hear the van firing up. The thought of her rushing through campus to meet me at the gym so she can gawk at my black eye has me wanting to throw up. Of course, if I throw up, that's a sign of a concussion, which will only make this rabbit hole deeper because I already had a concussion.

"I'm sure we can meet you at the office." I glance up at Coach and he nods.

"Okay, well, I'm on my way." By the time I end the call with my mom, the trainer is at my side, tilting my head up so he can shine a penlight in my eyes. The man is maybe twenty-two, and his degree is in exercise. He's not really qualified to diagnose head trauma, but I don't have any so I let him do his thing. I trace the movement of his finger as he draws it out then in again, and I promptly answer his series of easy questions, spelling my first and last names, and listing the last three presidents. *I wonder if our football players can pass this part,* I muse to myself.

Once I've satisfied his test, Coach pats my shoulder and helps me to my feet, still eyeing me suspiciously. I only hope he doesn't think Lucas or Tory punched me in the face. I wouldn't want to start that kind of scandal.

Coach sends the trainer along with me to make sure I'm all right during my walk to the office. He carries my backpack for me, but I keep my phone, texting Abby so she knows I won't need a ride home. She writes back instantly.

I'm here with your mom. I heard. You . . . fell?

I sigh, reading her text and typing my response.

Long story.

She shoots back a laughing emoji, but she has no idea what a mess this is.

My mom is standing at the front desk when I walk in through the side doors. She's wearing one of her cotton T-shirt dresses, so at least she changed from what I saw her wearing this morning, and her hair in a twisted knot on top of her head. When I step through the glass doors into the lobby, she rushes to me and holds both sides of my face, smooshing them with her purse and phone still in her hands.

"June Mabee, you have a black eye!" She tilts my head down and steps up on her toes as if looking at it from above makes it seem somehow less of an injury.

"I'm fine." I shake my head, glancing to the side to meet Abby's gaze. My friend's eyes are narrowed, but for a different reason. Abby's taken a punch or two in her life.

She's given her fair share of black eyes, too. She's not naïve, so I shake my head slightly once my mom lets go as a signal for her not to question—not right now.

I shift back to meet my mom's waiting stare. She's so broken, and I'm to blame for a lot of that.

"Kristen," Maggie Williams's familiar voice draws our attention to the main desk. My mom hesitates for a moment. In the past, when she's run into Maggie with me, there have been hugs. Right now, though, my mom is embarrassed. Here I am, black eye and all. It's awkward.

"I guess there's a form?" My mom moves around the desk to take the seat Maggie has pulled out for her.

"It's just a formality," Maggie says, sliding the already-prepared document around for my mom to review and sign. She leans into my mom and whispers loudly, "It's so you don't sue the school."

"Should I?" My mom leans back, holding the pen away from the signature line.

"No!" I blurt out.

I cover my face and Abby slides over to stand at my side.

"Well, I don't know," my mom continues. There's a deep wrinkle on her brow as she turns her focus to me. I can no longer tell whether she's serious about suing or using the threat to bait me into spilling my guts.

"Please," I beg. I'm sweating, which probably makes me look even more banged up, but it's because I really just want to be done with this.

My mom studies me for a few seconds then pinches one side of her mouth, clicking the pen in and out a few times before finally leaning forward and signing her name to the line.

"Thanks, Kristen. Hey, we should get together for real sometime, ya know? Like in a place where we can have booze!" Maggie's raspy laugh sparks a brief smile on my mom's lips and she agrees that sounds nice.

I walk out toward the parking lot, ready to bolt for Abby's car, but my mom is one step ahead of me. We barely get through the doors before she catches them behind us.

"June? The van," she says, pointing to where she parked along the curb in front of the office like an ambulance.

I breathe in long and deep but nod. My friend gives me a hug and whispers, "Call me" in my ear. I dump my bag on the back seat before climbing in the front. My mom is already waiting for me, and she eyes my movements like a hawk as I fasten my buckle.

"Do I at least get to know what happened to your face?"

It's hard to look her in the eyes. I tell her everything, basically. It's just that I have this horror that she hasn't been keeping up her end of the bargain. I can't fathom her keeping secrets from me, but a secret that big . . . she would have to.

"No," I answer, finally. Her eyes curse at me just before her mouth snaps shut in shock.

"Okay, then." She flips her gaze to the front, cranking the van and shifting into drive without hesitation. "I guess you can get used to me driving you to and from school for the next month."

Her tone is clipped.

"I guess," I say coolly, lifting my towel-covered icepack to my face and holding it in such a way that I block my mom's view of me.

This has to end. I need to tell her everything Lucas told me so she has the chance to either verify it, or not. Maybe she'll lie, but at least I won't be holding this feeling in anymore. Then I can tell her about my face and what happened with Ava, and about Lucas's interview today. I know she would be proud. My mom loved Lucas, to the point of teasing me when she knew I had developed a crush. Of course, now that I threw the little V-card announcement at her, she might look at him differently.

"I don't know what's going on with you, June, but I won't just sit back and let you fall into yourself. You can be mad. I'll give you time. I'll even give you a break about today. I'm not stupid, and it's pretty clear to everyone that you have a black eye. I just hope you aren't in a situation where someone . . ."

Her voice trails off and I know it's because the thought of me letting a guy hit me touches a raw nerve in her heart. My dad never laid a hand on her directly, but he threw things when he got angry. And from the few things she's told me about her high school boyfriends, I think she's faced worse than my dad's keys being thrown at her face.

"I'm not being unsafe," I finally say, relenting and dropping the ice pack from my eye as we pull into our driveway. My mom stops the van just past the curb, and I expect to find her eyes waiting for me as I face her. But when I look, I find she's not looking at me at all. Her focus is glued straight ahead and her mouth hangs open wide, anger reddening her cheeks and shaking her clinched jaw. I snap my gaze to her sightline, and at first what my eyes take in seems too enormous to be real.

The word WHORE is spray-painted in red across our garage door. The can used to create it is left abandoned in our driveway, its lid a few yards away. On instinct, I crank my neck to the left, searching the Fuller house for spying eyes. The garage is closed, as is the side door and all the shutters. But something this bold isn't Mrs. Fuller's style; she abhors confrontation. Asking her husband and son to ignore our existence seems more like her. The message written on our house, it isn't for my mom. It's for me. And I have an eye that matches it perfectly.

CHAPTER TWENTY

"Someone doesn't like me."

That's all I say as I exit the van, slamming the door closed behind me. I grab some acetone and some of my dad's old rags from the garage, then immediately start scrubbing the word off the garage door. My efforts fade the color, but the word is still there. It is still *very much* there.

My mom helps for a while. She keeps her promise of not prying into more today, though I can tell as she scrubs next to me that she so badly wants to. I can't really mask my tears, but I wear the grit on my face right along with the pain, which makes open, honest conversation less approachable.

That word isn't going away without paint. If I had my way, I would go buy a gallon of whatever's on hand and roll it on. My mom says she'll do it in the morning, after she drops me off at school.

She is still my ride, to and from, until I do something to make it otherwise.

Lucas will see it. I've been sitting in the center of my bed with the lights off for two hours, waiting for his practice to end. I only now locked my bedroom door. I want to make sure my mom won't try coming in, though if she does and is met with a lock, she'll flip her lid even more than she already has. She's worried. I'm worried, too. Somebody hates me, and somebody knows things meant to hurt me.

I can't quite see the full driveway from my window, but I see his lights spill across the ground. They stay on for several long seconds, even as I hear his door open and close. He's looking at the graffiti. It's strange how, even though I am nothing like that word, simply having it on my home makes me somehow feel dirty.

Lucas's lights flick off and his heavy door slams shut again. I don't bother going to the window. I've left it open, anticipating him. I'm not sure whether I want to pound on his chest and curse him for bringing this down on me or if I want him to hold me and make it better. I figure I'll know when I see him.

The skidding of his shoes on the roof shingles draws near, so I scoot to the end of the bed, my feet on the floor and my hands cupping my bare knees. I'm wearing my sleep shirt because it's the only thing that makes me feel comfortable. Now, I feel like that word, even though it's just a large cotton T-shirt.

"June." His voice is urgent as his hands wrap around the sill of the window. He lifts himself up easily, his hair wet from the shower he took after practice, his gray T-shirt sticking to his damp skin.

I ball my fists on top of my thighs, collecting the anger building in my veins, but as I prepare to pound my hands into his chest, he drops to his knees in front of me and gently cups my face. Tender eyes examine the bruising on my face.

"I'm so sorry," he says, repeating it three or four times until finally holding my gaze to his.

My hands relax and my palms grip at his shirt, and I cling to him like a bear cub, pressing the uninjured side of my face against his chest as I let out a silent sob. He lifts himself up to stand, holding me to him, one hand cradling my head while the other holds my weight. He turns to sit on the bed and I rest my weight against him. His palm runs up my back soothingly, and he tucks my face into the nook just under his jaw. He breaths out a soft hush into my ear.

"I know, June. I'm so sorry. I'm so fucking sorry." He rocks me with his words, slowly, lulling me into more normal breathing.

"She painted my house," I cry, my voice muffled against his body.

"I know," he says, his voice quiet and still at my ear.

For almost half an hour, I sit like this, hugged tightly in his arms, my face hot with tears while his fingers delicately tickle along my bare arms until the shaking in my chest calms. My house is silent beyond my door, and I'm not sure whether my mom is in her room or still sitting on the sofa, staring out the front window while she sips at wine and waits for whoever painted our house to show up and do it again. I told her they wouldn't, but she simply shot me a look indicating that if I was allowed to be left alone, so was she.

"How was the interview?" Even my whisper sounds

hoarse. Lucas's body shakes under me. He's fallen to his back, but keeps me cradled to him.

"There are more pressing things," he murmurs, finally moving his hand from my arm and up to my hair, combing his fingers through the long, tangled strands as he brushes them from my face.

"Not really," I sigh out. "I mean, if all this happened and you didn't get in, that would suck." I shift to look him in the eyes. He raises his chin to see me better. I do my best to wink out of my black eye but it's fairly swollen; maybe it looks like a tic. Lucas gives out a soft, sympathetic laugh anyhow.

He runs his thumb along my deep purple skin and I can barely feel his touch. His eyes land on mine after tracing the line he draws around my bruising.

"I'm in," he says, mouth closed tightly with an uncertain smile pushing up the sides.

I lift myself and push down on his chest, knocking the wind from him a little. He holds my wrists as I do.

"Shut up!" My shouted whisper breaks the silence and Lucas quickly cups my mouth and holds in his laughter.

"Shhh, I can't go to MIT if your mom shoots me first," he jokes.

I laugh with him then roll to his side, resting my palms on his beautiful strong cheeks.

"Lucas, I am so proud of you," I say, blinking wildly. There's a strong hesitation poorly hidden behind his eyes, the weight of this finally being real.

"He'll come around," I say, predicting that it's his dad he's worried about.

He shakes his head and looks down to where our legs are tangled, mine bare and his covered in his joggers.

"I don't even care. I'm going, and my mom said with the scholarship money I'll get, they can pay the rest."

I'm glad he's not looking me in the eyes right now, because his victory stings a little, and I'm not proud of feeling jealous. Not that I want to go to MIT, but I would love to go to one of the state schools. My grades are good enough to qualify for a few different tuition grants, but there are still so many expenses left to cover. Unless colleges let people camp in tents and eat from their garbage.

"My mom knows you helped," he says, his long lashes blinking up and uncovering his blue eyes as he peers up at me. For a short breath, I'm distracted from all of the sucky things in my life and just stare in wonder at them and the fact I can kiss them closed right now if I want.

"And she'll still let you go?" I joke. My laugh is short-lived, though. The way his mom glared at me flashes in my head.

"My mom doesn't hate you, June. She's just—"

"Hurt," I finish for him.

I get it. It's the same reason I haven't been to visit my father once since he left and moved in with Jamie—Jamie, who is only ten years older than me. Of course, he's only invited me to his condo once, so I guess I haven't had to reject him much.

"Yeah, she's hurt," Lucas says, breaking up my thoughts. "When she found out about the affair, she went through a pretty dark time."

"You haven't told her about the new one, have you?

The new affair?" I can't believe this is the discussion we have to have. Statistically, this many adults having affairs or getting divorced is actually not an anomaly. I know, because I checked on Reddit. Still, it seems impossible that this is where our adults all ended up. Weren't they all just drinking together in the Fuller back yard while we swam and lit sparklers on the Fourth of July?

"I haven't told her," Lucas says, moving close enough to touch his nose to mine. His eyes close, heavy with exhaustion. It's been a long stretch of days for both of us.

"Have you told Tory yet?" I ask.

He shakes his head, rubbing his nose softly against mine.

"I'm sorry about . . . the word. On the garage," he says. I let my eyes fall shut to lock out the pain of it.

"You told Ava about my mom and your dad," I whisper. I figure that's how she knew.

He doesn't affirm my question so much as he huffs out a breath and apologizes again. "I'm sorry. I don't even know why I did, but it slipped out once."

"*Shhh,*" I hum. I can't hear about her now. I don't care about their intimate secrets. And while I won't let him call her a mistake, I will let him feel as if he made a few. Trusting her was definitely one of them.

"I'm sorry, June. I'm sorry, I'm sorry . . ." His words fade.

I close the distance between us and press my lips to his. It's not a sensual moment, but rather a sweet one. His lips part slightly, as do mine, and we hold a chaste kiss between us for as long as it takes him to fall into slumber. My window is still open, and the air outside is cold. Our feet are covered by my turned-down blanket, so I gingerly reach to drag it up our bodies. As bad as I want to keep my eyes open, to stay present for this moment, I just can't. It's more than being tired. In the midst of all this awful, I think I'm also a little bit happy.

CHAPTER TWENTY-ONE

I'm not sure when Lucas woke up and snuck out my window, but by the time my eyes open this morning, he's gone. He left behind a little reminder, though, one he had to go back to his truck to get. I spent the first ten minutes of my morning just staring at it hanging from the back of my desk chair.

The sleeves of his letterman jacket make the same stupid crinkling sound they do when he wears it. My smile turns into a laugh as I sink my left arm in, then my right. The lining is cool, but I'll be dying of heat by lunch time, if I even wear this thing all day. Who am I kidding? I'm wearing this jacket for always. I'm probably never giving it back.

In a way, it makes me feel a little stronger for the day that lies ahead. I can't live like this, with secrets between me and my mom. And I won't let someone like Ava Pryor make me feel small. I mean, I am a senior now. I've grown up. I've grown . . . period. This jacket, it makes me feel a little badass—a little bit like Abby.

Embraced in the woodsy scent of the boy I think might really, truly be my boyfriend, I unlock my bedroom door and take in a deep breath. Today, I'm walking down those stairs. Honestly, I may never scale my roof again.

My mom is humming to herself in the kitchen, and I pause halfway down the steps to listen. I don't think she's happy, but maybe she slept a little. Or maybe she found her own symbolic jacket, something to make her feel a little bit badass, too.

"Good morning." I announce myself as I round the corner into the kitchen, and she turns, surprised to hear my voice. Her face is covered with dots of paint, as is her T-shirt. It's one of my dad's old ones she kept for things like gardening. She said it felt nice to ruin them. Well, this one . . . it's toast.

My mom puckers her lips as she leans over the counter and balances herself on her forearms, palms flat, her coffee mug between them.

"Are we talking now?" she asks me, her eyes surveying the jacket I wear.

I suck in my top lip and breathe in through my nose as I slowly nod.

"We're *starting* to talk again," I say. I can't unpack all of the garbage in my head during a short ride to school, but I can open the gates again. For a while after the divorce, my mom had this buzz word she used, something she got from the counselling sessions she tried. I throw it out there now, not to mock her, but to make her laugh.

"We'll . . . *dialogue,*" I say. She breaks into an instant

smile and eventually winks at me, turning around to top off her cup before grabbing her keys and purse to drive me to school.

I open the side door first, slinging my bag over my shoulder and glancing up in time to catch Mrs. Fuller's full view as she backs out from her driveway. Her tires screech to a quick stop, the jolt enough to fling her hair forward and force her sunglasses from her face. Rather than run, I maintain my pace and walk right to the passenger door of our van. I refuse to let my relationship with Lucas be shrapnel to our parents' failed relationships. I keep the jacket on even as I get into the seat and strap myself in. The jacket is really smothering and the fit is oversized, but I'm going to make sure I maximize the sightings of me in this garment. One hurdle is down already as Mrs. Fuller finally finishes backing out and pulls away. My next mission is the spray paint artist, Ava Pryor.

My eyes leave the rearview mirror and finally focus on my marred garage door. The pink and red stains of WHORE are gone, which explains the paint dots all over my mother's body. What I don't quite understand, though, is the enormous middle finger she painted in its place. My mouth is still hanging open when she gets in the van.

"You like it?" she asks. I blink once and turn my gaze to hers. There's a proud smile on her mouth, and I know it's partly there because mothers are alphas too. In many ways, they are the alpha-ist of them all. Instead of hiding and taking the abuse, my mom decided to let the world know the Mabee girls don't take shit from anyone.

"I do," I say, returning my focus to our freshly painted garage door. My smile pushes into my eyes, and that nervous thunder that's been abusing my chest for the last few weeks is a calm purr. "I like it a lot."

My cockiness sticks with me as my mom drops me off at the front of the school. Despite the itching desire to hunt down Ava and take a victory lap around her, I don't. I don't run to Lucas, either. Instead, I drag my feet on my way in, smearing a few chalk lines drawn on the front sidewalk to celebrate spirit week. I stop at my best friend's car and lean back, stretching out my arm so she can feel the thick leather of this very hot fucking jacket.

"Boom! Look who's running this shit now," Abby says, tugging on the sleeve then holding a fist out for me. I pound it and call her "bruh" just to mock the guys who usually walk around in these. That includes Lucas, and Tory, but over the last few weeks they've grown accustomed to me taking them down a peg.

"You sure I can't retaliate against her for that shiner?" Abby asks. She pops a piece of gum in her mouth and snaps it aggressively.

I told her the real story last night before Lucas came. She also knows about the garage. She hasn't seen my mom's artwork, though.

"It's fine. I don't even care about Ava Pryor anymore." My eye stings a little when I say it.

"Liar," she says.

"You're right," I admit with a laugh. "But I don't care quite as much."

The bell rings and I push off of the front of my friend's car, walking with a little swagger.

"My mom has to drive me home today, but you should come by and see what she's done with the garage."

She squints at me suspiciously.

"It's a worthy surprise," I add.

"Well, all right then." My friend reaches to the side and grabs my hand for a squeeze, and we part at the office doors.

I stretch to shove them open and suddenly a palm reaches over me and pushes the door open wide. I recognize his arm, the freckles that form the little dipper just above his wrist. I smell the coconut from his shampoo. To be sure, I pause my steps so his large body crashes into me from behind, and when his arms wrap around my midsection and he walks me forward, away from my independent study room, I give in with a teasing guess.

"Earl? Is that you?"

He spins me fast and catches my jaw in his palm, stepping in close as he towers over me with a kiss. It feels as though the whole world is watching, and it makes me smile.

"This public enough for you?" He runs the pad of his thumb over my lip and my body chills.

"It's getting there," I say. He holds on to my hand, but walks backward toward his class—the class I could still be in with him, but damn me and my pride. Maybe this is better, heart growing fonder and all. As he moves away, our fingers slip apart.

"This jacket is really fucking hot," I joke.

"You love it," he teases.

"I love you," I say.

Shit.

He stops moving. Maybe he also stopped breathing. His eyes are huge, mouth open, but maybe that's a smile on his lips? Maybe not. It's definitely an amused expression. I wonder if the whole world just heard that.

My eyes are definitely wide, I can tell by the air stinging them. My mouth waters a little bit too. It does that when I eat olives, because I threw up once on olives. I think maybe I throw up on *I love you's*.

Shit.

I drop a prayer, and it's quickly answered by the ringing bell and rush of students filing through the office doors behind me. My class is ten paces back, his is about a hundred forward. Why isn't he moving?

My black eye is threatening to leak so I blink moisture back into the surface and wave my hand as if it's a powerful eraser that can take back slips of the tongue.

"I'm really tired. I meant the jacket. I love your jacket. Oh, God, umm." I smile exaggeratingly huge, showing my teeth like a first grader waiting for the tooth fairy, and squeeze my eyes shut tight as I shout "Good-bye," then turn and actually run to my independent study room.

That's not how that was supposed to happen. Things like that, though, they seem to keep happening with Lucas.

Drowning in sweat from my embarrassment, I pull off Lucas's jacket as soon as I make it to my seat. I leave it on my lap because I like the security it offers me. I actually do love this stupid jacket.

I also love the boy.

I manage to make it through the entire day without seeing Lucas. I was prepared at lunch to explain away my blurted-out confession. I don't want to scare him. Even though I've known him for years, maybe it seems psycho to come right out with *I love you's* this fast. Or maybe not. Abby is no help because boys tell her they love her on a monthly basis. She's never said it once herself, though. Not once. Except to me and her mom. Lucas never showed up at lunch, though, so I was off the hook. He sent me a text when Abby and I were throwing away our trash and said he got called into the principal's office. My guess is it was something to formalize his scholarship offer.

My mom texted before school was over and warned me she would be twenty minutes late. I, of course, offered to go home with Abby instead, but her response was a cackling emoji face.

The traffic should be cleared out by the time she arrives, so I've been spared from standing near the bus line where chaos breeds more chaos every afternoon at 2:20. And since I don't have to wait in the normal pickup spot, I venture around the back side of the gym to the slope that leads down to the football practice field. The guys aren't doing much yet, just some stretching. Lucas is easy to spot; he's on his back at the sidelines with his right leg in the air. The trainer—the same one who assessed my lovely shiner —is leaning into his leg and holding it straight as he pushes it toward Lucas's body. It's amazing how inflexible these athletes are.

"That's a nice jacket you have there."

I swallow hard. It's been a while since I've heard Mr.

Fuller's voice. He's always had this dominant edge. I used to be afraid of it; when we were kids, he was always the parent I didn't want catching us doing anything wrong. Now, though, I recognize those tones and inflections for what they are—crutches to make a small man feel bigger than he is.

"Thanks. I think I'll keep it," I say, twisting to the side and offering him a closed, smug smile.

He chuckles and pauses his steps, sinking his hands into the pockets of his blazer and glancing down to where his boots meet the dry grass of the hillside.

"You know, people who live in glass houses shouldn't throw stones." He smirks, proud of his plagiarized idiom. I let him think he's won for a few seconds, just long enough for his ego to inflate a little bit more.

"That's a very good point, Mr. Fuller. No, they sure shouldn't." As the satisfaction of saying the perfect thing at the perfect moment seeps into my veins, I breathe in deep as this big, scary man shrinks a little before my eyes.

His scowl breaks through the façade he works so hard to maintain, and his mouth chews on his words. He wants to break me, but what he doesn't know is I've already been broken and rebuilt.

"Say hi to Mrs. D'Angelo for me," I say before turning and heading up the hill with the heat of his eyes scalding the back of my head.

I pushed down the first domino, and I know how these things work. The tumbling has begun, and there really isn't a clean way to stop it. The only thing left is to sit back and watch it burn.

I walk through the lot as it clears, and as I get closer to

the entrance, I pull my phone out to check my mom's location on our app. She's a block away, so I go ahead and call her.

"I'm almost there," she answers immediately.

"I know, I saw. I'm walking to meet you, so turn in at that parking lot right at the corner. I think I want some ice cream. My treat." I can't see her, but I can imagine the face she's making by the tiny breath she exhales into the phone. It's a grateful laugh, a short one that touches her eyes and makes her shoulders drop with relief.

"That sounds . . . really nice." She's right. It does.

We end up timing things just right, and I step up to my mom's van just as she pulls in. I hold up my palm for her not to lock the door and open the passenger side to peel off my jacket. I'll like this jacket more when it's winter and I'm standing in the bleachers watching one of Lucas's playoff games. It's strange because I don't only hope I'll be there doing that. I know I will. I have this strange, quiet confidence in us.

"So, when do I get to ask about the jacket?" She lifts a brow as I scrunch mine a bit.

"Maybe when I feel less embarrassed about my knee-jerk confession when I stormed past you at six in the morning?" I smile through gritted teeth, suddenly feeling the heat of telling my mother I had sex.

"Right, well . . ." She pulls the keys from the ignition and we meet at the front of the van.

"I won't dwell. I'm not *my* mother, but because I'm not, I need to be direct about a few things. You're being safe?" she asks.

"Yes. Oh, my God," I cover my face. There's an older

couple enjoying sundaes at a sidewalk table about four feet away. I want to die.

"And what you did, it was your choice?" she continues.

I nod, eyes still closed tight and hand shading my face.

"And you know that all it takes is once to—"

"Yes!" I cut her off before she has a chance to blurt out the word *pregnant*. I look down at my feet and usher us into the small mom and pop store called Jan's that has served scoops to my mom and me since it opened when I was six. I guess Jan was one of the owners' moms. I always forget which one, but she passed away shortly after they opened.

My cheeks cool from the freezers, and my nose perks up at the scent of pistachio and vanilla as soon as we step inside. The girl working behind the counter is new. A lot of the sophomores and juniors at Public get their first jobs here because it's so close to school. She's young, probably still fifteen. It's nice when the owners are working because they always know our orders the moment we walk in.

I step up close to the glass and lean in to make sure they have my cherry jubilee flavor. The carton looks loaded enough to give me a double, so that's what I order. My mom gets pistachio, and we both wait while the girl, who's tag says her name is Marylee, scoops our dishes. My mom takes our bowls to a booth in the corner, and I hand the girl my card to pay. She shakes her head no.

"You can have it for free," she says, a shy smile tugging up the corners of her mouth.

"Oh-okay. Thanks," I stammer, putting away my card. I turn to walk away, assuming she must be a relative of the owners or something and maybe recognizes us that way, but I stop on a hunch and turn back around.

"Umm, not to be rude, but . . . why?" I ask.

She shrugs and glances off to the side. "I don't know. Just, aren't you Lucas Fuller's girlfriend?"

An audible laugh flies out of my chest, and I have to apologize immediately because I think it freaked her out a little.

"I'm just not used to that . . . term, I guess?" A giddy laugh bubbles in my throat. "You know, I can still pay."

This free pass for the popular crowd thing is bizarre.

"No, really. I want to, to be nice." I can tell I make her uncomfortable, so I smile and nod.

"Thanks, Marylee. That's really cool of you." I commit her name to memory as I head to the booth to join my mom. I'll find her at school tomorrow and if she has our lunch hour, ask her to join me and Abby and Lucas, if he shows up, and the twins. And I'm going to make sure she feels as special as she made me feel right now. She probably deserves it a whole lot more. All I did was lose my virginity to a quarterback.

I'm still floating on a cloud of kindness when I slip into the seat across from my mom. She hands me a spoon and I immediately scrape away at the melted layer forming at the top of my ice cream. The milky part is always the best.

"So . . ." My mom always starts awkward conversations with me like this. She said the same thing when she told me about the divorce. And that same two-letter transition was how she asked about Lucas and his jacket. I'm guessing the graffiti incident is probably what's coming next.

"You wanna talk about the whole *whore* thing?" I quirk a brow and push a spoonful of ice cream in my mouth.

"I wanna talk about the whole whore thing," my mom reiterates.

I'm not sure there's a way to back into this topic delicately, though I've practiced a few times. I definitely don't want to start by asking her about the money Mr. Fuller gave her, or the affair they may or may not have had. I decide to go with plan C—talking about Mrs. D'Angelo—which was my favorite as of this morning.

"It's kind of a long story," I say.

"I've got time," my mom says, dragging her spoon over the surface of her scoops. The best part about this place is the massive size of the servings. I don't dare explore the calorie count. I much prefer the sound of two scoops to two-million grams of sugar.

"I've been hanging out with Tory D'Angelo a little."

My mom's face lights up as her lips close around her spoon.

"I remember that kid. He's one of the twins, right? Weren't they at your birthday party at the lake?" She's talking around her spoon, and it's nice to see her amused. It's going to make it hard when I have to crush her spirit.

"They were. Tory's the one who went skinny dipping." I grimace and my mom makes a sour face. We were nine at the time, but still old enough to make seeing a naked boy in a crowd feel uncomfortable.

"Right. Yes. So, he's the one you're hanging out with now. Interesting choice." She's teasing me a little, and I'm not sure whether she's trying to relax me or herself. The tension between us over the last couple of days has been strangling her.

"He's actually a lot nicer than I gave him credit for," I admit. A proudness plays out on her face at my words.

I gather my thoughts as I consume a large bite. My mom's gaze lifts to meet mine as she waits, expectantly.

"I was dropping some school things off at his house after the first day, and I saw . . . *something*." God, why is this so hard to say? Maybe because once I start pulling this thread, the rest will come out fast. So very fast.

My mom stops eating, deep interest in the direction of this story taking hold of her. I'm sure she expects another story about Tory, but I can't drag things out.

"I saw Mr. Fuller there, and they were kissing. It was pretty obvious, and it did not look like it was the first time they'd . . . *kissed*." I add weight to that word so my mom knows it means more. I can tell she understands by the heaviness that pushes down on her brow and pulls in her eyes. She pushes her bowl toward the center of the table, and I hate that I'm ruining her appetite. I'm also terrified that she's upset. Not because finding out something about your friends' parents is hard, but because she's jealous due to her own past with Lucas's dad.

"Did you tell Lucas? Or Tory?" Genuine concern is apparent in her tone.

"Lucas knows," I say, looking down at my spoon. I've started to draw patterns in my ice cream. What a waste of two perfectly good desserts this has become. "I'm not sure how to tell Tory, or even if I should."

My mom nods, seeming to understand. I feel sick

wading into this next phase, but I have to do it. I owe it to all of us to hear this one unheard side of the story.

"There's more," I say, licking my suddenly dry lips. I hold my front teeth together and flit my gaze to my mom's a few times, searching for strength to hold it. I can't, and if I look at her again, I'll chicken out. I bring my hands onto the table and weave them together, pressing my thumbs together as a distraction.

"Lucas said that wasn't his dad's first affair." I wait while those words sit in the air between us. I hold my breath and tune my ears for clues, searching for a gasp or some hint in my mom's reaction that what Lucas said is true. The longer her perfect quiet goes on, the easier it is to lift my chin and bring my eyes to meet hers. When I find them waiting with a cluelessness to the words I'm about to level her with, I loudly gulp in air and let my shoulders relax from the place they've been hunched up near my ears.

"Mom, Lucas thinks his father had an affair with you." I let that falsehood marinate for a while, let her mind make sense of it. I can tell by the short tic her face makes and the dent in her forehead that the mere thought of having an affair with Todd Fuller is ludicrous.

"He does," she finally says, a hint of ire in her words.

I nod.

"So does Mrs. Fuller," I add.

My mom lets out a gut-busting laugh that draws the attention of a couple ordering at the counter several feet away.

"Really?" She narrows her eyes, her open mouth caught in a look of disbelief.

"Lucas said she saw you two one night at his office . . . and he gave you money—"

She slaps the table before I can finish filling in the blanks, and tosses her head back in hysterical laughter. I look over my shoulder and give a short wave to the concerned couple, and to Marylee who mouths to me, "Is she okay?"

"That fucking asshole!" My mom slides from the booth and drags her cup with her. She marches up to the counter and I scramble to follow her.

"I'm so sorry, hon, but we have an emergency to tend to. Can we get to-go lids?" Marylee nods nervously and rummages around the bottom cabinets for lids to fit our cups. She hands us two and my mom slaps one on her ice cream. She hands me mine over her shoulder and stomps toward the door.

"Where are we going?" I'm pretty sure I know, but I want verbal confirmation that my mom is about to commit murder.

"We're going to set the record straight. And then, after the dust settles, me and you are going to enjoy our fucking ice cream." She's pointing at me while she spits out her words, and I'm both terrified and inspired by her strength.

CHAPTER TWENTY-TWO

I didn't even know my mom had a lawn chair.
Somewhere, from the depths of our garage, behind that enormous door painted with a huge F-U, she found one. It's lime green and aluminum, and she made sure to drag it across our driveway and into the Fuller's front yard without a single care for the scene it made and the atrocious sound it caused as it scraped along the pavement.

She's been sitting in that chair, legs crossed and venom ready to spew at her enemies, for the last hour. I vacillate between pacing behind her while I bite at my barely-there fingernails and staring at her from our kitchen window while I snack on random shit from our refrigerator. I'm down to pickles now, and not even spears. I've forked out at least a dozen dill chips. I'm nervous eating, which is the only reason I've held off from the ice cream—I want to enjoy it, not just angry-eat it.

I told Lucas to call me the moment he's heading home from practice. I want to be the one to tell him he had things wrong. My mom is going to set the record straight with fire and fury, but Lucas has had enough of that. It's not his fault he wasn't given the right set of facts. He just suffered from the lies. We both did.

The darker it gets outside without my phone buzzing in my palm, the more worried I become that I won't be able to warn him. Thankfully, the first set of headlights to light up the Fuller driveway don't belong to a man.

Without looking, I dial Abby and put my phone on speaker as I stare out at the scene unfolding in front of the Fuller garage.

"What's up? Did it all go down? Did your mom punch him in the face?" Abby loves a good fight. She also loves my mom, sometimes a little more than her own.

"I think maybe you should come over," I say while my mom follows the white Tahoe into the garage, stopping where the door slides closed. Her feet are purposely planted between the beams, making it impossible for Mrs. Fuller to close the door on her.

"I'm so there. Stay on the line; tell me what I miss," my friend says.

"I don't think I can. Just . . . get here," I demand. I end the call before she can protest and pocket my phone so my hands are free. I move to the side door, opening it enough to step into the frame, but I wait here for now. Of all the conversations about to happen, this is the one that has me most on edge.

The Tahoe's tail lights darken and the driver's side door opens. I can't see more than Shannon Fuller's legs. She's wearing black dress pants and black heels. My mom?

She's in flip flops and rolled up jeans. Fucking country mouse versus city mouse is about to go down.

Both women stand still, and though I can't see Lucas's mom's face, I can tell by the lack of movement that they are both silent. My mom nods her head, a quick tip of her chin as she folds her arms over her chest. Finally, Mrs. Fuller steps toward my mom, and when the two women are standing in a faceoff, bodies closed to warmth and affection, I move from the doorway. I cross the driveway to insert myself in this conversation on my mom's behalf.

"I don't want them dating."

Those are the first words I hear leaving Lucas's mom's lips. It's a crushing blow to the joy I felt earlier in the day. It's also the least important thing on the table.

"My daughter is an incredible person. He's lucky to have her love, and you do not get to belittle their feelings, especially since you've chosen to believe in lies." My mom's defense of me emboldens my self-esteem, though it still stings from Lucas's mom's words. The bad things always hit harder than the good, even when they aren't true.

"I have never, nor would I ever, sleep with another woman's husband," my mom continues. I take note of the words she's chosen and walk closer, and a bit taller, from hearing them. She's speaking them as a woman who has been hurt by other women.

"Kristen, I don't want to do this. I know what I know. And your daughter is here. She doesn't need to hear the sordid details," Lucas's mom says. I'm now only a few feet from them. My mom glances at me over her shoulder and reaches her hand out, urging me closer. I go, but a little reluctantly.

"You don't get to think she's not good enough for Lucas but too good for the truth. We are clearing this up tonight, and I'm not leaving this spot until we do. All of us. Todd included." My mom's voice is firm, teetering on the edge of angry but never falling off that ledge. It's weird to hear her call Lucas's parents by their first names. It reminds me how close we once were. I realize I'm not the only one who lost a friend in this web of lies Mr. Fuller spun. My mom and Lucas's mom did, too—they lost each other.

"Kristen, go home," Lucas's mom says, a pleading tone in her voice.

"I won't. Not until this is fixed," my mom says, and she weaves her arm through mine, locking me to her side.

Abby's car pulls along the curb in front of my house. I'm tempted to yell for her to stay inside, but that's not my friend's style. I see her moving closer in my periphery, and it doesn't take long for Lucas's mom to react to the growing audience.

"Oh, for Christ's sake, I'm not doing this," she says, her palm waving us away as she turns to head deeper into her garage.

"You sure? Todd just pulled up and Lucas is behind him. And I'm not moving. I'm going to say things that your husband needs to hear, and I am pretty sure you need to witness them!" My mom's words are grittier, and I can feel the rigid muscles in her arms. She's preparing to fight with more than words if she has to.

"Babe? What's going on here?" Mr. Fuller's gaze is locked on me and my mother despite the way he turns his head toward his wife. He looks like a fox sneaking away from the hens, and my mom is the farmer holding a rifle to his head.

"Our neighbors were just leaving," Mrs. Fuller says.

"June?" I twist at the sound of Lucas's voice, but stay where I am. My mom needs me here.

"We weren't leaving, Todd. We were just getting to the bottom of this big fat fucking lie you've concocted. That's what we're doing," my mom says. Most of the eyes in the area double in size, but not Mr. Fuller's. His shift and scan, looking for his next set of smoke and mirrors that enables him to keep having his cake and eating it too.

"Kristen, you don't know what you're saying," he says, but already I can tell from the cracks in his wife's expression that she's no longer sure she was ever given the truth.

"Oh, I know what I'm doing. I'm ruining your day, that's what I'm doing." My mom moves from her spot next to me, taking slow, methodical steps toward Lucas's dad. For a blip, Mrs. Fuller lurches as if she's about to step in front of my mom, in defense of her husband and the delicate story she's believed for two years. But she backs off, a worried scowl souring her expression.

"You never helped me with my divorce out of the kindness of your heart. You were setting up an alibi." My mom pauses a few feet from the witness she is about to badger, just shy of being able to poke his chest.

"Nicolas was going to leave you with pennies, Kristen. Of course I wanted to make sure your ex didn't absolutely ruin your life just because he had a lawyer and you didn't. I'm just sorry that you blurred the lines of my kindness. Babe—" Mr. Fuller turns toward his wife, his body rigid and fists at his sides. This is the posture of a desperate man. "She's twisting reality. And I'm so sorry you have to hear it. What happened was a mistake, but I guess to her . . . it meant more."

Mistake.

He has no idea how much of a trigger that word is.

"Is Mrs. D'Angelo a mistake too?" I expect the words to be coming from my mouth, but they aren't. Lucas has injected himself into this mess, standing up to his father and hitting him at his weakest point.

"The twins' mom?" Mrs. Fuller is catching on. She strides toward her husband and shoves at his shoulder. He desperately grabs at her wrist, catching it to block her swings, but she comes at him with another shove.

"Who told you that? Did she?" Mr. Fuller points at my mother, his finger a searing point right at her nose. It's a marvel my mom doesn't bite it off.

"I did," I step in. My body is trembling, but sometimes dominoes make a big quake when they fall. And the ones toppling now? They're enormous.

"Baby, she's lying. I mean, come on!" Todd Fuller's nervous laughter is paired with a whole lot of sweat. He's literally backed into a corner. The only thing left to do is to put him out of his misery. And the only person who deserves to do that is my mom.

"Tell me everything," Mrs. Fuller says, magic words that are about to change the face of her family forever.

The truth takes almost an hour to piece together between us, both me and Lucas's mom filling in gaps as my mom shares the true side of her story. When all is said and done, the illusion Todd Fuller worked so hard to create is a long-gone mirage, and the carnage left in its wake is irreparable.

As my parents' marriage was rapidly approaching a cliff, Mr. Fuller was just beginning to stray from his wife. It started during football camp our freshman year, when he and Natalia D'Angelo both volunteered as chaperones for the team trip down to Florida. Two weeks at a resort hotel while the boys were busy being molded for the gridiron gave them idle time, and I guess somewhere along the way, their fucking clothes fell off.

Lucas's mom was becoming suspicious, and when his dad caught her checking his phone, he panicked and changed the contact name from NATALIA, to ?MAYBE. His clever ruse sent her searching the wrong rabbit hole, and while the real texts my mother had with Lucas's dad were short, curt and confined to legal business, the fake ones were dirty and disheartening. That's because those texts were with Natalia, whom he has been sleeping with for almost three years now.

Mr. Fuller hooked my mom into his web by taking advantage of her despair. My parents were separated and my father was not going to pay to support me. Of course, he didn't really *want* me either. So when the kind neighbor whose name is on the letterhead for a fancy Indianapolis family law firm offered to help her out, pro bono, my mom leapt at the offer. It meant she sometimes had to drive downtown to meet him, and sit through after-hours negotiations with my dad's lawyer with Todd Fuller at her side. Not wanting to be a complete snake, when he negotiated a settlement of ten grand to cover my mom's legal expenses, Mr. Fuller gave that money to her. He handed it over in a seedy manila envelope, and he did it like that because he knew his wife was watching—or at least the private investigator she'd hired a month before was.

A spiraling drinking habit coupled with a prescription overdose led to a complete breakdown, and that's when Lucas's mom went into the hospital. My parents' divorce finalized that same week, and from her hospital bed, Mrs. Fuller begged her husband to end it with my mom. She played right into his hands, telling him she already knew everything. Of course she did. He made sure she knew what he wanted her to, which was nowhere close to the truth.

His long business trips while his wife struggled to find her mind weren't really about business. While Mr. Fuller snuck off with his son's best friend's mom, Lucas was terrified that his mom would never be the same. He spent every free moment with her in the hospital and then eventually at home when she was released. She didn't go back to work for three months, the demands of her ad agency job too much to handle. Her son held her together. And he made her promises.

He did whatever she asked. And when the ask came to cut me out of his life, he did it. I was already deep in my own shattered family crisis, helping my mom angrily pack up my father's things for donation and acting as the go-between for some of their phone conversations when he refused to pay bills he still owed her for. I didn't exactly reach out, but only because Lucas didn't either. The polarizing effect was a widening divide that made it easy for Lucas to buy into his father's lies. And since I was so used to being tossed away, I assumed Lucas and my dad were alike.

"Get. Out!"

Those two punctuated words, screamed by Lucas's mom, cut off Todd Fuller's litany of reasons and excuses. He stammers out a few more words, his face red and his arms flailing, fingers pointing. His fingers are always pointing—everywhere but to himself.

"Babe, you're not being rational," he says, belittling her in front of all of us. This time, though, instead of falling apart, she doubles in size and strength.

"So help me God, Todd, if you do not run upstairs and grab a bag full of your shit and leave this house right now, I will throw your things out the window and advertise free yard sale goods," Lucas's mom says.

Abby chortles over my shoulder, and I turn with my mouth wide. I almost forgot she's there. I am so rapt by the truth that I haven't looked around at all throughout the shouting. I'm too focused on inserting my facts where I finally discover they fit. Sometime, though, in the middle of it all, Tory walked up. He stays back to let the chaos roll, but he's definitely close enough to hear the heartbreaking facts that pertain to him.

"Tory," I croak. Lucas turns to see his friend. Abby shoots around on her heels. And the adults behaving like children let their shouting simmer into sudden quiet.

Tory's jaw is tense, a brewing anger in his eyes that's so opposite of the good-humored prankster that usually lives there. His glare is set on Lucas's dad as he moves forward, parting our small crowd. He stops at his friend's chest and places his palm flat over Lucas's heart, patting it kindly but firmly, a gesture that says, "I got this one."

It takes him approximately five more steps to square his body with Todd Fuller's, and even though Lucas's dad has about four inches on him, the youth and discipline Tory has in the gym make him no match.

"Leave my family the fuck alone," he says. "Oh, and your son . . . he's going to MIT. And you . . . you were a shitty football player."

The swing is hard and swift, Tory's fist landing in the soft cushion that separates Mr. Fuller's top teeth from his bottom along his cheek. The cracking sound is sharp and timed perfectly with the landing. A broken jaw is probably pretty painful. But even more so is an obliterated ego, which Tory puts the final nail in before walking back to his car and speeding away.

CHAPTER TWENTY-THREE

I've observed that a strange thing sometimes happens when you've gone through a divorce and survived it emotionally. You become a beacon of hope for others looking to do the same.

My mom hasn't called my father in a year. As long as his checks come, there really isn't a reason for them to talk. He sent her a text when he proposed to Jamie. She sent one back saying *OK*. Other than that small exchange, it has been radio silence between them. But when Lucas's mom came to mine, ashamed and humble and afraid for her livelihood, in search of a lawyer to go up against the man she was leaving, my mom knew the only worthy opponent was the slimeball who represented my father.

For two weeks, my mom has been Shannon Fuller's personal divorce route tour guide. Tonight, she talked Shannon into having a little fun down at her new studio. I guess boudoir photoshoots are an empowering thing for newly single women to do. After a shopping marathon at Victoria's Secret, my mom took her to have her hair and makeup professionally done. They've been at the studio shooting for four hours now, but they also took two bottles of wine. I have a feeling they'll be spending the night there.

Fine by me. It means Lucas and I don't have to talk in hushed whispers. Though I like the hushed whispers too, for entirely other reasons.

It's strange how fast time passes when we're together. He's climbed through my window almost every night since the episode we have affectionately labeled BFM for Big Fat Mistake. The only night he missed was the one when he helped me climb down so I could sneak out and drive up to Chicago with him and Tory and Hayden and Abby. Tory said he wanted to stand by the lake and look up at the skyline, and Lucas wants to erase his father's bad deeds and do right by his best friend. We made the three-hour trip in just over two and rolled back into the driveway just before sunrise. I told my mom about it afterward because I didn't want to start a new collection of secrets. Of course, she doesn't know about the nights Lucas is in my room. I have to have a few things, and as much as I want our bond to rebuild and grow, I also don't want to give up the feeling of having Lucas's arms around me when I fall asleep at night.

Or the feeling of having his fingertips tease along my midriff, as they are right now.

"So, about that date," I say, my eyelids lowered as I look down to where his head rests on my hips. His devilish gaze is focused on the work of his fingers that are slowly inching my shirt up my ribs.

"Yeah?" he hums without glancing up. His eyes close and he rolls his head to press a cool kiss on the skin next to my belly button. He opens them as his tongue takes a quick taste.

"Don't think you can use your typical ploys to distract me," I say, my hips already fighting to squirm because *fuck*, his ploys work.

"Okay," he hums again, this time dragging his tongue up higher, his bottom lip catching on my skin while his hand pushes my T-shirt up further. When his hand pauses at the spot where he should encounter my bra—but doesn't —his eyebrows lift.

"What's this?" His lip curls on one side, and I match with a smirk of my own.

"It's yours if you talk about the date you promised me," I tease.

He breathes out a laugh and inches higher still. I arch on instinct and he shifts so his weight is balanced on both elbows, his hands free to pull my shirt up the rest of the way until my breasts are exposed to the air.

"Ah ah," I say, barely getting the sound out as my breath hitches. I hold up a finger and waggle it in front of his face. "No dessert before dinner."

His lips tighten and curve on the ends, eyes hazing with all kinds of dirty thoughts. He moves his head forward enough to allow his mouth to close around my finger, his teeth gently biting the knuckle as he playfully growls.

"You are all dessert, June," he says, letting go of his hold on my finger.

"One. Date." I stand my ground, though I know all of

this is for play. The play is almost as arousing as the other things. Maybe even more.

"All right," he says, tipping his chin and kissing the skin just below my breasts.

I sharply suck in air and push my tits up, wanting more. Lucas ups the ante and kisses closer to the center of my pebbled peaks, a kiss for each curve of my breasts, all the way around, but never fully where I need his lips most.

"Homecoming," he says.

I laugh out because homecoming is *so not* either of us.

"What would I wear?" I question.

He lifts himself forward and flicks his tongue at the tip of my breast. I quake as he blows dry the cool spot he left behind, a tightly puckered smile playing on his lips.

"Black dress," he says, pausing to torture my other breast the same way. "I'll wear my black jeans, and that dark gray sweater over a shirt and tie." His cheek dimples with a tempting smile because he knows that look is my favorite. I asked him about that sweater last week.

"Okay. Black dress, and you . . . sexy as fuck. Got it," I say, knowing he likes it when I talk to him that way. His eyes flutter closed and he growls against my body, dragging his nose along the center of my chest and pausing with his lips brushing lightly atop my right nipple.

"Nothing under your dress," he says, his tongue taking another pass, a longer and harder one this time that bends my back into an arch that opens access for his hands to slide underneath, leaving him in complete control over me.

"That seems risky, me in a black dress at homecoming with nothing on . . . down . . . there." I bring one knee up and lift my hips, wanting to push myself into him and ease the building pressure.

"Those are my demands, June." He licks again and I bend to his will, my eyes barely able to remain open as I stare into him, calling his bluff. He isn't bluffing, though, and the thought of being out with him that way has me curious and hungry.

"I think I can do that," I say, my answer maybe surprising him a little. His right brow lifts higher than the left.

"So, it's a date?" He covers my right breast with his mouth and sucks hard, leaving nothing but the grip of his teeth, and ending with a gentle tug that has me wanting all of him. Now.

"It's a date. Now, please, Lucas. For all that is holy, will you fuck me?" I end my plea with a whimper and it amuses him more than normal. His eyes haze even more than they already are as he rolls my shirt up over my head, taking my arms along with it. He twists the fabric together, tethering my hands loosely above my head then sits up on his knees, my legs parted on either side of him. He's done playing games and teasing me, and his fingers curl around the band of my pink lace panties. I bought them with Abby with this night in mind, and I'm fairly certain they've done the job as the top of Lucas's cock protrudes from the band of his gray joggers. He rarely wears underwear, I've learned. A trait I have come to love for moments like this.

He slides my panties down my lifted hips, and I bend one leg at a time to free them completely. Lucas leans over my body, reaches for his wallet on the night table, and he pulls a condom out, clenching the packet in his teeth. His lips tick up a hint on one side, bringing his dimple back into play. I draw my knees up on either side of him, wanting him to ease the ache I have building desperately.

"You like it when I do dirty things to you, don't you, June?" he mumbles from between teeth gripping the wrapped condom.

I nod because yes, I do.

Lucas tears the packet open with his teeth and one-handedly pulls himself free from the band of his pants. He rolls the condom on slowly with the other . I lift my hips, begging him to stop the torture as he holds himself a fraction of an inch from where I so desperately need him.

He doesn't make me wait long, dragging the tip of his cock down my center twice then pushing inside me in a long, slow thrust. My legs automatically wrap around his waist, and he holds my hips as he works himself in and out of my body. This is the first time we've had sex without muffling our sounds against each other since the abandoned drive-in theater. I let go of some of the inhibitions that come with having to be painfully quiet in my room at night.

Obeying and leaving my hands over my head, I let Lucas drive my body toward climax, my hips holding steady to meet each push of him inside me. I've learned that I can give him pleasure with the smallest movement of my hips, so when I can tell he's starting to lose himself in me, I roll my body to tempt him closer to the fire. I know he's about to come when he falls forward and rests his forehead against mine, one arm holding his weight at the side of my head while the other hand holds my wrists together where I've left them tied in my T-shirt.

Every rock of his hips pushes me closer, his hips working harder and muscles clenching more. I cry out in pleasure against his bare shoulder, biting him lightly and squeezing my eyes closed as the first wave takes me over the cliff and sends me floating in a sea of satisfying riptides, wave after wave as my body clenches around him and I rock my hips up to meet every drive he makes into me. Finally, his body grows so tight, the feel of him so thick inside, that I know he's about to come. I pull his mouth to mine and kiss him harder than I ever have, my tongue probing, teeth tugging on his bottom lip, and soft whimpers falling from my mouth as his breath falls away and his body is nothing but sweat and sex and listless bliss.

He rolls our bodies together so his weight is no longer on me, and I toss my shirt to the side so I can move my fingers through his cool, damp hair, our bodies sticky and moist. I lie like this with him still flexing inside me for several long minutes, content to fall asleep with him there, locked together in a permanence that happens when someone is your first and you give your whole essence to them completely.

"Did I really just agree to homecoming?" He chuckles, and I love the crackling sound it makes in his chest, the slight tremors and vibration of his body under my touch.

"You did," I say, glancing up at him with a tempting smile. "And I agreed to nothing under my dress."

His mouth curls to match mine, a lustfulness touching the corners, drawing them up toward excitable eyes.

"You did," he says, pleased—and possibly aroused —again.

"I better get flowers," I add, knowing that right now, I could get anything I want. But as it stands, I pretty much have it all.

CHAPTER TWENTY-FOUR

M ost seniors endure a lot of impromptu photo sessions with their parents when they reach certain milestones. I've never gone to a homecoming dance, or *any* dance for that matter. Freshmen weren't allowed, and my Montessori school was too small to hold anything other than a craft fair. As far as milestones go, this is the first one I've had warranting photographs.

Of course, my mother is a professional photographer, so one session with her may make up for five or ten missed occasions.

The orders were clear, and we all obeyed. Me, Abby, Lola and Naomi arrived early and got dressed and did our hair and makeup upstairs in Lucas's mom's room. It was hard not to look around and notice the stark absence of anything masculine. Only Abby brought it up out loud, and only once. "I'm glad she's divorcing his ass," she said. That summed it up, and that's all we needed to clear the room of the bad energy and make way for magic.

While we dressed upstairs, Lucas, the twins and a few of the other guys from the team get dressed in my house, in my room. I did my best to hide things I thought might be embarrassing, but I feel better knowing Lucas is there. If Tory decides to go rummaging through my drawers, he'll throat punch him.

While we all get ready, my mom sets up a ridiculous amount of equipment—two umbrella lights, four different flashes, and a seamless paper backdrop hanging from some contraption she built out of PVC pipe. Nobody questions her, especially not me. The only photos I have of me and Lucas together are from before our bodies matured, when holding hands felt super racy and taboo. Oh, the things we've done to each other since then.

The main photos, of course, could only happen in one place. My mom has always been in love with the staircase inside the Fuller home. While our layouts are the same, our interiors are drastically different. My home would be what one might call the "base model," while Lucas's house is filled with the best upgrades. And the best feature, for both my mother and me, is the iron staircase that winds from one end of the house down to the foyer. This is why we had to dress here—to make a *grand* entrance that my mom could capture on film.

My mom bought about two dozen packs of fairy lights for her "vision," and she and Lucas's mom spent almost the entire day weaving the thin wires around the railing for a glittering effect. At one point, when I came by to drop off some clear tape, I overheard Shannon telling my mom that she wishes they had "done this a lot sooner." I didn't pry, and I didn't linger to eavesdrop, but I'm pretty sure she was talking about coming together and living with the truth.

The brash laughter from downstairs now that the boys have all come inside echoes through the high-ceilinged foyer and practically beats down Lucas's mom's door. I've been ready for almost an hour, but in that time, I've doubted every square inch of myself at least twice. Mostly, that I'm wearing a very short dress with nothing underneath. I've kept this secret from Abby; some moments are meant to be special and only shared between Lucas and me. Knowing he can touch me with one flit of my dress is one of those kinds of things.

My hair is pulled up into a loose ponytail that Abby curled into spirals that fall down my shoulders and back. The dress I bought is strapless with a back that scoops clear to the spot where my spine curves inward at my lower back. The amount of fabric that covers my ass is minimal, so my dancing tonight will not be bold and big. It's fine, though, because I intend on remaining in Lucas's arms most of the night.

"Here," Abby says, stepping behind me and dusting my shoulders and chest with a little bit of glitter. I barely recognize myself in the mirror, the gawky alt girl with long, dark hair almost looks like a princess. It's probably the glitter.

"He's going to lose his mind," she says, dropping her chin to my shoulder. I peek at her, looking away from our reflection and toward my friend who has always thought I'm beautiful. She holds her hand out and snaps a photo of the two of us together, and my smile stretches wider.

"For once, you caught a moment of me in a good mood," I say, laughing.

"Well, there was bound to be one," she says, snapping one more photo as I roll my eyes at her lame joke.

"And . . . there she is," she teases.

I reach for her phone in playful retaliation, but before I can catch her, there's a soft knock at the door. Lucas's mom slips in and holds her palms to her face. She shakes her head at the sight of the four of us, all done up as if we're heading to a royal ball.

"So, this is what it's like to have daughters," she says, genuine awe in her expression. I reach for her hand and squeeze it the moment she gives it to me. I still haven't let Lucas read the letter she wrote me after everything went down, but he knows she gave it to me. She spent two pages apologizing for believing I could be anything other than someone special. I cried when I read it, not realizing how much it hurt to have her think poorly of me because of something she believed my mom did. Her list of my best qualities was exhaustive, but it was also deeply personal and purposeful. She wasn't generic about a single thing, and described moments when Lucas and I were together as kids. She credited me for him finally finding his own voice, but I don't know that I did anything other than rip the tape from his mouth. Lucas was already near to breaking free of his father's expectations. All I did was give him a tiny shove.

"The guys are ready, ladies," she says, pausing at the door and lining us up to walk down one at a time. I know my mom's drill, and we will be repeating this sequence about eight more times to make sure she gets the perfect shot. But this first time will be the one that counts the most for me. It will be the first time Lucas looks up and sees me as more than the girl next door. A sexy, mature, driven and confident almost eighteen-year-old is about to walk down the steps and take his hand. I'll know exactly what our immediate future holds by that initial reaction. I'm ready for it.

Abby walks down the steps first, and we all giggle at the cat calls and whistles the boys deliver down below. We decided to go together as a group tonight since Lucas and I are the only *real* couple, but I know for a fact Tory sees Abby with the same colored glasses Lucas does me. He's just not quite ready to grow up and admit it.

Lola and Naomi go next, and I watch through the cracked doorway as they stop to pose on nearly every step. My mom is hysterical with laughter, but deep down, she actually thinks some of the poses they strike might work for commercial purposes. Her business hat is never far away.

My heart beats wildly the farther down the steps the girls go, and when the eyes staring from below all dart up to the doorway I'm hiding behind, my palms begin to sweat.

"I'm nervous," I whisper, giggling for Lucas's mom.

"You're stunning," she says. Without giving me more time to panic, she pushes the door open and steps back so I'm the only thing there for Lucas to see. He came dressed as promised, his straight black pants, dark gray V-neck sweater, crisp white shirt, and black tie. The preppy look may very well only work on him for me. It does work, though. It works without exception, and it works quickly. My insides shift from being anxious to being amorous. I step onto the landing, wrap my hand around the railing, and look down on the blue eyes peering up.

"You are beautiful," Lucas mouths, and my mouth stretches into a smile, the satin feeling of the deep red color on my lips making it easy to shine with happiness. He moves forward, away from the seven other guys here with him, and as I take the stairs one at a time, praying I don't fall in these shoes that are way too high for my novice feet to navigate in, he climbs to meet me.

My mother's cameras click rapidly, and as silly as I thought she was with some of this, I'm glad she's capturing this moment. If Lucas never looks up at me again, I'll always have the way he's looking at me now.

With only three steps left between us, Lucas takes one final stride, clearing them all until we share the same stair. He stands close, his hands bracing my elbows as I hold on to his biceps, not towering over me as he usually does thanks to the stupid amount of height added by my shoes.

"Look who's all grown up," he says through a playful smirk. His eyes are crystal waters against the dark gray of his sweater. I breathe in his scent and instantly am drunk on the warm vanilla and burning wood notes. Lucas takes advantage of my liquid state by tipping up my chin and possessively dropping his mouth on mine. His hand snakes around my back, landing low enough for his fingers to dip inside the fabric that drapes above my ass. He leans me back, and someone in the room whistles. I blush from being the center of attention, but I'm also rushed with heat from his touch.

I lean all of my weight into his strong hand as he holds me perilously over the cascading stairs, tethering us to gravity with his other hand on the banister. When he pulls away, I smile against his lips, happy to etch this moment in stone. One more heartbeat, though, makes it another milestone in my life.

"I love you, too," he says, his lips playfully brushing against the nape of my neck. He raises me and our gazes lock, his serious despite the flirtatious lilt of his lips, which are a little pink from my lip stick.

"I love you," I mouth, knowing nobody below can see me. His cheek indents briefly, a hint of his dimple appearing like a sign to let me know he read my lips . . . just as he heard me slip up and say those words before, way too early.

As I predict, my mom, the consummate professional, makes us repeat every single thing we do three more times, then she spends an hour taking shots of couples and groups on the stairs and in front of her plain backdrop. Before she shuts down her lights, though, I make her do one thing she hates but will thank me for down the road.

I drag my resistant mother outside to stand with me in front of our middle-finger garage door, and we stand together, embracing, her in her ripped jeans and Tommy sweatshirt and me in my two-hundred-dollar cocktail dress that my mom said I deserved despite my argument that it cost too much.

I had prepared Lucas's mom for the job, and from the digital proofs I checked on my mom's laptop, I'd say she came through beautifully. I will take that image of her and me together with me everywhere I go, and no matter how much life changes, my relationship with her will be my one true constant. My rock. That paint will soon be covered up, but the badass who did it? She's forever.

I expect attention when Lucas and I finally walk into the homecoming dance. Not because of the rumors swirling about everything that went down, but because of the epic performance he had on the field last night. His dad still showed up for the game, though his mother sat with us while his dad stood alone down by the fence. He didn't leave, because as broken as his relationship with his son is, he can't give up the high he gets from watching him do things he never could. Lucas is gifted on the field. He also happens to have a gifted mind, and for the boy I love, that's far more inspiring.

A few players stop us as we make our way toward the dance floor, handshakes and bro hugs take place with me at Lucas's side. But when the first slow song begins to play, everything—and everyone else—disappears. I find a home against Lucas's chest, and I intend on staying here until he takes me somewhere to be alone. The sensual touch of his hand on my bare back keeps my nerves firing no matter how slow or soft the song is we dance to, and I know we've been indulged when the DJ announces one more before he turns things up a notch. I don't quite expect this, though.

To most people in the room, this isn't a slow song. In fact, judging by the sneers and jokes, most people don't even know what this song is. But I know. Hayden D'Angelo knows. And now his twin knows, too.

"Did you set this up?" I say, leaning back and quirking a brow as "Midnight Hour" transforms our high school gym into a time machine right back to the nineteen-sixties.

"I thought you did!" Lucas laughs, flattening his hand on his chest and crossing his heart.

I narrow my eyes in thought, and scan the room in search of my suspect, but I don't have to look far. Tory leans proudly with his right elbow on the tower speaker near the DJ booth. He blows on his fingertips then runs them down the length of his lapel like a regular fucking Sinatra. My, I have taught him well.

The dance floor clears for the most part, but Lucas and I stay there for the entire song, singing along with the chorus, showcasing the worst of our vocal talents. When the DJ breaks through the end of the song asking the homecoming royalty court to step forward, I peel back so Lucas can join the other seniors standing near the platform set up under the basketball scoreboard. He instead slides back and out of the way with me, letting the twins and that guy Cannon walk up on their own. It's glaringly obvious he's not where he should be as three guys stand to the right of our principal and four girls stand to his left. Even more obvious is the disdain on Ava's face as she stares across the half court at me. There was a time when that small, insignificant action of hers would make me feel incredibly small, but tonight, it only serves as a source of amusement.

"She could not possibly hate me more," I say. Lucas bends his head down and claps through the reading of the nominees for king, including himself.

"Ava?" he questions.

I punch out a short laugh. "Yeah. She hasn't really bothered me since the whole spray paint and black eye incidents. What's weird, though, is I don't get why she hated me so much when you were dating her."

Lucas's eyes glimmer in his gaze, and a smirk paints his lips.

"Oh, I know why," he says, standing tall and not filling in the details just to torture me.

I clap through the list of queen nominees but keep my skeptical eyes on my boyfriend, my stare penetrating his ability to ignore it.

"Let's get out of here," he says, turning to the side to kiss the top of my head. I look up and meet his smile.

"But you're probably gonna win," I say.

"I don't really give a shit," he responds.

I give him side eyes for a moment, but it's easy to see he's telling the truth. I take his waiting hand and we weave through the crowd, having only stayed for four songs. They announce Ava's name behind us as we let the gym doors fall closed. It's a perfect way to leave her, on top of her completely irrelevant and fake mountain. It doesn't change the question I'm still dying to know the answer to, though. I hold my tongue until we get to Lucas's truck, patient a few minutes longer than I expect because Lucas quickly discovers I followed through with my promise in wearing this dress.

I sit sideways in his passenger seat with him standing between my legs. My body satiated from his touch, I peel away from our kiss and reach up to grab the knot of his tie. I tug it forcefully, and he grins.

"Tell me, Lucas Fuller. Why does Ava Pryor hate me so much?"

I may never be prepared for his answer.

"Because when she told me she was in love with me at her eighth grade birthday party I told her I was in love with you. And deep down, she knows I never stopped."

EPILOGUE

I t's strange to contemplate where we all started the year
—where Lucas and I started the year. There was a time
when I dreaded this day . . . graduation. I was so deep in
my own head that I thought the day would come and go
without things like parties, or friends. Certainly not
boyfriends. And yet somehow, I'm in a world where I have
all three.

In six hours, I'll walk across a stage and be handed a
ticket to my future. That future isn't as dim as I fear it
would be, either. My mom is an inspiration. She believes in
her work, and she works hard. That hard work has turned a
solo photography business into something that not only
pays the bills but also afforded her to tuck away enough for
me to go to Indiana East. It's not Notre Dame or Ball State,
but it is away from home, and an adventure. And it has a
really great liberal arts program, so maybe I'll be able to
figure out what the hell I want to be when I grow up.

Grow up.

It's funny to look back and remember those words Abby said to me when the year began: that we've all grown up. She was right. In many ways, we have. But we've also got a lot of growing left to do. I hope somehow we're lucky enough to still be together at the end . . . all of us.

Lucas leaves after summer for MIT. He's going to love it there, and I'm all right with that because I know he loves me too. I might lose him for a little while to that great big world he's going to experience. But his roots will always be here, on some tree-lined street about an hour from a big city, where a pair of driveways brought us together when we were young.

I trust him enough to know he'll always come back to me in one form or another, and we will always be in love, even if it's only first love. I can't help but believe there's a chance that me and him? We might be the real deal. The forever, and the always.

"Are you sure you aren't peeking?" Lucas shouts. He left me here at the bottom of his driveway about ten minutes ago with this stupid tie wrapped around my face. He tied it snug, so not only can I not see, I might actually be blind. He said he has a graduation gift for me that requires a little maneuvering. I'm nervous about what that means.

"I promise!" I shout back.

"Okay, you'll know when to pull off the blindfold," he says. I shake my head because I have no idea what that could possibly mean, but trust . . . I trust *him*. So, here goes nothing.

At first, all I hear is the slamming of a car door. I lose count how many seconds pass before another noise touches my ears, but when it does, yeah . . . he's right. It's time to pull off the blindfold.

"No fucking way!"

My dad's impossible project, the piece of junk I assumed my mom finally had hauled away, is backing out of Lucas Fuller's garage. On its own. Nobody is pushing it. It's being driven.

The rumble is like honey to the ears, and even though the body is in desperate need of a paint job, the form . . . my God, the form of that vehicle is sexy.

"I can't believe you got the Buick running!" I shout so he hears me over the deep growl spilling from the engine.

Lucas hops out, leaving the door open behind him. The seats are still torn, but the dash looks new, and the steering wheel is in the right position with a leather wrap around it. I palm my face and stare in shock as I walk closer, sitting inside briefly so I can touch everything. I step back out, closing the door behind me, and put my hands right back on my cheeks, tears forming in my eyes.

"I figured what good is an MIT degree if I can't get my girl a car to drive to college in," he says with a casual shrug. He acts as if this is no big deal but I know what shape that car was in. It was a shell. A ghost. He brought it back from the dead. And he did it for me.

I leap at him in an instant, arms wrapping around his neck as he catches me at the waist and swings me in a circle, my dress and graduation gown flowing around my body.

"You like it?" He dips his chin as he sets me on my feet and I step up on my toes to kiss him.

"I could not love a single thing more," I say, the smile

on my mouth aching as it stabs into my cheeks. This is what happiness is.

"I feel really bad," I say with a soft laugh.

His brow dents.

"Because I didn't get you anything that big," I say, glancing over my shoulder to take in the car still rumbling out its sweet sounding idle behind me. I bite my bottom lip and turn my gaze back to him, a little excited because while I didn't get him a car, I did get him something he'll like.

"That's a fairly sinister grin you've got there, June Mabee." His eyes lower and one brow lifts.

I let him stew with his thoughts and fantasies for a few seconds, then I tug his hands into mine and lead him backward toward the back seat of the car that is now mine. He follows willingly as I open the door and get in. He drops a knee on the seat between my legs and I slide until my back is pressed against the opposite window. He's wearing his dress shirt and dark gray pants, a black tie, and silver cufflinks on his rolled-up sleeves. I'm going to enjoy messing up his look later, but for right now, I feel he might just deserve a preview.

I let the sides of my graduation gown fall open and slowly unbutton the front of my dress one button at a time. My mom and his mom are picking up food. My dad won't show up until the ceremony, and his dad might not show up at all. We have a small moment alone to make a memory, and what I bought for him is meant to make an impression.

As my dress falls open, the thin white lace over my breasts and the matching panties come into view, and

Lucas's gaze scorches its way down my body. He leans forward without hesitation, and I open my legs to make room for him to completely crawl inside. When he shuts the heavy door behind him, I decide his pressed shirt doesn't have to be perfect to walk across a stage, and maybe it's all right if he gets a little messy now.

That's what life is. It's messy. It's sexy. It's ugly. It's brutally hard yet joyous all at once. And this life, it's all mine. Just like the boy who is making me feel like the woman I never thought I'd become . . . right . . . now.

THE END

PREVIEW OF BOOK 2 IN THE
VARSITY SERIES

By Ginger Scott

PREORDER THE EBOOK NOW:
Https://amzn.to/2zluA2u

A bby Cortez is a girl with goals, on the brink of
stardom. Falling in love isn't just something she
doesn't have time for—it's something she doesn't really
believe in.

Tory "Salvatore" D'Angelo loves falling in love. The
star basketball player at Public gives his heart away one

night at a time then takes it back when he's ready to move on.

But what happens when a jaded heart opens up to a free one? Is there a place where these two opposites might just be a perfect match?

Tory D'Angelo

I've never really gotten the appeal of flowers. I mean, one, they're super fleeting. Every time my mom's gotten flowers, I swear they're dead within three days. Feels like a major waste of money. Of course, my mom's flowers probably came from the man she was having an affair with, so it's entirely possible my perspective is tainted. Even so, what do flowers say about a person's feelings for someone else?

I like you enough to pop into the grocery store and pick up this pre-arranged bundle of plant clippings wrapped in plastic.

I mean, yeah. Flowers are pretty and shit, but there are a lot of things that are pretty. Cakes are pretty, and you can eat those. A perfect three-pointer drained within seconds, nothing but net . . . that's a thing of beauty. Art, a really hot red dress, or hell, a puppy! All of that is as aesthetically pleasing as a bundle of flowers. Yet here I am, clipping the stems off some weedy-smelling plant shit over my kitchen trash while my best friend June tells me what a good idea this is.

"She's going to love them," June assures me while she reaches toward my bundle, tugging on the stem of something. She pulls it free and dumps it into the trash with the stems I chopped off at an angle because "angles take in the water better" or whatever.

"She won't love that one?" I cock a brow and laugh. I'm still not sold on any of this.

"That one's dead."

I form an O with my mouth and drop my chin to stare at the drooping flower where it lies in the trash.

"Huh." I nod.

June giggles then wraps her hands around the bouquet, holding it steady so I can slip the giant band around the stems again. I never thought my best friend would be a girl, let alone June Mabee. I've pretty much picked on her since she got boobs, probably before that if I'm being honest. I still call her Maybe Mabee. June and I collided in epic fashion a couple months ago. We kicked off our senior year on a strange note, going through some really awful shit together. We're kinda honeymooning at the whole best friend thing, I guess, but she's not sick of me yet and turns out Maybe Mabee doles out some pretty solid advice. Though, I'm not totally sold on the whole flowers thing.

"You sure this isn't stupid? I feel really stupid." I'm sweating, and I've already showered from basketball practice, changed my shirt twice and put on a whole lot of deodorant. This is strange territory for me. To put it succinctly, I have a fucking crush. It's bizarre because hooking up with any girl at Public High—or in our whole town of Allensville, really—has never been an issue for me. June says it's because I'm used to being chased, and maybe that's true. But I also think it's because the girl I'm trying to impress has never, not once, shown an ounce of interest in my presence. In fact, if I had to make a guess, I would bet on her hating me.

"Abby is going to die . . . in a good way!" June's said that a lot, that little add-on of *in a good way*. Feels like a hedged bet to me.

Abby Cortez is June's *other* best friend.

Fine.

She's her *real* best friend, and I'm the new guy June hangs out with sometimes while she waits on her boyfriend, Lucas. *My* real best friend. Along with my twin brother, Hayden, we've become our own clique. Except for the little part about me being pretty sure Abby hates me. Oh, and me wanting to kiss her candy lips and wrap her legs around my waist just before I lay her back on the hood of my car.

This is complicated. But flowers is the key. June swears by it.

"You look amazing," June says, stepping into me and brushing something from the shoulder of my shirt. I went with a button down, mostly because this shirt is snug on my arms and chest, making me look a little bit beast-mode. I didn't need June to tell me how much Abby likes man candy. She was digging on the new guy, Cannon, for a while, and she noted his arms and chest a few times. Apparently, though, he's moody as fuck. Thank God!

"Where's your brother?" June asks.

"Job interview," I answer, bending down to catch my reflection in the glass front of the oven. I actually have product in my hair. *Who am I?*

"Wow. D'Angelo boys are going to work?" June mocks.

I shrug as I stand and face her.

"It's hard to be around here, and Hayden's had a harder time than I have. I think he wants something to fill the free time." June's eyes soften, but she's careful not to let them dip into pity. We don't do that around here.

My dad moved out a month ago. It's still pretty fresh for all of us. My mom was having an affair with Lucas's dad, and when it all came out, it basically blew up both of our families.

"Have you guys talked to your dad lately?" June asks. Our pops said we could go to Indianapolis with him if we wanted to, but this is our senior year. We're primed to win state this basketball season, and we both decided we couldn't give up on that. Staying here means sticking out the next few months in a house with a parent we pretty much have lost all respect for.

"Our first family therapy session is next week, with *both* of them. It promises fireworks," I say. June grimaces in response.

"You sure it's not weird, me forcing some double-date with you and Luc?" I squint through my question, and a small part of me wants her to let me off the hook. I've never been afraid of rejection, but with Abby, I put it at a solid fifty-fifty that she kicks me in the nuts when I ask her out.

"Stop," June protests, laughing at my nervous behavior. "It's sweet. And it will make you both more comfortable. Plus, it's Eight Lanes. Bowling is the easiest first date ever."

"Says the Eight Lanes employee who bowls a two-hunny," I say, one brow arched.

June's laughter ticks up but stops when we're interrupted by the familiar rumble of Lucas's truck in the driveway. I start to jump in place because he is supposed to bring Abby to the house with him and suddenly I'm full of enough energy to power a lightning bolt.

"It's go time," I say under my breath. June squeezes my arm and offers me a reassuring smile.

Lucas busts through the door first, and I puff out my cheeks to indicate how stressed I am. But something about the look in his eyes freezes me to the floor. My jumping stops, and my heart does too.

"Abort. Mission," Lucas says, pointing at me then staring intently into his girlfriend's eyes.

"What the—" My protest is cut short when Abby follows Lucas through the door in a rush, her hand gripped firmly in my brother's. My eyes see nothing else. I'm blatantly staring at the place where my crush and my twin are fused together.

What the actual fuck?

"I got the job, yo!" my brother says. At least, it sounds like his voice. I couldn't testify he said the words because I'm not looking at his mouth. I'm looking at the way Abby is holding his elbow with her other hand, bouncing with excitement. That's two hands she has on him now. Two. Hands.

"Did you hear me, bro? I got the job!"

I shake my head—*literally* shake my head—and force my gaze to meet Hayden's. We are nearly physically identical, but our personalities are vastly different. Where I'm loud, he's quiet. My confidence is offset by his reservation. I believe I can make any girl fall in love with me. And Hayden . . . he's never had a girlfriend. Ever.

Until—

"You're looking at the new host at Two-fers," my

brother says, holding up his new work shirt. It's bright red with two weenies embroidered on the pocket. It's ridiculous, and my natural instinct is to make fun of it, but I can't seem to find a single funny thing to say.

"Wow," I say, over-exaggerating this terribly small word.

"Right?" He pushes at my shoulder, pressing the shirt into me to take. I unfold it and stare at it while I fake laugh. I toss it on the counter and hold my hand up for him to slap, and we grip each other and pull in for a hug. My eyes catch June's over my brother's shoulder, and they are full of pity. *Motherfucking pity!*

"I hope it's cool that I invited Hayden to come with us?" Abby asks from somewhere behind me. I can't bear the thought of turning around and looking at her.

"Of course. Yeah, totally," I croak out. I cough to cover my weak-ass voice.

"I just gotta change, and we can go. What's with the flowers, dude?" my brother asks, pointing to my fisted palm that's nearly choking the bouquet to death with my grip.

"Oh," I say, lifting them and feeling suddenly numb. "I—"

"He lost a bet," June says, coming to my rescue.

Hayden nods, accepting her answer, then dashes up the stairs, leaving the rest of us here in this instantly shrinking space.

"That a new thing there?" June says to her friend in a half-whisper I wish I didn't hear.

"We've been talking a lot, with everything they're going through, and I don't know, it just sorta . . ." Abby's head waggles side-to-side, but it's the blush that colors her cheeks that has me defeated.

Just sorta.

The sudden need to rush from the room hits me, and I march across the kitchen toward June. "Here you go, a bet's a bet," I say, shoving the flowers I knew were a bad idea into her chest. She hugs them and lets out an "*oof.*"

I keep walking, making eyes at Lucas on my way out, knowing he'll follow me to his truck so I can scream obscenities and feel like a fool with only him as my witness.

"Wow, someone's a sore loser," Abby teases from over my shoulder.

I huff out a laugh, not even able to lob one of my normal comebacks because she's so dead-on. I *am* a sore loser. I'm also done catching feelings for some girl.

PREORDER NOW!
Abby and Tory's story continues in Varsity Tiebreaker, releasing July 23, 2020.
Now available for preorder here:
https://amzn.to/2zluA2u

ACKNOWLEDGMENTS

I'm gonna keep this short and sweet. This series is about the ride, about escaping our reality a little right now and living in between some angsty, fun pages, feeling some swoon then holding hands over our hearts. I wanted to write a world of characters to take us all away, and I wanted a dash of sports in the mix because hey...it's me! And I miss sports!

This series was started in the middle of a pandemic. Never in a million years did I think I'd write that statement. And it turns out that leaning on others when writing during the middle of a pandemic is crucial. There is no way I could have jumped feet first into this thing without my support team and without the readers holding out supportive hands ready to catch me after THE END.

This series has lived in my head for about a year, but shaking off the stress of the world today proved a little tricky. Thank you, Autumn, for telling 2020 to take a seat and shut up and let me write and edit. I always need you but this year, I need you a little more. My betas, Jen, Shelley, TeriLyn—I love you. Brenda Letendre and Tina Scott, bless you and your editing genius. And finally, my sweet Tim and Carter, my world, thanks for being the constant in the storm.

If you enjoyed this book, please consider leaving a review. The book market is daunting for us small authors, and getting the word out in this increasingly noisy world is becoming so hard. I am incredibly thankful to my readers and supporters for every boost they give. It's those viral shares, the recommendations to friends, that help get my stories seen, and I don't for one minute take any of that for granted. I get to do this because you give me your time and your passion—you tell others to give my books a try. So thank you all...to the moon!

And hey, don't worry...I'm in my groove now. You guys are going to love Varsity Tiebreaker and Varsity Rulebreaker. Take that, 2020!

ALSO BY GINGER SCOTT

The Varsity Series

Varsity Heartbreaker

Varsity Tiebreaker (July 2020)

Varsity Rulebreaker (October 2020)

The Waiting Series

Waiting on the Sidelines

Going Long

The Hail Mary

Like Us Duet

A Boy Like You

A Girl Like Me

The Falling Series

This Is Falling

You And Everything After

The Girl I Was Before

In Your Dreams

The Harper Boys

Wild Reckless

Wicked Restless

Standalone Reads

Cowboy Villain Damsel Duel

Drummer Girl

BRED

Cry Baby

The Hard Count

Memphis

Hold My Breath

Blindness

How We Deal With Gravity

ABOUT THE AUTHOR

Ginger Scott is an Amazon-bestselling and Goodreads Choice and Rita Award-nominated author from Peoria, Arizona. She is the author of several young and new adult romances, including bestsellers Cry Baby, The Hard Count, A Boy Like You, This Is Falling and Wild Reckless.

A sucker for a good romance, Ginger's other passion is sports, and she often blends the two in her stories. When she's not writing, the odds are high that she's somewhere near a baseball diamond, either watching her son swing for the fences or cheering on her favorite baseball team, the Arizona Diamondbacks. Ginger lives in Arizona and is married to her college sweetheart whom she met at ASU (fork 'em, Devils).

FIND GINGER ONLINE: www.littlemisswrite.com

facebook.com/GingerScottAuthor

twitter.com/TheGingerScott

instagram.com/authorgingerscott